SHADES OF SEPIA

ANNE BARWELL

THE SLEEPLESS CITY, BOOK 1

A found family of supernaturals protects humanity from
the stuff of nightmares.

Copyright © 2020 Anne Barwell

Cover design: © 2014 T.L. Bland
Publishing logo © 2019 T.L. Bland
http://www.thruterryseyes.com/
Cover art is for illustrative purposes only and any person depicted on the cover is a model

Editing: Desi Chapman
Blue Ink Editing
https://blueinkediting.com/

ISBN: 978-0-473-52892-8 (epub)

ISBN: 978-0-473-52893-5 (mobi)
ISBN: 978-0-473-52891-1 (print)

First Edition published by Dreamspinner Press, 2014

AUTHOR'S NOTE

This story was originally released in 2014 by another publisher. This edition has been revised and re-edited with the end result being a better, stronger story.

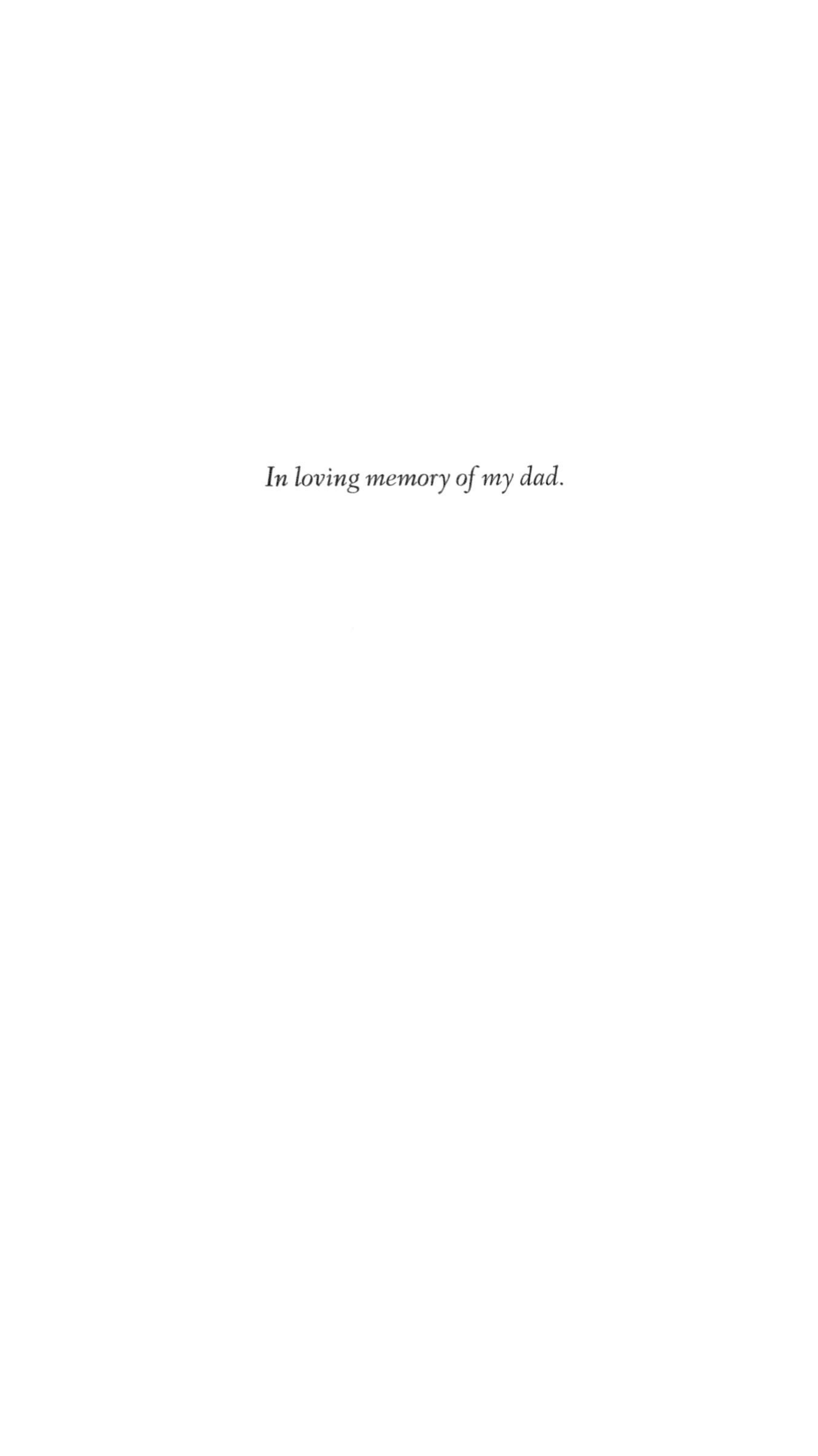

In loving memory of my dad.

ACKNOWLEDGMENTS

To Elizabeth, for all the hours we've spent brainstorming this series, and for beta reading. The Sleepless City grew from a chat we had about the fact we both had vampires we wanted to write more for. I've enjoyed the opportunity to let our guys interact.

To my writing and reading communities for your support and friendship, in particular RWNZ, and my Facebook groups Anne's Books and Brews, and Kiwi Authors Rainbow Readers. A special thanks to the New Zealand Rainbow Romance Writers group—you guys rock.

N.R. Walker for offering to format for me, and going above and beyond.

T.L. Bland for her wonderful cover art.

Desi for editing.

To my beta readers: Susanne, Ann, Lisa, Angela, Sharon, Calli, and Belinda. I appreciated all the time you've put into this story.

To my family. Love you

And last, but in no way least my friends at Upper Hutt Science Fiction Club and Hutt City Libraries.

CHAPTER ONE

"Ben? You there?"

"Yeah, just give me a minute, will you?" Ben Leyton called over his shoulder in the general direction of his laptop. He finished pouring milk into his tea and peered out the window for a moment. The street below was quiet and dark, apart from the soft glow of the streetlight in front of the bookshop.

"So how's it going?" Ange Duncan grinned at him from the computer screen. She'd always been one of his constants, a close friend he could talk stuff through with. They'd met at university, and something had clicked between them. "Not keeping you from your beauty sleep, I hope?"

"Nah, it's fine. You know I'm a night owl." Ben took a sip of his tea. Despite the time difference between the States and New Zealand, he and Ange had managed to keep up their regular Skype chats. During the six weeks he'd been in Boggslake, they'd tried different times before settling on late night for him, which worked out to be late afternoon for her. They both had flexible schedules that tended to shift a bit, so some weeks they caught up more than others.

"How's work going?"

"Fine." Ben rolled his eyes. "Well, fine, apart from Melanie. I swear I don't know how that woman got a job working in a café. Her social skills are zilch. One of the customers complained last week, and the boss had a word with her. She was over-the-top friendly for a couple of days before she started to revert."

Ange laughed, her gray eyes twinkling. "I think most work places have a Melanie, Ben, although so far we've been lucky." Ange worked at a community library part-time while studying for her PhD in anthropology at Victoria University in Wellington. "But mostly it's okay, yeah?"

"Yeah. It's sweet as."

"Apart from everyone asking you sweet as what?" Ange had been amused when she'd heard about that one. He'd had to explain the phrase the first time he'd used it. It was the little things that still tripped him up on occasion, although he was getting there slowly.

"I've got some of the locals using it now." Ben grinned. "Once I told them that there's no comparison, and that's the point, they thought it was pretty awesome." He sighed ruefully. "I suppose it makes up for all the stuff I've had to learn. I had no idea serving coffee could be so complicated." He'd referred to coffee with creamer his first day on the job as a flat white. The woman had looked at him blankly and asked why he was talking about house paint.

Ange pulled a face. "I don't blame you for taking your coffee black. The very idea of creamer, or cream for that matter..." She shuddered.

"I'm told it tastes good, but I can't get my head around

it," Ben agreed. Although he could ask for milk if he wanted, he didn't see the point in making a fuss.

"Hey, I got those photos you sent. I'll print them out later in the week and go see your granddad to make sure it's the right place."

"Thanks." Although many people traveled around a lot during their overseas experience—usually referred to as an OE—Ben had decided to settle in one place for a while and then go from there. Boggslake, a smallish city by Lake Erie in Ohio, seemed a good place, especially as his granddad had visited there years ago and spoke highly of it. "It looks the same to me, but it's hard to tell, as the trees would have grown quite a bit since the fifties. Granddad never mentioned the plaque on the park bench, so I included a close-up of it. I reckon that will help."

When Ben first became interested in photography, his grandfather encouraged it and loaned him his old camera to practice his skills. Before he'd left for Boggslake, Granddad gave him a copy of a black-and-white photograph taken in a park there. The use of light and shadows in it had fascinated Ben, and since his arrival, he'd spent a lot of time taking his own photos of that same park, playing around with different settings and effects. Spending time there also reminded him of his grandfather, with whom he'd always been close. Ben hadn't expected the homesickness to hit him this hard. Knowing he was somewhere his grandfather had once been helped in a weird sort of way. Sometimes he closed his eyes and just listened to the wind, pretending he was still home in New Zealand.

About a week ago, he'd reopened his eyes to catch a glimpse of someone watching him. He'd blinked, not sure whether he'd imagined it or not, but when he looked again, the guy was gone.

"Ben?" Ange's voice pulled him back to reality.

"Yeah, sorry. Just thinking for a moment."

The next night had confirmed Ben's imagination hadn't gone into overdrive. But as before, when he tried to make some kind of contact, the guy had disappeared. He seemed to have some serious ninja skills, and it was frustrating Ben no end. The few glimpses he'd had were of a brown-haired man of slim build, well-dressed, and very sexy.

"You've found someone and you haven't told me?" Ange teased him. She sobered slightly. "I hope you're being careful, Ben, and not having long conversations with strange men you don't know."

"I wouldn't do that!" Ben retorted indignantly.

"Yeah sure, of course you wouldn't." Ange rolled her eyes. "I've known you since we were both at uni, Ben. You talk to *everyone*."

"Do not!" He took another sip of tea, grabbed a chocolate biscuit out of the packet on the table, and dunked it in his drink. Perhaps he needed to approach this from a different angle. If the guy was determined to keep his distance, it didn't mean Ben couldn't at least take a photograph of him. Although it wasn't very logical or sensible, not knowing who this guy was and why he kept hanging around nagged at him. It wasn't just when he was at the park taking his photos either, which was one of the reasons he made sure he swung by that particular spot each night as he made his way around the wider area. But why was the guy always at the same place in the park? Perhaps because it was the first place they'd seen each other? It was as good an explanation as any.

"Don't give me that look." Ange had that intense expression on her face, which meant she was thinking. "You'd tell me if you were in any trouble, right?"

"I'm not in any trouble, Ange. Honest." Ben licked the tea off his biscuit, then popped the rest of it into his mouth. "And for your information, there's nothing wrong in making conversation. The customers at work aren't complaining, and it's a good way of learning about people, especially as I'm so far away from home." He attempted a pathetic kind of puppy dog expression.

She poked her tongue out. "Okay, whatever. I'm allowed to worry about you, though. That's what friends do." Her tone softened. "I miss you, you know."

"Yeah, I know." He smiled. "I miss you too."

The guy was there again. Ben was sure of it, though he was not going to draw attention to the fact he knew. He glanced around, trying to keep his demeanor as nonchalant as possible while he adjusted his camera.

He took a step back and to the side, making a show of being interested in one of the bushes to his left, held up his camera, then quickly spun on his heel and snapped several photos in succession.

Huh? The park bench was empty.

But the guy had been sitting there just a moment before. Ben could have sworn he'd seen him out of the corner of his eye just before he'd taken the photo. He scowled and checked his camera screen. Yep, the bench was empty. In reality and on film, or at least what passed for film in the age of digital cameras.

Wonderful.

"Fucking hell," Ben muttered under his breath. He grabbed his backpack and sat down heavily on the offending bench. Puffs of white floated in the air when he exhaled.

His jacket wasn't quite enough to keep out the cold, so he rummaged around in his bag for his thermos and pulled it out. Hot coffee would hit the spot perfectly and give him time to think about his next move.

The guy had to be somewhere near, right? Ben sighed and took a welcome sip of coffee. This was crazy. What if Well-Dressed and Sexy was some kind of stalker?

If he was, what did that make Ben?

"Is this seat taken?"

Ben looked up from his coffee and nearly choked when he saw who had spoken. "No," he managed to splutter as he struggled to catch his breath.

"My apologies," said the guy Ben had tried to photograph earlier, his casual tone implying the way he disappeared and reappeared, seemingly out of nowhere, wasn't unusual. "I didn't mean to startle you."

"You didn't," Ben said, then amended it at the raised eyebrow he got in response. "Well, yeah, you did."

His companion chuckled. "Unless you're in the habit of choking on your coffee?" He sniffed the air. "It smells good, so I'm presuming it wasn't the taste."

"Yeah, it does, and no, it wasn't." Ben mentally kicked himself for sounding so lame. Up close, it was harder to ignore his body's interest in the man sitting next to him. The English accent wasn't helping. Ben had always had a thing for English accents. He gripped his cup firmly in his left hand and held out his right. "Ben Leyton."

They'd been watching each other for nearly a week, so it seemed silly not to introduce himself. He ignored the warning whisper in the back of his mind that he'd maybe just given his name to some kind of stalker.

"Simon Hawthorne." Simon shook Ben's hand briefly, then shoved both his gloved hands into the pockets of his thick woolen coat. It looked expensive, as did the scarf and trousers he wore. Simon glanced down for a moment before clearing his throat, nearly catching Ben in the act of examining his equally expensive boots. When he looked up, Ben got a good look at brown eyes, several shades lighter than his own.

They stared at each other before Simon turned away. Ben gripped his cup tighter to hide his nervousness. It would be so easy to lose himself in those eyes.

This was crazy. He didn't usually fall for guys this fast. The only other time it had happened had been a total disaster, and he'd made an idiot of himself. "You're not from around here, are you?" Ben said finally. Simon frowned rather than answering, so Ben elaborated. "The accent, I mean. You're English."

"Oh," Simon said, "right. That. I was born in England, yes, but I haven't been there in many years. Boggslake is my home now."

"You must have moved here when you were a kid, then." Ben flushed, aware that Simon was staring at him in what appeared to be amusement. "I mean, you don't look that old, younger than I am, anyway."

So much for coming across as smooth and sophisticated. If Simon's upper-class accent and clothes were any indication, he was way out of Ben's league.

"I'm a lot older than I look," Simon said. "According to my driver's license, I'm in my thirties." Ben had been way off on that guess. He would have put Simon in his early twenties, perhaps younger.

"According to mine, I'm twenty-five," Ben countered, copying Simon's weird way of putting it. "You're not taking the piss, are you?"

"Excuse me?" Simon's eyes widened.

"You're not making fun of me, are you?" Ben translated. He should have known better than to use the expression, especially as it wasn't the first time he'd been asked to explain what it meant.

Simon shook his head. "No, I wouldn't do that. Thank you for the explanation, but I am familiar with the expression." He frowned, as though puzzled by the accusation.

Ben was definitely missing something about this conversation. "Look, maybe we need to get a few things straight," he said quickly. "You've been watching me. Why?"

"I... noticed you a few weeks ago." Simon shrugged. "I was curious." He paused for a moment, as though collecting his thoughts. "At the risk of being forward, I was wondering if I might buy you a coffee sometime, to make up for the fact I made you choke on yours."

"Are you asking me on a date?"

"I'm asking you out for coffee." Simon hesitated. "Unless I've got completely the wrong end of the stick, and if I have, I apologize."

"You haven't." Ben took a deep breath. "Got the wrong end of the stick, I mean. Coffee sounds great. Thanks." Something else Simon had said suddenly registered. "You said you noticed me a few weeks ago. I only spotted you about a week ago. Have you been watching me this whole time?"

"No." Simon shook his head. He shifted back toward the edge of the bench, putting a little more distance between them. "I've been... indisposed." He smiled a little at Ben's concerned expression. "Don't worry. It's nothing you can catch. Not now."

There was sadness, almost resignation, in his smile. Ben reached over instinctively and placed a hand on Simon's arm. Simon flinched, and although he didn't ask Ben to remove his hand, Ben did anyway.

"How long have you been in Boggslake?" Simon asked finally, a little too brightly. "You're not from around here either, are you?" He took his hands out of his pockets and placed them on his lap. "I've been trying to place your accent, but I can't."

"It's Kiwi." Ben laughed at Simon's blank look. "I'm from New Zealand. I've been here about six weeks. Finished my degree and decided to do the OE thing and see the world. My granddad spent some time here years ago, and I was curious to see the place for myself. I reckon I can always travel a bit farther afield once I've been here a while. It's as good a starting point as any."

"OE?"

"Overseas experience." Ben wondered how much time he was going to have to spend on explanations. Although he'd had a fair share of them since he arrived, this conversation was already beginning to set a record.

"You're a photographer." Simon seemed more relaxed than he'd been when they started talking. "I noticed your camera before. It's one of those newfangled computer things, isn't it?"

"Yeah, it's a digital. You don't know much about cameras, do you?" Ben fished it out of his bag and held it out for Simon to look at. Usually he wouldn't let anyone near his precious camera, but he had the feeling Simon would be careful with it. "Photography's not my day job. More of a hobby, but I'd like to do something with it, maybe sell some stuff to one of the local papers." He took a deep breath. "I'd love to get good enough to have something accepted for *National Geographic*, but that's probably a bit of a pipe dream. For now, I'm focusing on playing around with different effects, and twilight's good for interesting shots."

"If that's what you want to do, you should pursue it. Dreams are important." Simon took off his gloves and turned the camera over in his hand, examining it closely. His fingers were long and well manicured, his skin tone rather on the pale side, although not unhealthily so. "It's very small," he said. "My telephone has a camera in it, supposedly, but I've never used it. It took me long enough just to work out how to answer the damn thing."

"I can probably show you if you want," Ben offered.

"Don't you get tired of taking pictures at this time of day?" Simon handed Ben back his camera. "Everything's much the same, just different shades of gray and brown, especially once the light starts fading."

"I like that kind of thing." Ben shrugged. "Besides, that's when it gets interesting. Here, look, I'll show you." He brought up the menu screen and went back through the last few shots he'd taken. "See how the light through the trees is different between this picture and the one before it? It changes the whole feel of it, as though they've suddenly got a different story to tell. That's what I like about this stuff, the stories behind the pictures."

Simon leaned in closer. His fingers brushed Ben's. They were cold, but not unpleasantly so. A warm tingle ran through Ben where they'd touched. "I've never heard anyone talk about photography like this before, although I can see what you mean." He glanced up at the trees above them and then again at the picture on the screen. "It's like when you play a piece of music and let yourself feel it. Really feel it. That's what you're doing with the lighting, isn't it? You're varying the timbre, but instead of sound, you're using images."

Ben blinked. "I've never thought of it that way, but it makes sense, yeah."

"Sorry." Simon seemed embarrassed. "I don't usually put those kinds of thoughts into words." He reached for his gloves.

"You should do it more often," Ben told him. It had been a while since someone had got what he was trying to do, and he'd missed this kind of conversation. "Are you a musician?"

"Not a professional one, but I do play, yes." Simon smiled. "Piano. Classical mostly, although I occasionally like to play a bit of jazz. My uncle taught me many years ago."

"My grandfather plays. He's good too. He tried to teach me, but I suck at it. I prefer to listen." Ben ventured another question, hoping he wasn't being too nosy. "Do you see much of your uncle?"

"He's dead." Simon's expression flattened, as did his voice. He pulled on his gloves and started to stand. "He died a long time ago."

"I'm sorry. I shouldn't have asked, especially as we've only just met. It was rude of me." It was obvious he'd encroached onto a subject that was best avoided, although Simon had been the one to mention his uncle in the first place.

"It's fine, and you weren't," Simon said, but he avoided Ben's eyes. "I'd still—"

Ben's phone interrupted Simon. He ignored it, but apparently the damage was done.

"Is that your telephone? Perhaps you should answer. It might be urgent."

"It's just a text. She can wait." Ange had thought it funny to program his phone to play the opening bars of

"Slice of Heaven." At least it only did it when it was her number. The rest of the time it behaved itself with its original ringtone. She'd also pointed out that if he hated the sound of it that much, he could always set his phone on silent, a suggestion he'd chosen to ignore.

Simon's eyebrow rose. "She?" Something indecipherable crossed his face. "You should answer it. Ladies take offense if dismissed without good reason."

Ladies?

That sounded more like something Ben's granddad would say, rather than somebody Simon's age. He definitely had an old-fashioned streak about him.

"Okay, but can you get out your phone? We can trade numbers." Ben couldn't help but grin at Simon's blank expression. "I'll give you my mobile number so you can contact me. You promised me coffee, yeah?"

"Oh, right." Simon frowned. "I don't know how to do that. I was going to give you my card."

"Your card?" Ben retrieved his phone and flipped it open. He read the text and quickly sent a reply. "It's Ange," he explained. "We're going to Skype later, and she's letting me know she's going to be a bit late." No harm in letting Simon know he was expected somewhere later and would be missed if he wasn't there. Weirdly, Ben didn't get the feeling he had anything to worry about in that regard with Simon. His gut feeling told him Simon was someone he could trust, but he had no clue why.

Simon fished a phone out of his pocket and handed it to Ben. He then took out his wallet and gave him a card. "It's my business card," he explained. "In case my students need to contact me."

"Students?" Ben kicked himself for repeating what Simon had said yet again. He hoped he didn't sound too much of a dork. Glancing down at the card, he read it twice to make sure he hadn't made a mistake the first time. "*Professor* Hawthorne? Seriously?"

"I told you I'm much older than I look. I teach history at the university." Simon nodded toward his phone. "You were going to give me your telephone number."

"Oh yeah." Ben found the menu on Simon's phone and thumbed through different screens till he found the right one. "Nice phone." It was way out of Ben's price range and probably always would be.

"Thank you. My friend Forge persuaded me to buy it." Simon shrugged. "He's determined to drag me into the twenty-first century, however much I resist it." He lowered his voice. "I must admit, though, it is useful to be able to be contacted on occasion."

Ben reopened his own phone. "Your mobile isn't on your card, so I'm adding it to mine. That okay?"

"Of course. I was going to write it on the back of the card if you'd wanted it." Simon watched what Ben was doing with some interest. "You make it look very easy. Have you used one like this before?"

"I looked into them once, before I bought mine." He'd wanted to do his homework on everything out there, even the stuff he couldn't afford. "A friend had one and let me play around with it. They're quite user-friendly once you know what you're doing."

"That comment only serves to confirm that I have no clue what I'm doing with the blasted thing. Do you use your telephone to—" Simon stumbled over the word. "—Skype with your friend?"

"I prefer to use my laptop for that. The screen's bigger, and our conversations tend to go for a bit." Ben grinned.

"I'm thinking this Forge is right. You seriously need dragging into this century."

Simon scowled. "There's nothing wrong with being a little old-fashioned," he said, retrieving his phone.

"I kind of like it, actually," Ben admitted. He bit back the part about how having a mix of the two was better when he saw Simon's smile. It lit up his face, and there was a twinkle in his eye that hadn't been there before. Ben shifted slightly, glad he was wearing a long bulky jacket. "So," he said, his voice hoarser than he intended. "You'll phone me about meeting for coffee, then?"

"Yes." Simon studied him for a moment, then shoved his hands back into his pockets. "Or you could contact me?" He sounded almost hopeful.

"Okay." Ben went to grab his pack, stopping when a thought struck him. "Hey, before you go, could I ask you something?"

"Yes, of course."

"Can I take a photo of you?" Ben knew he shouldn't have asked as soon as he said it. He could have sworn he glimpsed something akin to fear in Simon's eyes, but then it was gone, to be replaced by a cold, flat expression.

"No." Simon shook his head. "I don't... photograph." He spun on his heel, and when Ben looked up again after hefting his pack onto his back, Simon was gone.

Ben sighed and mentally rolled his eyes. "I just wanted a picture," he muttered, not sure who he was annoyed with more, himself or Simon. "What is it with you and photographs? Anyone would think I was trying to steal your soul."

He hadn't handled that at all well. Simon stomped through the park toward the exit, his booted feet crunching dry leaves. He stopped to kick a stone, not realizing how much force he'd put behind the action until he heard it plop loudly into the pond some distance away.

Damn it!

The conversation with Ben had gone quite successfully, considering Simon had had to sidestep several questions he couldn't answer. Couldn't answer or wasn't prepared to?

Simon snorted. He didn't want to venture onto that subject just yet. If he could avoid it altogether, that would be just fine with him, although logically he knew it would have to come up sooner or later. He just wanted time to get to know Ben, to be sure he was the one before telling him the truth.

The wrought-iron park gates loomed just ahead. They were like him in a way, old-fashioned and left over from another age. He sat down on the bench just inside the park and closed his eyes for a moment, trying to pull his thoughts together.

But it wasn't just his thoughts that were the problem, was it? Simon groaned and shifted uncomfortably. Fuck, he was hard; more so since he'd accidently brushed his hand against Ben's. He'd thought he was going to come there and then for a moment, with the rush of excitement and need that had coursed through him.

Who was he trying to fool? Ben was definitely the one—Simon's soulmate. He'd been with other men before, but it had never felt like this. Hell, he and Ben hadn't even slept together yet. Their kind didn't react like this otherwise, at least not to this extreme, and Simon definitely didn't.

His thoughts wandered, his desires playing out in his mind. Kissing Ben, running his fingers through Ben's thick black hair. Simon groaned aloud, imagining undressing Ben, stroking his chest, tangling his fingers through more of that dark hair, Ben meeting his gaze, moaning softly as Simon grazed his neck with the tips of his fangs.

Simon loved touching, especially silky strands of thick hair under his fingers, against his tongue. His previous lovers had had dark hair like Ben, although Ben's eyes were a deeper shade of brown than either Stephen's or Albert's. Ben seemed so alive and excited about life, sharing his thoughts and dreams as though they were already lovers, instead of strangers who had only just met.

Other images flooded Simon's mind, jarring him back to reality, memories cutting through the moment, slicing apart the fantasy he wanted so badly. He opened his eyes quickly, wanting to be rid of them.

It was safe now.

Wasn't it?

Stephen lying in a pool of blood, his eyes open and staring, the sounds of shell fire breaking the silence of the still night air as Simon dropped to his knees in horror.

Years later, another World War had tempted him to lower his guard, to let someone in, only to rediscover all too clearly the consequences of doing so.

Albert screaming, calling for help, his breath choking off in a horrible gurgling sound as Simon arrived too late, just in time to see his lover's body slump in the arms of a man who was more monster than human.

"I'm not yours, John," he'd yelled at the vampire who had made him. Simon had grabbed Albert, claiming him, holding him close. "I don't want you. Leave me alone!"

Simon had vowed no more after Albert. He couldn't do this, couldn't allow anyone else to be hurt. Wouldn't let himself love, only to lose again.

Then why had he spoken to Ben? He should have stayed away, taken the fact he'd first seen Ben at the one time of year they couldn't be together as a hint from the universe, and carried on with his life. Their relationship had no future. Even if Simon's maker hadn't been heard of in fifty years, it didn't change the rather big difference between them.

Ben was human. Simon wasn't. Not anymore. No matter how much he wanted to pretend he was.

He hadn't lied when he'd told Ben his driver's license said he was in his thirties. It did, even if he wasn't. Physically, he was twenty-two. He had been for nearly one hundred years.

The town clock struck the hour, eight times.

This was ridiculous. He didn't have time to brood like this, to dwell on the past. It was dead and gone. Nor did he have the right to give in to a fantasy that would never be. What had he been thinking? He didn't do this, hadn't done this for a very long time. Pulling himself together, Simon strode briskly through the park gates and headed for home. A familiar hunger pulled at him. Perhaps that was what this was? He hadn't fed properly since the day before, so of course he'd be very aware of any human close to him. Ben's skin had been warm and inviting, his heartbeat, for the most part, steady.

For the most part? Ben's heartbeat and his breathing had sped up minutely when they'd touched. Perhaps the attraction was mutual? Unless Ben was in the habit of talking to strangers and accepting invitations to meet for coffee?

If he still wanted to do that after the way Simon had left. Stupid. He'd been so stupid. In allowing Ben to take his picture in the first place and then in telling him he couldn't be photographed. At least Ben didn't seem to realize Simon *had* been in front of the camera and he already had the picture he'd sought.

Why the fuck did Ben have to be a photographer? Even if they did see each other again, how long could Simon evade that particular issue?

Vampires didn't photograph. They didn't show up on film or on camera, so the fact Ben had one of those newfangled digital ones wouldn't make a darn bit of difference.

Edgelake Street and Boggs's Castle greeted him sooner than he expected. His thoughts had distracted him to the point he hadn't realized he was almost home. Walking had been a good idea. It had given him time to think, although it was doubtful his frustration would go entirely unnoticed. His friends were far too observant for that.

The word made Simon smile, despite his mood. The last fifty years had been good, apart from his bouts of loneliness. He had a home here in Boggslake, a job he loved, and people he dared to call friends. He'd take a deep breath and carry on. Just like he always had.

CHAPTER TWO

Simon's key in the door was greeted by silence, although he knew the other occupants of the castle would have heard it quite clearly. Just as they heard everything else that went on, even if they were too polite to mention it. Acute hearing had its disadvantages, but it was worth putting up with for the edge it provided.

Even if Forge did insist in playing that noise he called music far too loudly at times.

Muffled voices wafted through the heavy wooden door at the bottom of the stairs. Simon cocked his head for a moment, listening to snatches of conversation, his interest piqued. He removed his coat and scarf and hung them carefully on the coat stand by the front door before making his way into the kitchen they shared.

He swallowed, tasting saliva, and opened the fridge to study its contents. He'd eaten dinner before leaving the university, although he hadn't needed to. Human food, while enjoyable, didn't do much to satisfy him, especially when the steak was well cooked. He'd lost track of how many times he'd ordered it very rare, and doubted any comments about how the best part of it was the blood dripping onto his plate would be well received. Juliet, the teaching assistant the university insisted he needed, had for some reason decided it was part of her job description to ensure he ate properly.

It was annoying in some ways, but she meant well and stopped nagging him if he gave in, so for the most part, he made sure to eat at least some of his meals where she'd see him. He wasn't about to tell her that "feeding him up" was not going to make him put on weight, or give him the nourishment he required.

Something flecked in a mix of gray and red stared back at him from the fridge. Simon startled for a moment before peering at it more closely. Yes, those were definitely eyes. Was that fur? No, it was mold growing underneath the plastic wrap. Not for the first time, Simon was tempted to just buy Lucas a fridge of his very own and have it delivered to the top floor. His last polite suggestion had earned a confused look from Lucas. His experiments were well wrapped and not doing anyone any harm, he'd said, and this way he'd remember to keep an eye on them and chart their progress.

"One of the joys of living with the city medical examiner," Simon muttered under his breath. He decided to ignore what were probably bona fide leftovers on the same shelf, as they were also turning a strange green color.

The items on the next shelf down were in stark contrast to the one above. Everything was neatly packaged and well organized, and there was an assortment of different meats, vegetables, and salad foods. Two of each, but that was nothing new. Forge had been talking about doing the rounds of the sales on his way home from work.

Simon's shelf was almost empty, apart from something

that looked suspiciously like Lucas had left it there. He poked at whatever it was, then reached for the carton of milk. Eating wasn't appealing at present, and he only really needed to satisfy his hunger. He filled a glass with milk and ice cubes retrieved from the freezer. Chicken blood today, as he'd had beef yesterday. At least this way he could honestly tell Juliet he had a balanced diet.

A quick mix with a spoon had combined the two ingredients well enough, although the ice cubes were still crunchy. One of these days he'd go to the trouble of using the blender Forge had bought, but truth be known, Simon really couldn't be bothered. While Forge might enjoy his meals sprinkled with the frozen blood cubes and pretending they were icy croutons, Simon didn't see the point. He preferred to eat his food without the garnish of blood and get what he needed to survive this way. The taste of blood and milk together had grown on him over the years, and despite certain other people's rolling of eyes and expletives of disgust, it was better than what he'd had to do in the past to get his quota of animal blood in order to staunch his hunger.

He sipped his makeshift meal and headed for the basement.

"Hey, Simon." Lucas Coate glanced up when Simon walked into the room. He was sitting at his desk, peering at a collection of photographs. "Didn't get lucky, huh?"

"Like I'd tell you if I did." Simon looked over Lucas's shoulder to see what had got his attention. "You've received some new information about the case?"

He, Lucas, and Forge worked together investigating incidents connected to the supernatural community in Boggslake. Although supernaturals were not supposed to harm others of their kind, or humans, there were some who needed a firm reminder of that fact. Some of them also appeared to have missed the memo that they weren't supposed to flaunt their existence in front of humans. One thing Simon had learned very quickly after becoming a vampire was that, like humans, supernatural beings were both good, bad, and everything in-between.

Lucas grinned. "You did! I knew it!" He leaned back in his chair. "So Tall Dark and Sexy decided to talk to you, then? Or did you talk to him?" He sniffed at Simon, the photographs he'd been looking at quickly forgotten in light of something apparently much more interesting. "Did he touch you, or did you touch him? I can smell him on you." He repeated the action. "Yep, you smell faintly of human, and it's not someone I recognize."

"You honestly think he's going to answer that?" Jonas Forge asked from the desk next to Lucas's. He kept typing, his attention still focused on the screen in front of him. "Besides, the guy isn't tall. He's three inches shorter than Simon." Simon wasn't exactly lacking in height at six foot, but Lucas had an inch on him, and Forge had three.

"You ran a background check on him?" Simon didn't bother trying to sound surprised, as that would be a lie. Of course Forge had. It was his way of caring, or so he claimed. Some days he could swear Forge reminded him of the older brother he'd lost when the *Titanic* had gone down, but he'd never tell Forge that. Simon knew he should be touched by the gesture and thankful for Forge's centuries of experience, but occasionally, it could also be damn annoying.

"Yep." Forge frowned, his fingers still moving over his keyboard. "You've been drooling over this guy for weeks. Someone had to do something."

"You'll share, of course?" Lucas's ears visibly pricked up. His reaction got the attention of Forge's dog, Moose, who raised his head and barked but didn't move off his makeshift bed in the corner.

"I'm not sharing him," Simon said quickly before Lucas got any further into the idea.

"I meant the information, Simon. Honestly, what sort of guy do you think I am?" Lucas blinked, his eyes widening, his smile adding to the picture of innocence that still fooled most people who didn't know him. It was a practiced look and always reminded Simon of an overgrown puppy. Lucas was in his midthirties, although his unkempt hair, scruffy beard, and perpetual earnest expression made him look a lot younger.

"You're a horny werewolf," Forge answered dryly. He was older than both of them, having been turned during the Battle of Point Pleasant during the eighteenth century. Physically, he was in his early thirties. "You've been trying to convince Simon to go for a threesome with this guy since you first found out about him. Why change the habits of a lifetime now?"

"I'm wounded," sniffed Lucas. He brightened. "But hey, it was worth a go, right?"

"It's not going to happen," Simon confirmed. It was bad enough the two of them had teased him since they found out the reason he'd been going to the park every evening, but trying to keep secrets from them had never been easy. Both of them worked for the Boggslake Police Department, Lucas splitting his duties between the morgue and the field, Forge as a detective.

The air around them seemed to grow thicker for a moment before a middle-aged man in an immaculate white suit appeared in front of them, seemingly out of nowhere. "I'm sure Simon will introduce you to his young man when it is the proper time to do so. He still needs some time to court him properly. Such things should not be rushed."

"Thank you, Mr. Boggs." Simon inclined his head toward the ghost in thanks. There were times when Boggs was most definitely the voice of reason in comparison to Forge and Lucas, and Simon appreciated his support.

"Of course," Boggs continued with a smile, "once you and Mr. Leyton are officially courting, I will remind you that introductions are in order."

Had Simon been the last one to discover Ben's name? It was a rhetorical question. Not much went on without Boggs knowing about it.

"Of course," Simon confirmed, shooting a glare in Lucas's direction when his grin widened. If Forge could be thought of at times to be in the role of older brother, Boggs was definitely inclined to act as though he was their father. He was the ghost of one of the city's founders, and although they knew his first name, they always addressed him as Mr. Boggs. The castle had originally been his, and he was an important member of their team.

"Hey, listen to this." Forge tapped a couple of keys on his computer. "Switching on to audio, Blair, and putting you on speaker. Could you repeat what you just told me, please?"

"It's Alucard," Blair reminded him in a tetchy voice. He was a gifted computer hacker. Forge had tried to get in touch with a former FBI contact during a previous case, only to discover he'd died. His son, Blair, had come through with the information Forge had needed and worked for them ever since. He handled everything digital, while Simon took care of the more traditional sources of information. The university archives had proved very beneficial to several investigations, and between the two of them they had access to a wide range of resources. "How are we supposed to keep the whole secret identity thing secret if you keep using my real name?"

"Uh-huh." Forge grinned. He didn't switch on the computer's built-in camera. There was no point, as Lucas was the only one who would show up on it. Blair had never questioned their conversations being audio only, which was surprising considering the user name he'd chosen for himself was Dracula spelled backward. They'd all rolled their eyes, but Blair didn't seem to have figured out he was working with two vampires, a werewolf, and a ghost.

"Hey, guys," Blair continued, "everyone there in the Bat Cave?"

Simon felt a nerve under his eye twitch. Why, oh, why had that ridiculous name stuck when Blair had suggested it? Or worse still, why had Forge admitted they didn't have a name for their center of operations?

"Yeah, we're all here," Lucas called out. "How's it going, Blair?"

"Hi, Lucas. Great." Blair paused. "Well, not really. This case feels like it's two steps forward and one back."

"What do you have for us, Blair?" Simon asked before Blair decided to go off on a tangent, as he sometimes did.

"As I was just telling Forge, I've been looking for connections between the victims, and I thought I found something, but then it hit a dead end." Blair let out a sigh. "This case is a weird one, with the bodies always found together in pairs, so I figured I'd see if the sets of victims knew each other even indirectly. They don't."

He'd already told them that, so it couldn't be the information Forge thought they needed to hear.

"So anyway," Blair continued, "I dug a bit deeper and found out that some of the victims were blood donors."

"That's a step forward, yes?" Simon asked.

"Yeah, it would be, but that's just some of them. So even if someone was accessing those kinds of databases to choose these guys, it doesn't explain the ones who aren't."

Part of that explanation would most likely be that, while one of each pair of victims was human, the other was a vampire, but that was information Blair was not privy to and didn't need to be. Vampires also gave blood so there would be some available when they got injured in case they needed a transfusion, but the vampire blood bank records were only accessible to a select few.

"You still haven't told Simon and Lucas the other thing you told me," Forge prompted Blair.

"Oh yeah, sorry." Blair cleared his throat. "After hitting a dead end in Boggslake—crap, sorry, that kind of slipped out. I didn't mean any disrespect to the people who have died, you know?" He sounded very young all of a sudden.

"It's fine, Blair," Simon told him. "Keeping going, please."

"Yeah, okay. Thanks." When Blair spoke again, he sounded more confident. "Anyway, I got to thinking what if what's happening in Boggslake has happened in other places, so I did some more digging and found something interesting. About six months ago, there were half a dozen unsolved murders in Seattle."

"That's the same number there's been here," Forge said. "You think it might be the same guy? Seattle's the other end of the country. Why come here next?"

"If I was murdering people and the authorities were closing in, I'd want to get as far away from the original crime scene as I could," Boggs pointed out, although Blair wouldn't be able to hear him. He frowned. "If this isn't his first time, this killer is far more dangerous and organized than we first thought."

"That's the weird thing," Blair said. "You guys have two bodies found at each crime scene, right? In Seattle there's only one, or so someone wants us to believe." He paused dramatically. "I found something I think proves someone's been covering things up, and there were actually two."

"What makes you think that?" Lucas asked. There were other cells such as their own, who had taken it upon themselves to work together to keep the population of their city, human and otherwise, safe from supernatural threats. Supernatural beings, just like humans, were both good and bad, and often abused the power they possessed. Seattle's supernatural community had a reputation for cleaning up fast and efficiently. If Blair had found something they'd missed, his research skills were impressive.

"A couple of police photographers put their gear in to get checked because they were convinced their equipment was faulty. Not just the cameras were gone over thoroughly but some of the shots they'd taken. I found the reports. One of the photographers was super insistent something weird was going on, although I couldn't find exactly what. Apparently he'd taken a film camera to one of the crime scenes and developed the photos himself."

Most photographers who attempted to photograph vampires and questioned the results were usually persuaded to dismiss their suspicions. In Boggslake, it usually never got that far, as they'd learned to contact Lucas to let him know there was another one of those "weird things" he was interested in. Mostly they seemed happy to leave it to him to investigate further. Those who weren't, quickly changed their mind.

"What happened to this guy and his photos?" asked Forge.

"That's the weird thing," Blair told him. "After pushing for answers, he suddenly decided he'd made a mistake. Then about a month later, he took off with his family on vacation to stay with his wife's sister in San Francisco. I took a look through his financial records. This guy was in debt. One of his kids had been sick, and he was struggling to pay the medical bills. Someone took care of it anonymously, with a bit extra."

"You think he was paid to keep quiet about whatever he saw?" Simon asked. "I have a colleague in Seattle. I'll contact him and see if he knows anything." Ray was a vampire who taught history at one of the high schools in Seattle. They'd met briefly during a case in the fifties.

"You have contacts in Seattle too?" Blair asked. He'd already learned enough to have worked out they had contacts they could call on outside Boggslake, so no harm in confirming it.

"Yes," Simon said.

"Cool. I knew you guys were like the Justice League or something."

Lucas laughed. "I was going more for the Legion of Super Heroes, actually."

"Yeah, but the League has Batman in it," Blair began, "and the Legion is—" Luckily, whatever he was going to say was interrupted by the sound of a telephone ringing. Once he and Lucas started on one of their comics conversations, they'd go for what seemed forever.

"Aren't you going to answer that?" Forge asked Simon.

"What?" Simon glanced around for the source of the noise. He didn't get telephone calls and presumed it was coming from wherever Blair was.

"You're the only one around here who insists on that horrible ringtone," Forge pointed out, "so it's obviously your phone." He'd complained about it ever since Simon had explained—quite logically he'd thought—that if he was to carry a telephone, it made sense for it to at least sound like one.

"Try your pockets?" said Lucas helpfully.

"Oh, right." Simon fished his telephone out of his pocket. Its screen was flashing with the name of the caller. Simon stared at it.

"You're supposed to answer it, not stare at it," Forge said. "Or have you forgotten how to again?"

"I know how to answer it." Simon poked at the appropriate button, then held the telephone up to his ear. "Simon speaking. How can I help you?"

Forge snickered. Simon glared at him, thought for a moment about retreating to somewhere more private, then realized it would be a waste of time. Damn vampire hearing. Not that werewolves and ghosts were much better.

"Hey, Simon. It's Ben."

Perhaps he was calling to say he'd thought twice about meeting for coffee. But why would he take the time to do that? Surely if that were the case, he'd just not contact Simon again at all?

"Hello, Ben." Simon took a couple of steps toward the door, half turning his back on the other occupants of the room.

"I rang to apologize," Ben said, his words tumbling out over each other.

"Apologize?" Simon frowned. "Why?" If anyone should be apologizing for the way in which their conversation had ended, it should be him.

"I obviously upset you, and I'm sorry."

"You didn't," Simon reassured him. "I overreacted. I do that sometimes." He reached for his glass of milk and took a long drink. Feeling a little calmer, he collected his thoughts before breaking the silence. "Would you still like to meet for coffee?"

Lucas and Forge high-fiving was something best ignored, as was the smug expression on both their faces.

"Yeah, sure, that would be great," Ben answered very quickly. "When and where? I'm working a long shift tomorrow, so that won't work, but I don't start until eleven on Thursday."

After mentally consulting his calendar, Simon nodded. "That would be fine. I don't have lectures on Thursday mornings. Do you know Hunter's on West Thirteenth Street? We could meet there at nine."

"I haven't been there, but I'll find it," Ben said. "See you at nine then on Thursday?"

"Yes. Goodbye, Ben."

"Bye, Ben," called out Lucas.

"Bye." Ben paused. "Hey, who is that?" His voice took on a rather suspicious tone. "Simon, is there someone listening in on us?"

"Unfortunately, yes," Simon said. "I share my... building... with some friends who don't understand the concept of privacy. That was Lucas. I'll explain on Thursday."

"Okay. Bye."

"Goodbye," Simon said again, this time to a darkened telephone. He shoved it back into his pocket.

"He sounds cute," said Lucas. "I like the accent." He grinned. "Can I come too? I want to hear how you explain me."

"As much fun as it will be," Forge said, "I think we probably need to leave Simon to do that on his own. He's a big boy now and doesn't need either of us tagging along."

"Later?" Lucas asked, wearing the puppy dog expression again.

"You guys still there?" Blair interrupted. "What did I miss? Does Simon have a date or something?"

"Or something," Simon mumbled. He grabbed what was left of his milk and headed for the door before Boggs decided to start asking questions about the conversation too. "I have assignments to grade. It's probably going to take the rest of the evening."

Once he reached the relative privacy of the kitchen, he stopped and allowed his thoughts to catch up with him. He loosened his tie and rinsed his now empty glass several times before putting it in the dishwasher. The last time he'd gone on anything resembling a date had been nearly sixty years ago, and that had been a disaster. At least this time his prospective romantic interest wasn't straight—that wasn't a mistake he was in a hurry to make again anytime soon.

Frank hadn't been his soulmate, but despite that, Simon had still allowed his feelings to grow to the point he'd acted upon them to steal a kiss. Frank had been very polite about it, almost apologetic, and at least they'd parted as friends.

He'd lost so many during the years, not only to death, but to time and distance. It was easier not to take those chances, to keep people at arm's length, and to talk about subjects that really didn't matter.

One meeting and he'd already crossed that line with Ben. But being near Ben was different. It was as though the barriers he'd erected were beginning to erode even before they'd met, and he didn't know how to stop it. He'd heard stories about knowing one's soulmate was near, of the overwhelming physical need that came with it, but he hadn't truly believed it.

Until now.

Simon sighed, glad he couldn't see himself reflected in the glass window above the counter. What the hell had he done? Even if this did work out, how would Ben react when he found out what Simon was? As soon as they got close, he wouldn't be able to keep it a secret like he had before, as the soulmate bond would see to that.

He'd have to keep his distance, and his emotions under control. He groaned and leaned heavily against the counter. God, he wanted Ben so badly, wanted to touch and taste him, and it was only going to get worse. He knew it would.

Run. But I'll always catch you. There's no escaping what you are. What I've made you.

A low growl escaped his lips. He felt his fangs start to descend, but this time his hunger wasn't for blood but for something very different.

"Shut up, John," he muttered in response to the memory. "I'm not you. I'm not like you. I'll never be like you."

Simon turned and ran up the stairs into the haven of his apartment and slammed the door. He leaned back against it and closed his eyes.

"I can stay in control. I'm still human. I can do this."

He was meeting a potential friend for coffee. That was all.

Dark brown eyes, crinkling at the edges as Ben smiled. Black hair, curled through his fingers.

A wet kiss, lips parted, inviting.

He crossed the room, opened the lid of his piano, and began to play the first movement of Beethoven's "Moonlight Sonata."

Focus on the music. Focus.

He'd played this sonata so often he knew it by heart.

I suck at it. I prefer to listen.

Simon smiled at the recollection of Ben's words and felt himself begin to calm. His fingers moved over the keys, his emotions taking solace in something familiar, something safe. Although it was in a minor key, he'd always found comfort in the melancholy mood of the piece, especially in the slow, repeated rhythm of the opening.

They were only meeting for coffee. There was no harm in it. They'd share conversation and enjoy each other's company.

His mistakes were in the past. History. And that was where they'd stay.

He wasn't strong enough to walk away. Not again. He wasn't sure he could. This was a compromise, for as long as he could cling to it, until the façade cracked completely and Ben discovered the truth.

Surely it was better to have some time together as friends than an eternity alone.

CHAPTER THREE

Simon glanced at his watch for the third time in as many minutes. Ben was late. They'd arranged to meet at nine, and it was already three minutes past the hour. Had he changed his mind? If he had, Simon wouldn't blame him.

Another check of his telephone confirmed he hadn't missed any calls. Damn it, he should have given Ben's name to Juliet and told her to put him through to the telephone in his office if he'd called. She did have a tendency to screen calls from anyone not on the list he'd already supplied her with. He'd do that when he got into work later, if it wasn't already too late.

The front door of the café opened. Simon heard the almost inaudible click of the door before the bell rang cheerily. He looked up and smiled when Ben stepped across the threshold and looked around. Ben's worried expression quickly changed to a somewhat sheepish grin when he spotted Simon and walked over to his table.

"Sorry I'm late," Ben said, pulling out the chair opposite and sitting down. He was breathing heavily, as though he'd been running. "I got my directions mixed up and ended up in the wrong place."

"It's fine," Simon assured him. "I haven't been here long." He signaled the waitress. "I'll have the usual, please, Carole. What would you like, Ben? Have you eaten?"

"Yeah, I've had breakfast, thanks." Ben peered at the menu for a moment. "I'll have a coffee, please." He pulled out his wallet.

"My treat, remember? I'll take care of the check when we get that far," Simon reminded him. "Thank you, Carole."

"Always a pleasure to see you in here, Professor." Carole smiled at both of them, her gaze lingering for a moment on Ben. "I'll be over with your order very shortly." She was a middle-aged woman and always very polite and friendly.

"Are you a regular?" Ben asked. He brushed a dark strand of hair back from his forehead. Simon watched it flop forward again, seemingly with a mind of its own.

"Yes. The house blend is excellent, and at this hour of the morning, it's usually not too crowded either."

"Good coffee's important," Ben agreed. He wasn't dressed in the jeans Simon was used to seeing him in but instead wore dark trousers. The navy collar of a shirt peeked out over his sweatshirt. He slid the messenger bag he carried onto the floor next to his chair, positioning it so it leaned against one of his legs.

"Do you have far to go from here to get to work?"

Ben shrugged. "It's no biggie now I've worked out where I'm going."

The side of Simon's mouth twitched. "Well, I would hope you know where you work. It's going to make for an interesting day if you don't."

"Yeah, right." Ben rolled his eyes. "So... who is this guy Lucas? You were going to tell me about him. He's your flat-mate or something?"

"You don't waste time on small talk, do you?" Simon was rather pleased about that. He'd had enough of that kind of thing growing up but still found himself falling into the habit a little more easily than he liked.

"I figured we'd chat about the coffee and the weather later and get the other stuff out of the way first." Ben shrugged. "Besides, it's been driving me crazy. His voice sounded kind of familiar, but not enough to place it."

"You think you might have met him?" Simon raised an eyebrow and inwardly groaned. That figured. Ben was good-looking, and Lucas had a tendency to flirt with anyone who took his fancy. Not that Simon held it against him, as it was a part of who and what he was. Werewolves had a very different mindset than humans and vampires when it came to dating, let alone taking a mate.

"I don't know. I meet a lot of people at work. He might have called in once or twice. It was difficult to hear over the phone too." Ben was thoughtful for a moment. "There's a guy called Lucas who comes in every Monday."

"Does he flirt with you?" Simon asked, his eyes narrowing. He felt his fist clench and hurriedly put his hand under the table, where his reaction would be less obvious. "Where do you work?"

A wave of emotion rushed over him, annoyance rising to anger at the idea that someone else would dare flirt with Ben. Simon took several deep breaths and willed himself to calm. They were merely meeting for coffee. He had not claimed Ben as his, nor had they consummated the soul-mate bond. Ben could go out with whomever he wished.

Possessiveness was part of the bond and its drive to mate. Logically, he knew that, but he hadn't expected it to be this strong. Nor this soon. Hell, they hadn't done anything yet.

Nor were they going to.

"He tried, but I told him I wasn't interested." Ben was watching Simon's reaction with interest. He held up his hands. "Hey, I don't make a habit of going out with people I don't know. Besides, he flirts with *everyone*."

"Thank you," Simon said. "I'll take it as a compliment that you made an exception for me."

"Yeah." Ben met Simon's eyes across the table. "I'm not usually one for talking about this kind of stuff with people I don't know either. You're very easy to talk to." He lowered his gaze and shifted awkwardly in his seat. There was an earnestness about him Simon found very appealing.

"I don't usually speak of it at all," Simon admitted. "I'm a little out of practice. It's been a long time since I... met someone for coffee."

"Here you are," Carole said, interrupting the conversation. She placed their cups in front of them. "Enjoy your coffee." She smiled and disappeared again before Simon could recover his composure enough to say thank you.

Ben took a sip of his coffee and smiled appreciatively. "This is good." He peered over at Simon's cup. "Cappuccino," he noted, looking smug. "I figured it would be."

"Excuse me?"

"You struck me as a guy who drinks cappuccinos," Ben explained. "I like guessing what people like to drink. It's kind of a weird thing with me. I can look at a person and work out their coffee or tea preferences."

"Just coffee and tea?" Simon swallowed his sudden

wave of panic. He didn't want Ben to have any clue of his other drinking preferences.

"Yeah." Ben shrugged. "So if you're a closet drinker, I'd have no clue. You're not, are you?"

"I don't drink much in the way of alcohol." There was no point as he couldn't get drunk. It was one of the drawbacks of being a vampire. That, and the fact that he still got carded on occasion. He wasn't sure which of the two was more annoying.

"Neither do I." Ben seemed pleased by the answer. "I like the occasional beer, but that's about it really."

"You were going to tell me where you work," Simon prompted, shifting the subject onto safer ground.

"Oh, yeah." Ben glanced around and lowered his voice. "Miller's Café on Willow Street, do you know it?"

"It's by the university, so yes, I know it." Simon frowned. "I haven't seen you in there, and it's another place I visit regularly." It was also one of Lucas's favorite haunts, so it was very likely he and Ben had already met.

"I work different shifts, so we might have missed each other. I often work the shifts others don't want since it doesn't really matter to me as long as I have enough hours. They're trying to work around lectures and study and stuff. I'm not." Ben took another sip of coffee. "It happens."

"It does," Simon agreed. It had been a few weeks since he'd ventured near public places, apart from the university, and even then he'd been careful. He hadn't wanted to take any risks while he was contagious. Contrary to popular myth, vampires were only able to turn humans for a short period each year, on the anniversary of when they first became a vampire themselves. "I'm often in there early mornings."

Ben grinned. "I haven't had many of those, thank God. So not a morning person, although I'll work them if I have to. I swear it's only the caffeine holding me up on those shifts, especially at the beginning of them." He shuddered.

"I don't mind mornings. I've always started my day early. Habit, I suppose." Simon had been brought up that way, and it had stuck, like a lot of other things. One day, he'd move with the times, but up to now he'd never seen the appeal of it.

"So you and Lucas live in the same building? Are you flatmates or something?" Ben was like a dog with a bone on the subject. He certainly seemed curious. "Does he always butt in to your phone calls like that?"

"Lucas's... mindset can be quite unique at times. It's just how he is. You get used to it after a while, although sometimes it can still be bloody annoying." Simon paused, unsure as to how much information he wanted to share about his living situation. He took another sip of coffee before coming to a decision. "The building I live in has several floors. Lucas, Forge, and I have one each, although we share a kitchen and some of the other facilities. It works well, for the most part."

"Forge? You mentioned him before. He's the guy who convinced you to buy your phone?"

"Yes. He's an old friend. We've known each other for years." Simon was not about to tell Ben exactly how many. He'd met Forge briefly in a bar in France a few months before he was turned but hadn't known what he was then. Afterward, when he'd run from John with no clue what was happening to him, Forge had found him, helped him through the change, and given him a place to hide. They'd lost touch for a few years after that, before working together in Europe during World War II with Declan, an old friend of Forge's whom Simon had met shortly after he'd been turned. Although it was Declan who had originally written to Simon in the late 1940s to suggest he settle in Boggslake, it had been Forge's home for many years before that.

Staying seemed the sensible thing to do, and it had been too long since Simon had had a place to call home. He'd lived at the castle ever since.

"Back home, I shared a house with a couple of uni students. As crazy as it sounds, I miss the noise sometimes. Don't get me wrong, I love my apartment, but it's not the same."

"You don't have neighbors?"

Ben shrugged. "It's a smallish apartment over a bookshop. Not a lot of noise, although the guy who runs the shop likes to play music at odd hours. He's got the apartment on the other side of mine."

"What bookshop?" Simon felt his face burn when he realized what he'd just done without thinking. "Sorry," he mumbled.

"And here I was thinking you were subtly asking for my address." Ben sounded amused.

"I wasn't. I mean, not unless you want to give it to me." Simon dropped his gaze. It wasn't as though he'd be able to just walk in unannounced anyway, at least not without being invited over the threshold first.

"You gave me your card. I know where you work, and I've told you where I work." Ben shrugged. "Tell you what, I'll tell you my address if you tell me yours."

Simon stared at him for a moment, unsure how to take the comment. "I live at Boggs's Castle on Edgelake Street," he said.

"Above Scribbles Bookshop on High Street," Ben replied. He grinned. "See, that wasn't so hard, was it?"

"I suppose not, no." Simon smiled. Something about Ben put him at ease, more so than he'd felt in a very long time. He really wished, though, that Ben hadn't used that particular adjective. Hard was exactly how Simon was feeling at the moment. He swallowed and licked his lips. "Do you want—"

A familiar sound interrupted his question as to whether Ben would like to go out for dinner later in the week. Simon groaned. Whoever had rung him needed to be hanged, drawn, and quartered.

"Excuse me," he said, pulling the offending object from his pocket. He scowled when he saw who it was. "What do you want, Lucas?"

"What? No greeting or what can I do for you?" Lucas didn't have the grace to sound apologetic.

"I'm busy, and you know I'm busy." Simon allowed some of his annoyance to creep into his voice. "What is it? Can't Forge deal with it?"

"No, he can't, or I would have phoned him." Lucas let out a loud sigh. "He's been up all night and threatened to kill me if I disturbed him, so I figured I'd phone you instead." He lowered his voice. "It's about the case, Simon."

"Excuse me a moment, Lucas." Simon gave Ben an apologetic smile. "I'm sorry, Ben, but this is a business call I have to take. I'll be as quick as I can."

"No worries. Take your time."

"There's been another killing," Lucas told Simon. "One of the crime guys at the scene phoned me. Apparently, it's one of those weird things I like to know about."

Simon nodded slowly. He had a fair idea what was coming next. "It's the same as before?" He frowned. That meant a higher body count in Boggslake than in Seattle. Why hadn't the killer stopped at six like he'd done there?

"Yeah. One of them isn't showing up on camera. Look, Simon, it's only a street over from where you are. Can you wander over and see if you recognize either of the bodies? There's no ID on either of them, and you know if it's one of you guys it won't be easy to find out who it is. I'm also hoping there might be something else at the scene you might notice that someone else wouldn't."

"All right." Simon drained his coffee, hoping like hell it wasn't anyone he knew. He listened while Lucas gave him the exact location. "I'll get over there straightaway." He hung up without saying goodbye.

Ben was staring at him. "Everything okay?"

"Yes." Simon pulled out some notes from his wallet, enough to cover the bill with a good-sized tip. "I'm sorry to cut this short, but I need to do something for Lucas. Can I contact you again? Perhaps we could meet for dinner?"

"I can walk with you a way if you'd like, if you're still heading to the university." Ben didn't seem to want to finish their conversation just yet.

"It's better if you don't, and I'm not. My first lecture isn't until two." Simon hesitated, unsure as to the correct way to take his leave.

"Okay." Ben was still studying him closely. He leaned over before Simon had the chance to move out of the way and planted a soft kiss on Simon's lips. "Phone me."

Then he was gone, leaving Simon feeling rather dazed.

Ben had kissed him. He'd kissed him. And Simon hadn't kissed him back.

Bloody hell.

It had felt good too. Simon wet his lips with his tongue

and stood for a moment before reality struck him like a ton of bricks.

He couldn't think about this now. He had to get to the crime scene before the forensics team had the chance to complete their work. Pulling himself together, he retrieved his coat from the stand inside the door and psyched himself up for what he was probably about to see and smell.

If the vampire had fed off the human victim, as the previous autopsies had suggested, there would be a strong smell of blood. Human blood.

The light outside was brighter than he'd expected. He fumbled inside his coat pocket for his sunglasses and put them on. Although sunlight, for the most part, didn't bother him, his eyes were sensitive to light. The glasses also served to hide his eyes when they became completely brown. Humans didn't react well to someone with no white in their eyes, and he didn't want to interact with them and attempt to explain, as the change was a sure sign his vampire nature was much closer to the surface than usual.

By the time he got to the crime scene, people were already milling around, trying to see what was going on. Police had taped off the area and were standing guard. Simon walked past slowly. He didn't need to be close in order to find out what he needed, as his senses were much more refined than those of a human.

In this case, it was more of a curse than an advantage. The reek of blood hit him first, as he'd known it would. He felt his breathing speed up and his fangs start to descend. Just the smell of it was enough, a temptation of something he couldn't allow himself to taste. Not again.

Simon dug his nails into the palm of one hand, using the pain to center himself. He could do this. He didn't need to taste, didn't need the high that came with it. Not anymore.

He would not lose control like that again.

Edging closer, he focused on his other senses, dismissing the low conversation of the plainclothes officers bending over one of the bodies as something he already knew. Small puncture wounds in the neck of the human victim, his companion's face a taut canvas of pain, her eyes open and staring.

Simon jerked back. Bile rose in his throat. It couldn't be. Oh Lord, no. He forced himself to take another look to confirm.

It couldn't be her. Cynthia was a friend. He'd known her for over fifty years. She was one of the oldest of their kind here and at least a couple of hundred years older than Forge. She wouldn't feed on a human, let alone attack one. She hadn't touched human blood in centuries.

His stomach churned. He ran until he reached the privacy of a deserted alley and dropped to his knees, shaking, trying to scrub the image from his mind.

She was dead. She'd killed a human.

A sob ripped from his throat. He struggled to his feet.

"Simon?"

He spun, barely keeping the vampire in control and out of sight. "Get out," he hissed, not wanting to see anyone, not now, not like this.

"I'm sorry." Ben took a step forward. How much had he seen? "You knew one of them, didn't you?"

"Ben? What are you doing here? You should leave."

"You're upset. I saw you run." Ben edged closer still. He put his hand on Simon's shoulder. "I want to help."

Simon leaned into him, his world narrowing for that moment to the two of them. He groaned, his need for Ben threatening to overwhelm him. Raising his head, he kissed Ben's forehead, warm skin against the heat of his lips.

"I knew *her*," Simon whispered. He refused to look at Ben, to take the chance the man he wanted so badly might see what lurked not far beneath. Dark glasses only hid so much. "Please, Ben. I need to be alone." Simon turned away.

"I can stay if you want me to," Ben said softly.

"No." Simon pulled himself together with some difficulty, forcing the vampire to retreat although he could feel it just below the surface. "Thank you, but no. I'll be in touch."

He buttoned his coat, his fingers shaking, and began to walk. Quickly. Away from Ben, not looking back.

There was no reply. But then he hadn't thought there would be.

Be home, please be home.

Ben booted up his laptop and signed into Skype. He put the kettle on and kicked off his shoes while he waited. The day hadn't gone fast enough, and Melanie's stupid-arse behavior at work hadn't helped. He'd seriously wanted to give her a piece of his mind but held his tongue at the last moment.

Trying to focus on his job after watching Simon walk away from him had been next to impossible. How the hell did he help someone who so obviously wanted to be alone? While Ben knew he probably shouldn't have followed Simon after leaving the café, he hadn't been able to help himself. Something about that phone call had made Ben uneasy, a feeling that Simon might be in some kind of trouble.

He was falling for the guy. Hell, he'd already fallen

headfirst. Ben wasn't in the habit of kissing someone on the first date. He still wasn't sure why he'd done it. Simon's lips against his had felt so good. It had taken all Ben's willpower not to pull Simon closer, take him into his arms, and deepen the kiss.

The cup he was holding slipped from his fingers to smash onto the floor. Ben ignored it. Just thinking about being with Simon like that made him hard as hell. What was it with this guy? Ben couldn't get him out of his mind; it was as though something drew him to Simon, a connection between them that could not be ignored.

Ben sighed and began to clean up the broken crockery. He knew next to nothing about Simon, and he wasn't a fool. Simon had steered the direction of their conversation several times to avoid whatever it was he didn't want to share. Then to see him upset like that.

Of course he'd be upset if a friend had been killed. But it seemed more than that, although Ben couldn't explain why he thought that.

A gut feeling?

"Hey, Ben. You there?"

Ben turned the kettle off and sat down in front of the computer. "Hey, Ange. Just making a cuppa. Be there in a couple, okay?"

"Okay." Ange frowned. She raked her fingers through her messy short blond hair. "Then you're going to tell me what happened, right? I figured it must be important when you texted me at work."

"Right." Ben was thankful to turn his back on the screen while he made his tea. While coffee was his drink of choice when he was out, he tended to drink tea in the evening, especially when he was upset. It was a comfort thing. Like the cheesecakes Ange used to make him when they shared a house together during their university days.

"Did that guy do something to upset you?" Ange's eyes narrowed, her expression confirming what Ben already knew. If Simon had, it was a good thing Ange was still in New Zealand on the opposite side of the planet. She was very protective toward those she cared about.

"No." Ben took a sip of the hot sweet tea and took a deep breath. "The coffee date went really well. Simon's a nice guy. I like him."

"But?" Ange prompted. She raised one eyebrow. "Hang on a moment. Date? I thought you said it wasn't a date. You didn't do anything you shouldn't, right?"

"Ummm." Ben felt himself blush. He hated the way he did that and had been teased mercilessly about it for years. At least when they texted or spoke on the phone, she couldn't see his rising color. Skype, for all he loved it, had some major drawbacks.

"You did!" Ange leaned in closer to the screen.

"I might have kissed him," Ben mumbled.

"You what? What am I missing? What's going on?" Her eyes narrowed. "He didn't slip you anything, did he?"

"Of course he didn't!" Why *had* he kissed Simon? The need to touch him had been overwhelming. Ben couldn't stop thinking about it, about him.

"Did he kiss you back?"

"Kind of." He hadn't given Simon the chance to, but he'd kissed Ben on the forehead before he'd walked away. That was a good thing, right? It meant that they'd see each other again. "I'm worried about him."

"Why? What happened?" Ange glanced at something to the side of her screen. "You haven't told me much about him, just that he teaches history at the local uni. I still haven't got a photograph either, which is odd for you. You take photos of everything, especially guys you're interested in. It's one of the signs you are."

"He doesn't like his photo being taken." It sounded even more peculiar when he spoke the words out loud. "He got upset when I asked."

"Some people are just camera shy." Ange frowned. Ben could see her mind going into overdrive. "Look, I'll do some digging on him in case there is something up with him. See if I can find out who he is exactly."

"You can't do that!" Ben stared at her in disbelief.

"Sure I can. What if he's some kind of drug dealer or something?" Ange tsk-tsked. "You're not in Guatemala now, Dr. Ropata."

Ben snorted and rolled his eyes at the *Shortland Street* reference. Ange was way too addicted to that show. Ben had never seen the appeal of it, even if it had been running on New Zealand television for over twenty years. "I'm not starring in a local soap opera. This is real life, remember?"

"Of course it is." Ange blinked innocently. Ben wasn't fooled for an instant. "So... what happened? You still haven't told me."

"One of Simon's friends was murdered today." Ben said the words as calmly as he could. "At least I think she was a friend. I asked him if he knew her, and he said yes. I saw him at a crime scene. When he saw one of the bodies, he looked really ill and bolted. I followed him. He was really upset."

"Oh no. The poor guy." Ange's hand went to her mouth. "Has he got someone with him?"

"I don't know. He lives with some friends, so I'm hoping they're there for him." Ben sighed. "I offered, but he pushed me away and said he wanted to be alone. I don't know whether he and the woman who died were close, but I'm guessing by his reaction they were." He frowned, his mind replaying what had happened.

"What?" Ange asked. "I know that look. What aren't you telling me?"

"I'm not sure. I just get the feeling there's something else going on with this guy." He held up one hand before she could interrupt. "I trust him. I'm not sure why, but I do. It's weird. We talk, but I get the feeling he's hiding something. A couple of times I could have sworn he was scared I'd find out whatever it is, but he hid most of his reaction really well."

"Hmm." Ange scribbled some notes. "Look, Ben, I'm going to see what I can find out about him." She glared at him when he opened his mouth to protest. "If he has nothing to hide, there's nothing to worry about, right? But if he has, either we need to help him or you need to get the fuck away from him. I have some resources I can call on, and I know Josh will help me if I ask nicely."

"There's no need to get Josh involved with this," Ben told her. Between the library and university and her hacking skills, she had access to information on just about everything. Josh was her partner in crime at the library and a "damn good researcher." Ben had teased her once about their friendship being something more, but as Josh was gay, it wasn't going to happen.

"Let me worry about that, okay? Josh is discreet. He knows how to keep secrets. Now that's all under control, tell me everything you know about Simon." She grinned. "So I can research this properly, of course."

"Of course." Ben rolled his eyes. "Umm, there is another thing I haven't told you."

"Hmm?"

"I'm falling in love with him." Ben took a deep breath. Love at first sight and the notion of soulmates was something they'd talked about ages ago, but he'd dismissed both of them as romantic fantasies. Now he wasn't so sure. "There's something about him, a connection I can't ignore. I think Simon's the one, the guy I want to be with, my soulmate."

CHAPTER FOUR

Simon knocked at the front door and waited. While nowhere near the size of the castle, the house was still fairly large by Boggslake standards. The immaculate garden hadn't changed much since the last time Simon visited, although the tree in the front garden was somewhat taller.

This meeting was not going to be easy, but he needed to do this for his own peace of mind. He also had to find out whatever information he could about what had happened to Cynthia. He owed her that much, at least.

The more he thought about it, the more he was convinced someone had set this up to make it look as though she had killed the human found with her. Cynthia Wyatt was not a killer and never had been. There was always an alternative, she'd told him once, when he was struggling with his own lust for human blood. She'd been a calm influence, a rock when he'd needed one. Declan had turned to her for help during that dark time in Simon's life. While Declan had brought Simon back from the edge of hell, Cynthia had shown him a way to stay far away from it.

Cynthia's murder the previous day had shaken him

more than he'd admitted to anyone. By the time he'd reached home, he was almost composed, although Forge wasn't fooled for an instant. He'd always seen through Simon's masks, just as Simon could see through his.

Even so, Ben was the only one who had seen him so close to the edge. Yet Ben had still wanted to help. That had scared Simon more than his near loss of control.

If Cynthia could lose control, what hope did Simon have of keeping his?

Lucas was wrong. It had to be a setup of some kind. Simon had shaken his head when Lucas quietly said Cynthia had definitely fed off her human victim. There was human blood in her mouth and more partially digested. He'd offered to show Simon the autopsy results, but Simon had refused. They didn't prove anything. There was an explanation for it somewhere; they just weren't looking in the right place.

"Can I help you?" The young man who answered the door eyed Simon up and down suspiciously.

"Hello, Richard. I'm here to pay my respects to Mr. Wyatt," Simon said. Forge had offered to come speak to Hugh, but Simon had insisted he do it. Although Hugh knew both of them and who they were, Forge was a cop and Simon wasn't, so Hugh might be inclined to speak more openly. It should also be easier for Hugh this way. He'd been through enough with having to identify his wife's body the day before.

"Please come in, Professor Hawthorne. Sorry, I didn't recognize you at first. It's been a while since we last met." Richard gave Simon a curt nod.

"Yes, it has," Simon agreed. He lowered his voice. "I hope Mr. Wyatt has not had too much in the way of unwelcome visitors."

"Oh no, Professor." Richard shook his head. He ushered Simon inside and took his coat to hang it on the rack in the hallway. "The... authorities have been most helpful and supportive. Now if you'll excuse me, I'll let Uncle Hugh know you're here." He'd always referred to Cynthia and Hugh as his aunt and uncle.

The vampire community took care of its own. It was doubtful Cynthia's identity, or any of the details about the crime, would be made available to the press. Whoever was behind this needed to be found and dealt with quickly before there were any more human or vampire victims.

This feeling of community was one of the reasons Simon had settled in Boggslake. The supernaturals and humans who lived there had a mutual understanding. While discretion was still required on the part of those who, while not human, could pass for one, the humans turned a blind eye to things that would otherwise raise questions. Simon had taught at the university for over fifty years, and no one questioned the fact he hadn't aged during that time. It was just one of those things that wasn't spoken of. In return, he and his colleagues kept the city safe from the more unsavory supernatural elements.

There were people within their wider supernatural community who took care of driver's licenses and other such things that would betray who and what he really was.

"Hello, Simon. It's good of you to come."

Simon turned at the sound of Hugh's voice. He walked briskly over to him so Hugh didn't have to cross the distance between them. "Hello, Hugh. It's good to see you again too, although I wish it was under more pleasant circumstances."

"So do I." Hugh leaned heavily on his stick but held out his other hand for Simon to shake. "You're looking good, my boy." Hugh had always called him that, despite the age difference between them. When they'd first met, Hugh was in his thirties, and although Simon was much older, he didn't look it. Discovering the truth had changed the term into a private joke between them.

"Thank you." Simon linked his arm through Hugh's. Hugh leaned on him as they walked into the nearby sitting room. They hadn't seen each other for several months. Hugh looked as though he'd aged several years during that time, and for the first time since Simon could remember, his old friend looked every bit of his eighty-five years.

Richard hovered by the doorway, ready to lend a hand if needed. Hugh waved him away. "Professor Hawthorne will take good care of me, Richard. Perhaps you would be good enough to prepare some tea for us?"

"Okay, Uncle Hugh. I'll be right back." Richard left the room as asked but glanced at Simon again before he did so.

"He's a good boy," Hugh said after Simon helped him into his chair. Despite his physical frailty, his eyes were bright and clear. "A little overprotective at times, though, especially of late." He smiled. "He reminds me a lot of his grandfather."

Richard's grandfather, Samuel, and Hugh were cousins. When Frank, Samuel's friend and traveling companion, had returned home to Australia, Samuel had decided to settle in Boggslake. Cynthia had offered him a place to stay, and even after Samuel had moved out when he'd married, he and his family had been frequent visitors to the Wyatt home.

Simon nodded. "Samuel was a good man. I was sorry to hear he'd passed on. Cynthia told me at the university dinner last month." He waited a moment to make sure Richard was out of earshot. "He knows? We can speak freely?"

"Yes." Hugh frowned. "It's been a long time since you've been a guest in our home, hasn't it, Simon? It always seemed easier to meet over dinner out or to catch up at those social functions she loved to attend."

"Ten years, give or take," Simon said.

He glanced around the walls, smiling at the painted portrait of Cynthia and Hugh together. He remembered Hugh hanging it when they'd first moved in, and he had recognized Declan's artwork immediately. Declan was a talented artist and forger and also provided portraits that could pass for photographs to vampires who needed them. This age had a fixation with photographic identification, which was a problem for older vampires who had been born before it was in common use. At least the younger ones had photographs of themselves, which could be altered using computer software to pass for something more modern.

Hugh had been about Ben's age when he and Cynthia first met, and Cynthia had appeared a few years older, as she'd been turned when she was thirty. Declan had captured the early years of their relationship perfectly in the portrait. Hugh had his arm around Cynthia's waist, and she was smiling, her brown eyes crinkling at some private joke, her blond hair curling around one ear. She'd worn it short for years, but the first time Simon had seen her, it had reached down to the small of her back.

"We meant to do something about that but never did." Hugh shook his head. "I always thought we'd have more time." He chuckled, but there was no humor in it. "That probably sounds amusing coming from me, considering how short a life span I have compared to you."

"It's not," Simon assured him. "You should have had more time. We'll get the bastard behind this, Hugh. I promise we will."

"She offered to turn me, you know, but I didn't want it, not then," Hugh said. "I thought we'd have forever, but as I grew older it struck me that one day I'd be leaving her alone. It never occurred to me that I'd lose her first." He nodded his thanks when Richard reentered the room with a tray. "Leave it, Richard. We can serve ourselves. I'm not quite that old and decrepit yet, you know."

"I never presumed you were, Uncle Hugh." Richard glanced at Simon, his earlier formality gone or at least discarded for the time being. "You won't wear him out too much, will you? He's a stubborn man and doesn't take care of himself well enough."

"The stubborn man isn't deaf and can hear what you're saying," Hugh told him. "You can fuss over me again once my friend has gone. There's really no need to stay."

Richard stared at him for a moment. He bit his lip before replying. There were tears forming in his eyes. "Call for me if you need me. I won't be far away." He retreated quickly, but not before shooting Simon a look that suggested not looking after Hugh wasn't an option.

"This is difficult for him," Hugh said softly once Richard was gone. "He was very fond of her." He smiled. "We couldn't have children, of course, but that doesn't mean we don't have family. It's important to have a place and people to call home, don't you think?"

It was all Simon had ever wanted, and everything he'd lost by becoming what he now was.

He nodded slowly but didn't comment. He might have felt that way once, but not so much now. He had friends and a home. An image of Ben came into his mind, and he couldn't help but smile.

"I need to ask you about what happened to Cynthia," Simon said softly, pushing Ben from his thoughts. As much as he enjoyed Hugh's company, this wasn't merely a social call. "I don't mean to be insensitive, but it's important we catch whoever is doing this before he or she strikes again."

"Cynthia wasn't the first, was she?"

"No." Simon poured them both some tea and handed Hugh a cup. He took it with a shaking hand. "I think she was as much a victim of whatever this is as the person who was found with her."

"I know what it looks like. Dr. Coate was very kind, but he was also honest with me, which I appreciate." Hugh added a spoonful of sugar to his tea and stirred it thoughtfully. "He's not one of you, though, so I didn't want to say anything out of place." He looked up at Simon. "I've heard about the animosity between vampires and werewolves. Besides, I wasn't sure he'd understand about the bond Cynthia and I shared."

"Your soulmate bond," Simon prompted when Hugh grew silent again. Such a bond wasn't commonplace between vampires and humans. Vampires often took mates, but not everyone was fortunate enough to find the missing part of their soul, the person they needed to feel truly complete.

"I felt her die." Hugh's tone was flat, almost matter of fact. He shivered. A look of pain crossed his face, an outward sign of his inward struggle to contain his grief. "She was in agony, and she was scared." He banged his cup down on the table next to his chair with more force than Simon would have thought him capable of. "My Cynthia was a good woman. She didn't deserve to die. She did what she could to help people, to make the world a better place." He swallowed and began to shake. "I should have been there. She shouldn't have died alone, feeling like that. I felt her." Hugh looked up at Simon, tears flowing down his wrinkled face. "She reached for me, Simon. I felt her brush against me, and then she was gone. But it wasn't her. There was something there I'd never felt before."

"Something you hadn't felt before?" Simon leaned toward Hugh and placed a comforting hand on his knee. Hugh had always been so strong, just like Cynthia. Simon couldn't remember the last time he'd seen Hugh cry.

When Hugh finally spoke, there was fear in his voice. "I knew what she was, just as I know what you are. I never believed all the stories about vampires or why people might be scared of you. I never was."

"Until now," Simon said quietly. A cold chill spread through him. He didn't want to hear what Hugh was going to tell him, even though he had a fair idea of what it might be.

Hugh nodded. He swallowed. Simon sat back in his chair, feeling the need to put some distance between them. It would be difficult enough for Hugh without someone who was a reminder of what his wife had been close by.

"I felt darkness, like I was being swallowed by a deep black hole where light couldn't reach. And hunger, raw need that was so overwhelming I couldn't think straight. It wasn't her. I'd seen glimpses of her vampire before, but nothing like this. She was always so in control of it." Hugh's voice wavered. "For that moment, I truly felt scared of her. And that, more than the fear itself, terrified me." One hand gripped the arm of his chair. "It wasn't her, though, was it? Please tell me it wasn't her."

"I..." Simon stared at Hugh for a moment, wanting to find the words, needing to hear them himself. The description he'd given was one Simon knew all too well. After he'd lost Albert, he'd been that creature Hugh had felt. He'd killed so many people, driven by a bloodlust he couldn't control and didn't want to stop. It had dulled the pain, but not only that, it had felt good.

"Simon?"

Simon forced himself to focus, not to lose himself in the past. "It wasn't her," he said, his voice sounding strained. "Whatever did this to her, it wouldn't be because she wanted it. Someone made her lose control. That's the person who is to blame for whatever happened, not her. She loved you, Hugh. She would never have done anything to hurt you or anyone else."

He wanted to believe that. Perhaps Lucas was right. The autopsy report had shown she'd fed off the human found with her. No one forced Cynthia Wyatt to do anything against her will; she was too stubborn for that. Unless... Simon glanced at Hugh, then turned away. No. Not even threatening Hugh would ensure her cooperation in something like this. She'd have to know the consequences, and that it would most probably be the end of what they had together.

"I still love her, you know." Hugh sounded stronger. His voice had an edge to it, a firmness in his conviction Simon envied. "Even knowing what she might have done, I still love her, and I wish she was here." He fell quiet for a moment, the ticking of the clock on the mantelpiece loud in the silence between them. "You'll let me know when this is over, won't you? I'd offer to help, but I'm not as young as I used to be."

"I'll let you know." Simon started to stand, but Hugh shook his head.

"Stay for a while. Talk to me about old times, about her. There's so few people to listen anymore. Everyone's like me, grown old." Hugh smiled a little. "I saw your expression earlier when I spoke of the importance of having someone or something to call home. Have you met someone?"

"You're changing the subject," Simon said, keeping his tone light.

"Humor an old man, my boy." Hugh took another sip of tea. "I want to think about good things. It helps me forget the other."

"Can you tell me more about your soulmate bond?" Simon began after a few minutes. He shook his head. "My apologies. I shouldn't be asking you about this now. It's insensitive of me."

Hugh smiled. "It's fine. We had a good life together, Cynthia and I. I do admit I really had no idea what it would be like to become a part of her world, but I wouldn't have given it up, no matter what. We had a good marriage, and I've had a good life. If I passed over tomorrow, I wouldn't change anything, apart from the last few days."

"You don't regret you refused her offer to turn you?"

"No." Hugh shook his head. "If I was a vampire, I'd be facing several lifetimes without her. This way I know I'll be with her again soon. It's easier." His expression softened. "She was beautiful, wasn't she? Forever young, but that's not what drew me to her. It was who she was inside, her passion for life, the way she felt so deeply about everyone she came into contact with. She truly cared and saw her immortality as a way to make a mark on the world, to try to make it a better place." He stared at his hands. They were wrinkled, with age spots, fine skin that looked as though it would bruise just by brushing against it. "She looks at me as though I'm still young, still like we first met. It's like she sees past the physical me and into my soul." A tear ran down his cheek. He seemed unaware he was using present tense, and Simon wasn't about to correct him. "If you have the opportunity to be with someone like I was with her, grab it, Simon. Grab it and hang on to it tightly."

Simon nodded slowly, although he wasn't sure he agreed. He'd grieved for so many friends and for those he'd loved and lost. Could he go through that again without losing something of himself? Albert's death had sent him over the edge. He still had nightmares about it.

"We didn't need the soulmate bond to be happy, but it added something I never thought possible." Hugh continued talking, his eyes glassing over as though he was losing himself in his memories. He pulled out his handkerchief and blew his nose. "I thought once she was gone, I'd just keel over and die. That's what your legends say, isn't it? It figures, doesn't it, the one bloody story I need to be true, and it's not."

"I'm sorry." Simon had been surprised to learn it hadn't happened. According to the stories surrounding the soulmate bond, if one partner died, the other followed shortly afterward. Perhaps it was different when it wasn't two vampires?

"When I found out about it, I was angry. She should have told me what she was. It wouldn't have made any difference. I still wanted her. That wasn't why I was upset. Why hadn't she told me the truth? There aren't any secrets once you cross that line. As soon as she let her guard down, as soon as we kissed that first time and I told her I needed her, I knew. I knew everything." Now that Hugh was talking, the words kept coming. Had he ever spoken about it to anyone else before like this?

Hugh grimaced.

"Well, almost everything. Apparently when it's between a vampire and a human, the bond isn't as open or as strong. I'm not sure whether that's a good thing or not,"

Hugh continued. "I made the mistake of asking her if she'd bewitched me, if the fact I couldn't stop thinking about her and I was driven to be with her was some kind of vampire thrall. I still remember the look on her face, the hurt expression. How could I have thought that? That's when I found out it was much stronger for her. She offered to walk away if I didn't want this. I took her into my arms and held her tightly, told her I loved her and I believed in her. I still remember the first time we were together. From then on, I could feel her in my mind, in my heart, even when we were apart. It was as though I could reach out and touch her, although she wasn't in the room. I couldn't always tell what she was feeling, but I knew she was there." His gaze lingered on his wedding ring. "When she marked me—" A loud sob ripped from his throat. "She's gone. She's truly gone, hasn't she?"

Simon nodded. He didn't know what to say. His mouth went dry at the thought of marking Ben.

It took a few moments for Hugh to regain his composure. "Pour me a glass of brandy, will you?"

Simon did what he requested. One glance at Hugh confirmed that asking whether he should be drinking was not a good idea. He'd lost his wife; he said he'd had a good life. What the hell did it matter if he did something that might not be good for his health?

"Do you need me to stay?"

"I need you to find this bastard and deal with him." Hugh took a large gulp and gestured for Simon to leave the decanter on the table. "Thank you for coming to see me." He looked up and met Simon's eye. "Goodbye, my boy. It's been a privilege."

"Goodbye, Hugh." The way in which Hugh had

phrased it sounded suspiciously final. Perhaps it was. "I'll let you know when it's over," Simon said quietly.

Hugh nodded but didn't say anything.

The hallway was empty when Simon collected his coat, but he knew better than to believe he was alone. "Look after him, Richard," he said. "Mr. Wyatt is a good man, and he's been through enough."

"I'll stay with him, Professor." Richard appeared out of the shadows. He had been standing just outside the room for most of their conversation, ready to go to Hugh if needed. His ability to not be noticed was impressive, but Simon had heard his heartbeat and breathing and known exactly where he was. "He'll not be left alone."

"Thank you." Simon closed the front door silently behind him, put on his sunglasses, and began walking to his car. He'd almost reached it when an uneasy feeling came over him, a sensation of being watched. He turned quickly, scanning the street from all sides, using all of his vampire senses to do so, but there didn't appear to be anyone there.

That was odd. At first, he'd thought Forge might have asked someone to keep an eye on Hugh's house, in case his wife's murderer decided to tie up any loose ends, but there was no obvious police presence there or in the vicinity. Unless they were plainclothes officers? No, that was unlikely. There would be no point in going after Hugh. He was an old man, and killing him would not fit with the pattern of these murders.

Another scan also brought up nothing, apart from a young woman walking her dog. Listening to her heartbeat confirmed she wasn't a vampire, as otherwise it would have been a lot slower. This was a quiet neighborhood, and with it being early afternoon, most of its residents were either out at work or elderly and indoors.

Simon relaxed. This whole thing had him on edge, as did Hugh talking about the soulmate bond. Simon had meant what he'd said about catching whoever was behind this, and that was where he needed to focus his attention. Glancing at his watch, he noted the time and then pulled out his telephone. It was answered almost immediately. "Lucas? It's Simon. I have some information for you. Do you want to meet somewhere over coffee?"

It was often the easiest way to trade information. Most of the local cafés had a quiet table where they could talk without being overheard, and it was better than waiting until Lucas finished work. Simon had always stayed clear of the morgue and Lucas's office, as it would take too much in the way of explanation, and his involvement in anything police related was most definitely off the record.

"Sure. I can be at Miller's in fifteen. See you there." Lucas hung up before Simon could reply.

Miller's? Why did he have to choose Miller's? Simon stared at the phone and sighed. Perhaps Ben wasn't working today. Or maybe, a small voice whispered, perhaps it would be a good thing if he was.

CHAPTER FIVE

Ben wiped his hands on the towel, relieved to finally be done with the enormous pile of dishes. He glanced at the clock and grinned. "Going on my break now," he called out, stopping by the coffeepot to pour himself a cup. The freshly brewed coffee aroma had been tempting him for the past ten minutes, and he'd been stuck in the kitchen for most of his shift. A generous amount of milk completed the near perfect cup of coffee, and he made his way to the front of the café, looking for a free table.

A familiar voice caught his attention, and he smiled. Lucas was at his usual table, and he'd know how Simon was. Ben had hoped Simon would have been in by now. It was one of the reasons he'd offered to swap shifts with Raewyn, who usually worked the early one.

Lucas had someone with him. Ben hesitated, suddenly unsure. Perhaps he'd leave asking after Simon for another time or phone him directly after a few more days. The man with Lucas turned. Ben's breath hitched. He froze.

Simon's expression was hard to read, a reaction that

could have been either surprise or shock. Ben rather hoped it was the former.

"Hi, Ben. Come sit with us." Lucas broke into a large grin. He indicated the cup in Ben's hand. "You're on your break, right?"

"Yeah." Ben slipped into the empty seat next to Lucas.

Simon was staring at Ben's cup. "I thought you took your coffee black," he said.

After everything that had happened the day before, that was the best he could come up with?

"I don't like creamer, so when I run out of milk, I drink it black," Ben said, trying to keep his reply calm and to the point. He took a sip and pulled a face. The decision to drink it again with milk had been a big mistake. "Definitely tastes better that way, or maybe I've got used to it."

Lucas glanced from one to the other. He sighed loudly and dramatically, as though making a point. "I knew your voice sounded familiar on the phone, but I didn't make the connection that you were Simon's Ben until I saw his reaction when he saw you just now."

"I'm not *his* Ben," Ben said.

"Of course you're not." Lucas winked at Simon. "Not yet, anyway."

"I'm surprised Forge didn't tell you," Simon said, "considering he would have already known."

Lucas sniffed. "He's like you, doesn't always share. You're not like that, though, are you, Ben? You'd share, right?"

"No, he won't," Simon said a little too quickly.

"Bite me," Lucas retorted. Simon's eyes narrowed. Ben could have sworn he heard a low growl. Then Simon laughed.

"Not even if you ask nicely." Simon took a long sip of

coffee, ignoring the hurt look on Lucas's face, which disappeared quickly to be replaced by another grin.

"Oh well, it's always worth a go." Lucas turned to Ben. "Wouldn't a three-way be a great idea?"

"No!" Ben snapped at the same time as Simon. What the hell was Simon's relationship with Lucas? Weren't they just friends?

"Whatever." Lucas seemed unperturbed by the refusal. "Well, if you change your mind, you know where to find me." He stretched. "I need to use the little boys' room, so if you'll excuse me, I'll be back in a few." Ben shifted to let him out. "Take my seat, Ben. It's nice and warm, and it's closer to Simon."

Ben stared after Lucas but took the seat he'd vacated.

"That was almost subtle for him," Simon said dryly. "I hope he's not usually that forward when he's in here."

"No, he's usually quite polite, actually." Ben shrugged. How was he supposed to start this conversation? There was so much he wanted to ask, to say. "How are you?" he said finally. "I was worried about you."

"I'm fine." Simon looked up at him. "I'm sorry for running out on you yesterday. Cynthia's death hit me rather hard."

"You don't need to apologize for that!" Ben reached over, put his hand over Simon's, and squeezed it. Simon smiled and blushed. He looked so young when he blushed, and the smile had a shy quality to it that Ben loved already. "It's difficult losing someone. I wanted to help, but I suppose I should have just minded my own business. We've only just met, and I stepped over a line, I guess."

"You were showing your concern, and I appreciate it. Perhaps we should try this again? What time does your shift finish today? I could take you out to dinner. If you'd like to, that is."

"I'd like to," Ben said. "You've already bought me coffee, though, so this should be my treat."

"Let him pay." Lucas sat down on the seat Ben had vacated. "Knowing Simon, you'd probably never be able to afford where he wants to take you, and besides, letting him pay will make him happy."

Ben opened his mouth to point out that any relationship he was going to enter into was going to be an equal one, thank you very much, and he'd always paid his share, when he spotted Melanie heading over toward them. She'd obviously returned from her break without him noticing.

"Oh crap," he said.

"Professor Hawthorne!" Melanie said. "How nice to see you in here again." She frowned when she saw Ben sitting next to Simon. "Shouldn't you be out back dealing with that pile of dishes?" she asked him.

"Already done, and I'm on my break," Ben told her. He felt Simon's hand tighten around his. Melanie noticed the movement, and her eyes widened.

"I asked him to join us," Simon said. "Is there anything I can help you with? We're still enjoying our coffee, so you can come back later to clear the table."

Ben bit back a smirk at the annoyed expression that crossed Melanie's face. "Well, if you're sure, Professor," she said, making a point of glancing at her watch.

"I know I only have a few minutes left," Ben pointed out to her, "but thanks for the reminder anyway."

"We'll send him back in one piece, Melanie," Lucas said. "Unless you want to keep him, Simon?"

"No, I wouldn't keep him from his work, but a memento would be nice." Simon leaned in and brushed his lips against Ben's, lingering for just long enough to give Ben a taste of what he knew he badly wanted more of. "I owe you that from yesterday," Simon said when he broke the kiss.

Melanie stared at both of them. "Oh," she said. "I'm sorry. I had no idea." She turned and fled toward the kitchen, her face bright red.

"What? Huh?" Ben's cheeks heated, his blush at least several shades deeper than hers. He licked his lips, still tasting Simon on his skin. His body felt on fire, and he struggled to think straight. The kiss had felt good, more than good. Ben didn't tend to use the word *awesome*, but it was the only one his lust-fogged brain was supplying.

"Oh, didn't she know you were gay, Ben?" Lucas put his hand to his mouth, feigning shock, an over-the-top gesture that swiftly brought Ben back to reality.

"Yeah, she knew, so I don't think that was it." Ben took a gulp of coffee. He couldn't take his eyes off Simon. If that was their second kiss, he couldn't wait for their third.

"I think I might have just outed myself," Simon said dryly. "She's in one of my classes at the university and flirts with me constantly when I come here. I suspect she's just realized she was wasting her time."

"You could be bi," Lucas pointed out helpfully.

"I'm not," Simon said, "and besides, I'm already taken..." His voice trailed off.

Already taken? Ben swallowed. Simon couldn't be serious, could he? What the hell was he playing at, kissing him like that if he was with someone else?

Lucas elbowed Ben in the side, none too gently. "Earth to Ben. You still there? Simon, I think you'd better tell him again, and ask nicely this time so he understands what you're saying."

"Simon?" Ben managed to croak. Ask him what? "What's he talking about?"

"I... um..." Simon cleared his throat. "I'm not interested in her, Ben, or anyone else. I'm interested in you. That's what I meant when I said I was already taken. By you. Is that all right?"

"Oh."

"So is that a yes?" Lucas glanced between them. "Put me out of my misery, here."

"That's a yes," Ben said. At least for now, while they figured out whether this relationship had the potential to be something more long-term. "Oh, and, Lucas?"

"Yeah?"

"Could I talk to Simon please? Alone."

"Oh, right. Sure." Lucas stood. "I should probably get back to work anyway. Dead bodies await and all that. Thanks for your help, Simon. See you when I get home, and..." He leaned over and whispered something in Simon's ear.

"No," said Simon firmly. "I don't think so. Definitely not."

Lucas shrugged and grinned, pulled on his jacket, and walked away. "Spoilsport. You never want to share any of the details."

"Is he always like this around you?" Ben asked, by now certain he would have noticed if this was Lucas's usual behavior.

"Yes. Do you mind?" Simon shrugged. "He feels comfortable around you, and this is his way of saying he approves."

"It's fine." Ben saw Melanie peering over at them from behind the counter. Her embarrassment hadn't lasted long, and now she'd be his long-lost best friend so she could find out for sure whether he and Simon were an item. "So, dinner tonight? Do you want to pick me up at home or meet somewhere else?"

"I'll pick you up at home. The restaurant is some distance away, so it's best if we take my car." Simon hesitated for a moment. "You can invite me in."

It seemed an odd way of putting it, but Ben wasn't about to comment. For all he knew, it could be another one of those cultural differences he wasn't aware of. "Yeah, sounds good. About seven, then? I'd better get back to work before I get into trouble."

"I'll see you at seven." Simon stood and retrieved his coat from the back of his chair. He wore suit trousers, and an expensive-looking gray cardigan that matched his tie finished the ensemble.

Ben tore his gaze away with some difficulty. Simon was not only a sexy guy, but his sophisticated dress sense was a real turn-on. "Umm, what should I wear for this place?"

"Surprise me. I'm sure you'll look good in whatever you decide to wear." Simon smiled. "See you tonight."

"See you tonight." Ben watched him go for a long moment, only realizing he'd forgotten to ask him something else when the doorbell chimed with their next customer.

What the hell had Lucas meant by that comment about dead bodies awaiting?

Simon climbed the staircase leading to Ben's apartment. Scribbles Bookshop was one he frequented fairly regularly, as they had an interesting range of books and a well-stocked classical music CD section. Ben had said he'd been in Boggslake for six weeks. He must have moved in here just after Simon's last visit to the shop, so they'd just missed each other.

The closer he got to the door of Ben's apartment, the more different scenarios began to replay in his mind. What if Ben didn't invite him in so many words and just expected him to be able to enter? How could he explain he couldn't without telling Ben the real reason why?

You have to use my name when you invite me in. I'm a vampire.

He could see the shock on Ben's face now, and the fear. Simon shivered. He'd never had to tell Stephen or Albert the truth. Stephen had died before Simon had been turned, and John had killed Albert before Simon had the chance to tell him he was a vampire.

Or rather, found the courage to tell him.

Sixty-nine years later and he still struggled with that one. Perhaps if he and Ben got to know each other first it would help, and he'd be more likely to accept Simon for what he was. They had the luxury of dating and spending time together in conversation, something he and Albert had never had. At least he didn't have to hide his feelings toward Ben in public, as gay relationships were accepted now for the most part. Simon had met Stephen in France during the First World War, and they'd had to resort to meeting after dark in no-man's-land. It was dangerous, but getting caught even kissing would have been too. That hadn't changed by the time he'd met Albert in Europe, just over twenty years later. Humans took such a long time to accept anyone who was different, and the superstitions and fears regarding vampires did not help.

He had already begun to make slips of the tongue, like telling Ben about needing to be invited in. Simon didn't want to make an impression of being rather weird even before Ben found out about the rest of it.

Simon still remembered his father's reaction when he'd found out his son had become a vampire, the look of disgust on his face and the contempt in his words. Better that Simon had died in the Battle of the Somme five years before, like his family had been led to believe, than that he had turned into this monster.

His father was long gone now, dead for over eighty years, yet Simon had never been able to shake the memory of the final words between them. He'd fled his family home, never to return, his hope that his beloved uncle, Edwin, would have at least accepted him also dashed, as he'd died of influenza three years before.

He didn't see the point in dwelling on all of that now. Either tonight would be one of hope for the future or it wouldn't. Forge had told him once that he needed to move on. Not everyone would react the same way, and besides, how did Simon expect others to accept him for what he was if he didn't accept himself?

Forge had made a good point, but it wasn't one easily rectified.

There was only one door at the end of the hallway—the other apartment had access from inside the shop, as it was occupied by its owner—so Simon knocked briskly and waited for a reply.

Ben answered after a few moments. He wore very form-fitting black trousers, and the buttons of his shirt were still undone. Simon tore his gaze away from the dark chest hair and flat stomach with some difficulty and cleared his throat.

"Hello. I'm sorry. I'm a little early." Simon went to take a step forward, then caught himself in time. Bouncing off the invisible barrier that prevented him from entering a private dwelling uninvited was something best avoided as it would be embarrassing, to say the least. Only very old vampires could cross a threshold without an invitation. "Do you want me to wait outside while you finish getting ready?"

"You're not that early, and I'm running late. I had a difficult customer at the last minute, so I got held up." Ben waved his hand to invite Simon in. "If you make yourself comfortable, I won't be long."

"Umm..." Simon froze. Ben hadn't said the words, and a gesture wouldn't suffice. What the hell was he going to do now? "I can't..." The explanation died on his lips. He couldn't do this, not now. Not tonight. Maybe not ever.

This was a mistake. He started to turn away, to run. Better that than Ben's reaction when he discovered the truth.

"It's fine, really." Ben kept talking. "Come in, Simon. I can give you the five-second tour if you'd like. With the size of the place, that's about how long it's going to take."

Simon heaved a sigh of relief. "That sounds good, thank you," he said, walking into the apartment. He really hated that stupid rule. Of all the things that were believed of their kind, why did that need to be one that was actually true?

"You look like you've seen a ghost or something. I know it's a little messy in here, but it's not that scary, honest." Ben finished buttoning up his shirt. "Do I need to wear a tie, or do you think I'll do as is?" He sat on the sofa and began pulling on his boots.

"You'll do very nicely as is," Simon told him. He'd dressed down a little for their dinner date so there was less risk of Ben feeling out of place once they arrived at the restaurant. Simon had dined regularly at Braedan's Restaurant since it opened thirty years ago. It was one of the few places in Boggslake that served his steak rare enough for his liking, and their chocolate dessert reminded him of the one Grandmother Beatrice's cook used to make.

The apartment was small, as Ben had said, but it seemed comfortable enough. Unlike the hallway, the walls inside were freshly painted in a neutral cream color, which made the space seem bigger than it was. A large free-standing bookshelf stood in front of one of the walls. There were a few books on it—none of the titles were ones Simon recognized—and what appeared to be a pile of graphic novels. A medium-sized coffee table was apparently used in lieu of a dining room table, as there was a closed laptop on it and a notepad and pens next to it.

"Feel free to borrow anything on that shelf," Ben said, noticing his interest. "I keep the stuff I'm in the middle of reading in the other room. I didn't bring much in the way of hardcopy with me because of having to lug them, but I've picked up a few since I got here. I mostly read on my tablet because that's what I have with me, but nothing beats the feel of paper."

"I've never really seen the appeal of graphic novels," Simon admitted, "but then I haven't made much of an effort to read any either."

"I'll have to introduce you to a few of my favorites, then, and you can tell me what you think. It's easier when you have someone to talk to about it afterwards."

A dartboard hung on the wall next to the bookcase. Several darts had found the bullseye. Simon moved closer, curious. Other darts sat in an open box on one of the shelves.

"I'm keeping in practice," Ben explained. "I don't suppose you know of anyone who plays locally? I've asked around but with no luck, but Mr. McKay has said it's okay if I add a dart board to our games corner in the café."

"Sorry, no. You're good at the game by the looks of it."

Ben grinned. "Pub champion for the last couple of years so don't want to lose my touch." He walked over to the kitchen area, which consisted of a counter, an oven, and cupboards all in a long row. There was a container of milk still on the counter, which he put away in the fridge. The container of brown powder he left on the counter. "Milo," he explained in response to Simon's raised eyebrow. "It's a kind of chocolate drink mix, very popular at home. I brought some with me, as I wasn't sure I'd be able to get it here."

"Can you?" Simon didn't remember ever seeing it.

"I haven't tried yet." Ben shrugged. "I can live without it if I can't, and besides, my mum said she'd send me a care parcel if I want anything I can't get here."

"There are import stores we can try if you'd like. The British one is only about an hour's drive away. I've been meaning to visit it again soon, so you could come with me."

"Thanks," Ben said. "Sounds like a plan. Tell me the name of the shop, and I'll take a look online and see what they've got."

"You can do that?" Simon had never considered the option. He had resigned himself to the fact he was expected to use a computer at work, but as it was a frustrating experience, he'd never bothered purchasing one for himself. The few times he'd needed to use one at home, he'd used either Forge's or Lucas's.

"Yeah. I can show you how when we get that far." Ben pulled on a dark brown sweater, then retrieved a leather jacket from the sofa. The shade of the sweater brought out the color of his eyes. His hair was still damp from the shower, and the ends of it clung to the back of his neck. "Okay, I'm ready."

"You promised to show me your apartment first," Simon reminded him. The distraction would help his growing urge to touch and taste Ben. An image of Ben against one of these walls, writhing under Simon's touch and gasping his name, entered his mind, and he swallowed, nearly missing Ben's reply.

"Yeah, I did, sorry." Ben indicated the room they were in, seemingly oblivious to Simon's reaction. "There's not much to show, really. This is most of it." He walked over to the door on the right side of the room and opened it. "This is the bedroom, and the other door is the bathroom. The apartment's compact, but I like it that way, as I don't have to spend a lot of time cleaning."

"You don't enjoy cleaning?" Simon peered into both rooms, noting the lack of possessions, although there was another pile of books on the nightstand next to the bed, which was neatly made. The bed was a double and looked very comfortable and sturdy.

He shifted slightly, hoping his hardening erection wasn't too obvious.

"I don't mind it, but I'd prefer to spend the time doing other things." Ben locked the apartment door behind them and followed Simon down the stairs. "What time did you book the restaurant for?"

"Not until eight, so we'll still be there in plenty of time." Simon preferred to be early. He'd had it drummed into him as a child that tardiness was something that would not be tolerated. As much as he was annoyed by it at times, he found himself still living much of his life by his father's ideals. It was ironic, considering he'd never have his approval and told himself he didn't need it. He'd never told his father he preferred the company of men, and it was doubtful his father would have been happy about that either.

The cool night air was somewhat of a relief after the warmth of the apartment. Simon stood for a moment and took several deep breaths, letting it brush against his heated skin. Despite his slow heartbeat and cooler body temperature, he still blushed like humans did and felt the heat that came with arousal. He also felt extremes of temperature, but the cold didn't bother him as much as the heat. Contrary to popular myth, he was not about to combust in sunlight, although too much time spent in it was not advisable, as vampires dehydrated a lot faster than humans.

"How far away did you park?" Ben asked.

"I'm right here," Simon said. He walked over to his car and ran a hand over her. She was one of the luxuries he'd allowed himself, having decided if he was going to drive an automobile, he'd be comfortable and purchase something that reminded him of home.

Ben's mouth dropped open. "That's an Aston Martin, isn't it? Like James Bond drives?"

"I suspect his car is a little newer than mine, but yes." Simon had bought the car ten years ago from a local dealer who had been more than happy to ship in whatever he wanted from the other side of the country after he'd mentioned how much he was prepared to pay.

"Aren't those—" Ben broke off whatever he'd been going to say and looked very uncomfortable.

"Expensive?" Simon said softly, guessing what was going through Ben's mind. "Yes, but I have money, so I like to live comfortably. It's the way I was brought up."

"I can't keep up with anything like this," Ben mumbled. He shoved his hands into his jacket pockets. "I want our relationship to be equal, and I'd like to be able to take you out to dinner somewhere nice too."

Simon sighed. He placed one hand on Ben's shoulder and turned him so they were facing. "This isn't a competition, Ben, and I want a relationship that is equal too."

Ben met his gaze for a moment, then shrugged.

"One thing I've learned is that wealth comes in many forms. It's not just about how much money you have. Father taught me about finances from an early age. He was convinced it was the most important lesson I would ever learn in life. He was wrong."

"It's not the most important thing." Ben frowned. "Sure, you need to know what you're doing with it, but it's not what life is about, except when you haven't got enough of it so you're worrying where your next meal is coming from."

"That's it exactly," Simon agreed. He let go of Ben's shoulder. "You said you were worried about not keeping up with me because you couldn't afford what I can. Did it ever occur to you that I worry about not being equal to you in some way?"

"How do you mean?" Ben asked slowly. He took a step back so he was standing farther away from the curb and folded his arms, eyeing Simon somewhat warily. "You're not much older than me, yet you seem to have done a lot more with your life. You're already a professor at a university, and you've made your fortune."

Simon could not help but chuckle. "You make it sound so easy." He shrugged. "It was in some ways, but not in others. My family came from old money, so I had somewhat of a head start."

He had his niece, Clarice, to thank for that. Claiming what was rightfully his hadn't been a simple matter. Not only had he miraculously returned from the dead, but his father had disowned him on the spot. Clarice had been more sympathetic, yet Simon had refused to take anything she might need. She'd never married or had a family so had insisted on leaving him a sizable amount in her will, naming him as a distant cousin so as not to draw attention to his true identity, which would have been difficult to explain. Luckily, he'd also had some private accounts of his own that his father hadn't been able to touch which hadn't been closed because his mother didn't want to believe her husband's claim that their son was truly gone.

"One of the first things I thought when I saw you was that you were probably out of my league," Ben mumbled.

"*One* of the first things?" Simon raised an eyebrow.

Ben blushed. "Yeah," he said. "I think you're kind of hot." He swallowed. "You said you were worried about not being equal to me? How so?"

"You think I'm hot? Seriously?" Simon felt himself start to color and moved the conversation on quickly when Ben nodded. "One of the first things I noticed about you was your enthusiasm for life and the way you're not afraid to talk to others, especially about what interests you. The way you spoke about the photographs you'd taken stayed with me long after that first discussion we had. I'm not always good at that kind of conversation, and it takes me a while to talk to people about what really matters. It's very easy to resort to small talk and use it to sidestep subjects I want to avoid."

"You've done that with me a few times," Ben pointed out, "and I'm not entirely sure what you've described me doing is always a good thing. It's got me into trouble a few times, especially as I don't always know when to shut up and let things be."

Simon flinched. "Yes, I know I've done that with you."

He'd probably have to do so again too. Telling Ben the truth wasn't an option he wanted to contemplate just yet. "There's a lot about me you still don't know, and I'm not sure I'm ready to share all of it yet." He took a deep breath. "If you want to walk away, I'll understand."

"I don't want to walk away," Ben said. "We've only just met, and we're still getting to know each other. Feeling comfortable enough to share the important stuff takes time. There's a lot about me you still don't know too." He grinned. "Just because I tend to rabbit on doesn't mean I expect you to. Just be honest, though, okay?"

At least as much as I can be for now.

"Okay," Simon agreed. "A word of warning, though. I do tend to dwell on the past somewhat. I've been told I need a kick up the ass on that one on occasion." He deliberately pronounced the word *ass* with an American accent to highlight the fact he was quoting someone else.

Forge had a way with words at times, but maybe he was right, as much as it pained Simon to admit it. He'd tried so many times to move forward, but it always seemed as though his past caught up with him and dragged him back. This time could be different, couldn't it? He would make sure it was.

"You sound like an old man," Ben teased. "You've still got the rest of your life ahead of you, so why not leave all that stuff for when you've got a few more years to look back on."

"Some days, I feel like one." Immortality wasn't always as great as it was cracked up to be. Yet, Simon had to admit, it had also given him opportunities he'd never have had the chance to explore if he'd been limited to one lifetime of experiences.

Opportunities he'd never asked for and at a price that had been far too high at times.

"Is this one of those moments I should be kicking you up the arse?" Ben seemed more relaxed than he had a few moments ago, so hopefully he'd taken some of what they'd talked about to heart. If not, Simon would have no qualms about reminding him. The difference in social standing between them was not something he'd expected to be an issue and would be the least of Ben's concerns when he found out what Simon was.

"Probably." Simon opened the passenger door of the car for Ben. They'd been standing on the sidewalk talking for several minutes, and he preferred they continue their conversation inside the car where it would be more private. "We can keep talking while I drive. Otherwise, we'll be late for dinner."

Ben seemed surprised Simon had opened the door for him but climbed in with a quick thank you nevertheless. He ran one hand appreciatively over the wooden dashboard. "She's a beautiful car, Simon. How long have you had her? It is 'her,' right? I know ships are, but I've never been sure about cars."

"Referring to my car using a feminine pronoun is fine." Simon turned the key in the ignition, and the car purred into life. "I've always thought of her like that, but I get teased enough about the car and the fact I wanted a right-hand drive, so I've been careful not to say it out loud."

"Forge?" Ben guessed.

"Yes, and Lucas. According to them, she's my 'pride and joy.'"

"Nothing wrong with that," Ben said. He settled back into his seat and peered out the window as Simon pulled out into High Street. "I've been really looking forward to this evening, especially after that last customer I told you about. He was past annoying, one of those people who notice you're wearing a name badge and then work your name into every single sentence."

"That sounds very annoying," Simon agreed. "Does he come into the café often?"

"This was his first time, thank God." Ben grimaced. "His only redeeming feature was his accent. It reminded me of you."

"Of me?" Simon hoped his voice didn't sound too strained. He felt a chill crawl up his spine. "What did the man look like, Ben?"

"Do you think you might know him?"

"Maybe." Simon hoped not. "Describe him for me."

"Let's see." Ben considered for a moment. "He had these piercing blue eyes, like they'd see right through you, but there was no warmth in them at all. Something about his manner gave me the creeps."

Simon slammed on the brakes. His hands were shaking. No, it couldn't be. John was dead, or he was supposed to be. Behind them, someone leaned on their horn. Simon jumped and pulled the car to the curb so they were off the road.

"Something's wrong, isn't it?" Ben placed a hand on Simon's knee. "What did this guy do to get you so riled up?"

"Blue eyes and what else?" Simon failed to keep the tremor out of his voice. "How old did he appear to be?"

"He was an old guy," Ben said. "About sixty, I reckon, and he had red hair, although it was kind of blond in places, which might have been the gray showing through. He was skinny as, too, like he hadn't had a decent meal in ages."

It wasn't John. Simon let out a sigh of relief. He let go of the steering wheel, pulled Ben close, and held him tightly. While it was possible to change one's appearance, John had always been too vain to bother with disguises. He'd never pose as someone that old and was rather proud of the fact he'd been turned when he was barely twenty. His apparent youth was one of the things that made him so dangerous, as he wasn't above using it to his advantage.

"Simon?" Ben asked again when Simon finally let go of him. "What did this guy do to you?"

"It's not him," Simon said. "It's not John." John was supposed to be dead, he repeated to himself. "Promise me something, Ben, and do it now."

"Sure. What?"

"If you ever see a young man with piercing blue eyes and dark hair, with an accent like mine, who shows any interest in you at all, don't wait to talk to him, just get out and get as far away from him as you can."

"Okay." Ben frowned. "One thing, though. Who is this guy you're so afraid of?"

He's my maker, the vampire who made me.

Simon opened his mouth to say the words, but nothing came out. Instead, he swallowed and avoided looking at Ben directly. He couldn't lie to him, but he couldn't tell the whole truth either.

"His name is John Wells," he said finally, "and once, many years ago, we were a couple, or so John wanted to believe."

"Wanted to believe? You mean you weren't?"

"No." Simon shivered at the memory. "Definitely not. I never wanted anything to do with him."

CHAPTER SIX

Simon quietly closed the door to his office before he pulled out his telephone and called Declan. He needed this conversation but couldn't risk someone listening in. The previous night's dinner had been an enjoyable one. Ben was good company and very easy to talk to. Simon had caught himself a few times about to say something that would invite far too many questions.

"Good evening, Simon." Declan picked up after a couple of rings. Hearing his deep rich voice with its hint of a not easily defined European accent evoked a smile from Simon, and he settled into his chair. "Or rather good morning, as it's still morning for you, isn't it?"

"Hello, Declan, and yes, it's still morning." Simon loosened his tie. "I hope I'm not disturbing you?"

Declan chuckled. "An hour ago, you would have been, and I would be ignoring your call."

"A dinner date or something more? I hope it went well."

"Purely business, mon ami, but yes, it did. The countess is a beautiful woman."

"I'm sure." Simon mentally rolled his eyes. "How much is she worth?"

"I'm shocked, shocked that you would ask such a thing." Declan sounded more amused than anything.

"I know you, remember?"

"I wine and dine her, and then I collect payment," Declan said. "She was kind enough to invite me out to her estate tomorrow evening, and her security system is sadly lacking in its efficiency. I would be shirking my responsibilities if I didn't test it properly for her."

"I don't know why you take these kinds of risks."

"I enjoy the challenge, and practice makes perfect. Becoming bored would be more of a crime, yes?" There was a rustling noise at the other end of the telephone, and then Declan spoke again. "So are you going to tell me the real reason you called? It's not like you to waste time with small talk. I know how much you detest it."

"Am I that obvious?"

"We've known each other a long time, so to me, you are, yes." Declan poured himself a drink, or so the sound of liquid hitting ice suggested. "So come on, what is it? Have you been carded again or mistaken for one of your students?"

Simon scowled. "Why are you bothering with that drink I can hear?" Some days he wished there was still a point to consuming large amounts of alcohol. He missed being able to get drunk. "It's not as though it's going to do anything."

"There doesn't have to be a point to everything. Some of us drink because we enjoy the taste of it. You should try the concept sometime." Declan clinked his glass against something, presumably to make a point. "Stop changing the subject. You know better than to phone me and think I won't call you on whatever bullshit you have going on. Come on, surely it can't be that bad?"

"Not bad, definitely not bad…" Simon trailed off, suddenly unsure whether this was a good idea. He sighed.

"So are you going to tell me about him?"

"Bloody Forge. He's been talking to you, hasn't he?"

"He has, but not about whoever has you this worked up." Declan's chair creaked, the springs adjusting to his weight. "That sigh was a dead giveaway, and it didn't sound related to your current case." His voice softened. "It's time you started to live again, mon ami. It's been a long time since you allowed yourself to love. There's no point to this long life we've been given if we don't embrace and enjoy it."

"Considering what happened last time, do you blame me?" Simon shrugged. "Ben's a good man, and he has an enthusiasm for life I haven't seen in a very long time. He believes in people, and he's not afraid to say what he thinks and to reach out and show he cares."

"That's not a bad thing," Declan reminded him.

"What if being with me makes him lose that?" Simon stared at the ceiling of his office.

"You haven't told him, have you?" Declan made a *tsking* noise. "You can't build a relationship on a lie. I hope you're not intending to try."

"There's not much chance of that," Simon said. "If this is what I think it is and it goes much further, he's going to know everything whether I want him to or not." He'd deliberately made their good night kiss a chaste one, but it was becoming more difficult to hold himself in check rather than let go and allow himself to enjoy the sensation. He wanted to take Ben in his arms, to touch him, taste him properly, and fuck him hard. "I'm fine," he said. "I'm fine." Simon groaned aloud.

The telephone dropped from his fingers to land on top of the pile of papers in front of him.

"I can tell," Declan said. "So have you thought about the possibility that this Ben is your soulmate? Or are you too busy being fine to acknowledge what's right in front of you?"

"I've thought about it."

It figured that Declan would put two and two together and work out why Simon was so frustrated. Declan had encouraged him to pursue his feelings for Albert and listened to Simon's fears about doing so then too. Although Simon had loved Albert, this felt different, and his physical need for Ben was much stronger. Declan had been the one who'd told Simon about vampire soulbonds, but he'd been evasive when asked how he knew so much about it.

"You know this frustration you're feeling is just going to get worse, yes?" Declan poured himself another drink. "If you think you can continue to control your need for him and keep seeing him, you're an idiot."

"Thank you for the vote of confidence." Simon propped the telephone up against another pile of papers so he could continue the conversation without having to hold it. He laced his fingers together.

"You can't deny the soulmate bond. No one can. It's a part of who we are." The springs of Declan's chair groaned again. Simon heard footsteps. It sounded as though Declan was pacing. He did that when he was thinking.

"Are you suggesting I tell him?" Simon shook his head even as he said the words. "That would solve the problem, wouldn't it? I'll tell him what I am, and then keeping my distance won't be an issue at all."

"If he loves you, it won't matter to him." Declan

hummed something softly. It sounded suspiciously like some romantic song that claimed love solved everything.

Simon laughed. It sounded bitter and cracked to his ears. "Of course, it won't." What he wouldn't do for a decent drink. He licked his lips. They were dry. He swallowed, a growl escaping his lips. He was hungry too. "He already knows I'm hiding something from him." He waited a moment before continuing. "I told him about John."

"John is dead." Declan stopped pacing. "You're the only one keeping him alive."

"Am I?" Simon glared at the telephone. "Ben saw someone who might have been John yesterday. I had to explain to him why I'd needed to make sure it wasn't him."

"You're certain it wasn't?" Declan's tone had an urgency to it Simon hadn't heard in a while. "No one could have escaped that fire."

"I chained him to that pipe with the handcuffs he'd used on Forge," Simon said very quietly, lowering his voice so only another vampire could hear him. "I still hear him yelling at me to release him, Declan." He shivered. Killing was not something he enjoyed, apart from when he was driven by bloodlust. Then his thirst could not be quenched.

Simon walked over to the side table where he kept a water jug, poured himself a glass, and drained it. The liquid did nothing to quench his thirst. His fingers shook. Bloody hell. He needed to get home and feed—no, he wouldn't use that word. It wasn't that. It would never be that. He had to take supplements to stay healthy because other food couldn't do that for him. That was all.

"He got what he deserved and more." Declan changed his tone to match Simon's. "He hurt Forge. Hurt him badly. The man is—*was*—a *monster*. A sick psychopath who needed to be dealt with. If you hadn't done it, I would have."

Forge's screams shattered the stillness of the cold night air. Declan and Simon had glanced at each other and sprinted into the building, not caring for their own safety. By the time they'd found their friend, he was slumped forward and barely conscious, the silver in the restraints holding him burning into his skin like acid.

"He reasoned he was justified in what he did. He was impossible to argue with, and believe me, I tried."

Hitting John that night had been very satisfying. If he closed his eyes, Simon could still hear the crack of his fist against the jaw of the vampire who, after turning his life into a living hell, had dared to claim it was in the name of love.

John didn't know what love was. All he knew was power and possession, of taking what didn't belong to him by force.

"This man Ben saw. You know for certain it wasn't him?" Declan asked. Despite his earlier comment, it was becoming obvious he wasn't sure John was dead either.

"I'm fairly sure it wasn't him." Simon clenched his fists. "I intend to confirm it, though." He'd trace the man and see for himself. He couldn't risk John getting anywhere near Ben.

"There's something else, isn't there?"

Simon nodded, although Declan couldn't see him. "This case we're working on? Lucas has found scars on the wrists of... some of the victims."

"Silver scars?" Declan's breath hitched. "Like the ones Forge has?"

Silver not only could be used to restrain a vampire, but the physical effects from being in contact with it took a long time to heal and often left scarring. Sixty years later, Forge still had scars on his wrists from that night. He probably always would.

"Yes." Simon had gone cold when Lucas told them. Forge had hidden his reaction better, but he'd still shivered almost imperceptibly. Hours spent in John's company tended to have that effect on people. Simon had survived several days after John had caught and turned him and still wasn't sure how he'd managed to escape with his sanity intact. If Forge hadn't found him and offered to help and hide him when he had...

"There are others who are not vampires who know about the effects of silver on us. It doesn't mean anything."

"I know that." Simon narrowed his eyes, picked up his glass, started to drink, then remembered he'd already emptied it. "Maybe it's not John but someone else. Whoever it is, this can't be allowed to continue."

If whoever was responsible came anywhere near Ben, Simon would take matters into his own hands, and to hell with the consequences.

"I hope you're not thinking about going after this killer on your own."

"Of course not." Simon kept his tone light. "I'm not an idiot." He ran his finger around the edge of the glass. His voice hardened. "I will, however, do whatever it takes to protect Ben. If and when whoever is behind this becomes even a hint of a threat, I'll bloody kill them myself."

Declan sighed. "Yes, you are an idiot. I can understand you want to protect him, but you're not going to be of much help if you end up a pile of dust at his feet, are you? Promise me you'll be careful?"

After a long silence, Simon shrugged.

"Simon? Was that a yes? I can't hear you."

"No," Simon said, "that was a maybe."

Ben glanced up from wiping down the table. Ron, the café owner, was walking toward him, and he had someone with him. Ben frowned. The man with Ron had been in the café for the last hour or so, talking to both staff and customers, but he hadn't come near Ben as yet.

It looked as though his luck in avoiding whatever was going on had just run out.

"Ben, this is Detective Forge of the Boggslake Police Department. He has a few questions." Ron smiled. "Take whatever time you need, Detective. I'm sure we can spare him for however long this takes."

Forge? As in *Simon's* Forge?

Had something happened? Ben forced himself to remain calm.

"Thanks, Mr. McKay, I appreciate your cooperation." Forge pulled out a chair at the table Ben had been cleaning and sat down. He was a tall guy in his thirties and had at least four inches on Ben. Reaching across the table, Forge offered his hand to Ben, who shook it and then sat opposite him. Forge had a strong grip, and his skin was very cool to the touch, like Simon's. "Jonas Forge. And you're Ben Leyton, right?"

He was definitely Simon's Forge. Jonas wasn't exactly a common name, and he hadn't consulted any notes when he'd used Ben's full name, nor had Ron introduced him using it. Besides, how many Jonas Forges would there be in the city in the same occupation? Simon hadn't mentioned a description or that the guy was easy on the eyes. Not that Forge was Ben's type, but it didn't hurt to notice stuff like that. However, where Simon had an air of being almost olde worlde—for want of a better description—Forge didn't in any way. His dress jeans and leather jacket were very different from Simon's usual attire.

"Yeah." Ben hesitated for a moment, then decided it was better to be up-front. "You're Simon's friend, right? He's okay, isn't he?" They hadn't seen each other since dinner on Monday evening, although they'd exchanged a few texts. It was now Wednesday. Ben figured Simon was busy with work, as he hadn't come into the café in the last few days, and he'd been evasive when Ben suggested they meet again on the weekend.

"You'd know that one better than I would." Forge grinned. "I figured he's probably mentioned me." He had dark brown hair, almost auburn, and his blue eyes were intense, his gaze suggesting he didn't miss much. "He's definitely mentioned you."

"Oh." Ben felt himself blush. Forge's grin widened. "So what did you want to talk to me about, *Detective*?" If Forge wanted to tease him, he could do it somewhere else, not while he was at work where he would probably get flak for it later.

The change of subject got a nod of what appeared to be approval from Forge. "I was hoping you might be able to help with a current investigation," he said, the humor disappearing from his voice. Forge pulled a photograph from his pocket and laid it on the table between them. "I believe you've met this man."

Ben peered at the photo. His eyes widened, and a chill ran through him. It was the customer from the other day, the creep who had rattled Simon. He chose his words carefully. "He was in here on Monday. He's not a regular, and I hadn't seen him before. He hasn't been in since either."

"He talked to you." It was a statement, not a question. "What was the conversation about?"

"Nothing in particular. Just the weather and that kind of stuff, and he noticed my accent." Ben frowned. "Has something happened to him?"

"We believe he was murdered." Forge studied Ben as though he was looking for a reaction. "I was hoping you might have some information that could help track down his killer."

"Murdered? Shit." Ben's frown deepened. "Does this have anything to do with Simon's friend being killed?" The neighborhood was beginning to feel distinctly unsafe. However much of a creep this guy had been, no one deserved to die.

"How much do you know about that?" Forge seemed surprised. It appeared Simon hadn't shared that bit of information.

"Not much," Ben admitted. "I only found out because I was with him and saw his reaction. He was upset. He said they'd known each other a long time."

"Yes, they had," Forge confirmed. He studied Ben a few more moments. "Are you sure there's not anything else you want to tell me?" He smiled, as though trying to put Ben at ease.

Ben pointed to the photo. "If it's any help, he had a British accent like Simon's." It was information they wouldn't get from a corpse.

"That's interesting." Forge's eyes narrowed, not the same reaction as Simon's, but still a reaction. "Anything else? You're sure your conversation with him was just about the weather?"

"Yeah. Pretty much." Ben shrugged. "He struck me as a

bit of a creep, but we get all sorts in here. It's certainly not enough to kill someone over."

"You'd be surprised what motivates someone to kill," Forge said. "Sometimes it doesn't take much." He picked up the photo and studied it for a moment. "Did you mention this guy to Simon?"

"Why do you want to know that?"

"What was his reaction?" Forge lowered his voice. "Look, I'm not accusing anyone of anything. I just want to know. You're not in trouble."

Ben's heart started to race. He gripped the edge of the table. Surely, Forge couldn't think Simon had anything to do with this guy's death? The idea was crazy. Simon wouldn't do anything like this, and besides, they'd already sorted out this guy wasn't his ex. "Does this guy have a name? Or aren't you allowed to tell me that?"

"We haven't identified him as yet," Forge said. "Did he mention anything personal, like a name or something that might be a clue to where he lives?" He cocked his head to the side as though listening to something Ben couldn't hear. "It's not John Wells."

Ben raised his head with a start. "You know about John?" He realized how much of a stupid question it was as soon as the words were out of his mouth. Simon had said he'd known Forge a long time. Of course, Forge would know about John.

"I've had the displeasure of meeting him, yes." Forge's expression suggested he'd just tasted something foul. "Consider yourself lucky you haven't." He tucked the photo away in his jacket. "Did Simon think this guy might be John?"

"He wasn't," Ben said somewhat sharply. "You said so yourself."

"That's not what I asked."

"I don't know anything else about this guy that I haven't already told you, Detective," Ben said. He glared at Forge. "He had a passing resemblance to John, that's all, and Simon knew that." He stood, ready to leave the conversation. He'd had enough of it. Why was Forge asking about Simon's ex? This guy wasn't him. Surely he couldn't think Simon had anything to do with this? "Go do whatever it is you do, and catch whoever did this, rather than wasting time asking questions about someone who *thinks* you're his friend."

"Sit down, Ben," Forge said. He sneezed a couple of times.

"Why? Are you going to arrest me if I don't?" Ben turned to go. He wasn't going to listen to any more of this.

Forge chuckled. "No. Simon would have my ass if I did, and you haven't done anything wrong." Something in his tone made Ben hesitate. "Sit down, Ben. Please."

"I can't help you with your investigation. I've told you everything I know," Ben repeated.

"I don't want to talk to you about that. Consider me off duty for the next few minutes if that helps." Forge sneezed again. "Damn allergies," he muttered.

Ben sat down. A couple of customers were staring at him. He ignored them. "Okay, but any more crap and I'm going back to work."

"Firstly, let's get one thing straight," Forge said. "Simon's my friend, and he's saved my life more times than I can count. I've known him a lot longer than you ever will, and I'm not accusing him of anything. I just wanted to be sure of your feelings toward him."

"You could have just asked. It doesn't piss people off so much that way."

"Yeah, but it doesn't give me your gut reaction, does it?"

Forge looked more than a little smug. "Words are sometimes just that, but there's no mistaking how you feel about him with the way you just spoke to me."

"It wasn't personal," Ben said. It probably wouldn't do to anger Simon's friends, especially if Forge was just doing what he claimed.

"Yeah, I get that." Forge glanced around. The café was fairly busy, but most of the customers and staff seemed focused on their own affairs, now that Ben's temper was receding. "Simon's a good guy, and I haven't seen him let himself care for someone like he does for you in a very long time."

"I care about him too."

"I can see that." Forge leaned forward. "You already know about John, so I'm not telling you anything new when I say Simon's been hurt badly in the past."

Ben sighed. He had a feeling he knew what was coming. "You're going to give me the 'hurt him and I'll kill you' speech, aren't you? It's really not necessary, you know. I don't intend to hurt him, and I'll be pissed at myself if I do."

"You're a bright guy," Forge said, "and direct with it. I can see why Simon likes you. And yeah, that's pretty much it in a nutshell. Hurt him and I'll find you." He stood, their conversation apparently at an end. "Welcome to Boggslake, Ben, and remind Simon he needs to bring you round some-time." He pulled a card out of his pocket and handed it to Ben. "Take care of yourself. Stay away from anyone you don't know, and don't invite anyone into your apartment. Okay?"

"Okay. I'm not about to do anything stupid." Ben wondered if the two murders were related. Forge's last comment seemed to suggest a risk that whoever was behind them might not be done yet.

"That makes one of you, at least. If you think of anything else, call me. My cell's on the card." Forge inclined his head. "Good to finally meet you, Ben." He headed to the door, shoving on a pair of dark glasses before he stepped out of the café into the sunlight.

"Yeah," said Ben softly. "Good to finally meet you too."

~

Simon put down the history magazine he was reading and drained the rest of his coffee. To say his focus was somewhat lacking would be an understatement. It was completely shot. Instead of the words on the page, he kept thinking about Ben and the dinner they'd shared several evenings before.

He'd said far too much to Ben, but he'd also not said enough. Declan was right. It was going to be more... difficult to ignore this soulbond the longer he tried.

A groan escaped his lips. Apparently his cock hadn't got the memo that he was deliberately avoiding the use of the word *hard*. His hand drifted lower, and he stroked himself, his eyes closing.

"Don't let me interrupt you. We can talk when you're finished."

"Bloody hell, Forge." Simon's eyes snapped open, the words jerking him back to reality like cold water. "Haven't you heard of knocking?"

"You're in our shared living space," Forge said with a grin. "I don't need to knock." He sat down on the couch opposite Simon's and put two cups down on the coffee table between them. "Coffee for me, and I figured you'd want some tea."

"Thank you." Simon didn't see the point in mentioning he'd been drinking coffee. "How's the investigation going?"

"They found another body this morning," Forge said, sipping his coffee. He seemed to be watching Simon, as though waiting for some kind of reaction.

"Body as in singular, not plural?" Simon asked, raising one eyebrow.

"Yeah. The guy was definitely killed by a vampire, though." Forge met Simon's gaze. "Good thing I know you don't hunt anymore, or I might have thought you'd done it." Although his tone was light, it didn't hide the underlying seriousness in his voice.

"Why would you have thought I'd done it?" Simon shook his head. Although Forge had said Simon hadn't, he'd apparently entertained the notion.

"Does this guy remind you of anyone?" Forge retrieved a photograph from his pocket and dropped it on the table.

"No, should he?" Simon peered at it more closely and frowned. Actually, come to think of it, he did match the description Ben had given him.

"That's what I thought," Forge said, watching his reaction. "Add the fact he had an accent like yours *and* had been chatting up your boyfriend, and hell, I might have been tempted to go after him myself."

Simon scowled. "How did you know about that?" His eyes narrowed. "Please tell me you haven't involved Ben in this."

"He's already involved. He met the victim and might have had some info we could use to find whoever is behind all this." Forge shook his head. "If there's even a chance your psycho ex is still out there, don't you think Ben needs to know what he's dealing with?"

"John's not my ex," Simon corrected, shivering. His

teacup shook, and he put it back on the table. The memory of John touching him and the endearments whispered in his ear still made him feel ill.

"Ben thinks he is." Forge's voice was calm. "He's a bright guy, Simon, and he's already figured out there's something more going on with you than you're telling him."

"Did he tell you that?"

"Nope, but it doesn't take much to see it." Forge took a long drink of coffee. "He's protective of you too." He seemed thoughtful. "I implied you might have had something to do with this murder, and he wasn't having any of it. Interesting for someone who doesn't really know you, don't you think?"

"You have no right to talk to him about any of this." Simon glared at Forge. "It's safer for Ben if he doesn't know what's going on."

Forge snorted, then sneezed a couple of times. "Like hell it is. I'm investigating a crime, so I have every right to talk to him about it. We have bodies piling up, and suddenly one of the murders breaks the pattern and the victim just happens to have been chatting up Ben a couple of days before. Think about it."

"It could have been an isolated vampire killing," Simon said, knowing how weak the argument sounded. He handed Forge a box of tissues. "And take your bloody allergy pills. You know how you get when you don't."

Forge took a tissue and blew his nose, but ignored Simon's comment about his allergies. "When was the last time we had one of those in Boggslake? That's the whole thing with living here, remember? There's an unspoken treaty with the humans. We don't hunt them, no matter how tempting it might be."

"Maybe the killer got disturbed before he could finish

off the vampire responsible, so he or she is still out there, and that's why there wasn't a second body." Simon didn't believe what he'd said for a moment. Maybe if Cynthia hadn't been one of the vampires involved, but even so... All vampires in Boggslake knew that hunting humans was not tolerated and the Supernatural Council would send someone to deal with any perpetrators if they dared step out of line.

This case had the council rattled, something that didn't happen often. That was a worry in itself.

"Maybe." Forge didn't look convinced. He glanced at the magazine Simon had discarded. "What are you really afraid of? Keeping Ben safe or his reaction when he finds out you're a vampire?"

"That's none of your business." Simon stood. If Forge was in this kind of a mood, he'd finish his reading elsewhere.

"It's definitely my business." Forge's eyes narrowed. "You're my friend, Simon, and I care about you. I know what you've gone through in the past, but don't you think it's time you stopped living there and started thinking about the here and now?"

"How dare you?" Simon's voice rose, but he didn't walk away. To hell with letting Forge say what he wanted and think he was going to get away with it. "This is my life, Forge, and I'll do what I bloody well want with it." He swallowed. His mouth was dry. "I know the past is gone, I'm very aware of that, so there's no need to point out the obvious."

"The way you talk about it, sometimes I think it's where you'd prefer to be, clinging to what's happened rather than what might be. You're not the only one who's lost someone. We all go through that, but you need to let it go, let them go. What you're doing won't bring anyone back, and not only that, it's dangerous as hell no matter who is behind all of this."

Simon sat down again. He clenched his fists. "I'm not living in the past," he said quietly. "How could you think that?"

"If you don't give it up, that's all you're going to be left with. You have a nice guy who wants to get to know you, the real you. Ben cares about you. With everything going down, don't you think you owe him the truth? Isn't it better to be honest and give him the choice to at least walk away with the knowledge of how to defend himself against vampires, than to keep yourself safe and have something happen to him?"

"What if something happens to him anyway?"

Forge made a frustrated noise. "Go on, justify it to yourself all you want, but that doesn't make it right. Give him some credit. You're a good guy underneath all that baggage you cart around with you. Stop being a jackass and let him in."

They glared at each other for a moment, and then Simon lowered his gaze. Forge shrugged, grabbed his coffee, and stalked out of the room.

The air shimmered and then solidified into Boggs. "Simon," he started to say, but Simon shook his head.

"I don't need you to tell me something I already know," he said, getting to his feet and heading for his apartment. "Forge has done that in spades. Just leave me alone. Leave me *alone*."

CHAPTER SEVEN

"You're worried about something. Anything you want to talk about?" Ben asked. He'd noticed Simon's nervousness grow into agitation since they'd finished their coffee. "Is this something to do with whatever happened last night?"

Simon had phoned him late the previous evening and asked if he wanted to meet. His tone suggested something was up, but he'd denied it when Ben asked, then apologized for not contacting him sooner.

"What makes you think something happened last night?" Simon shoved on a pair of dark glasses as they walked out of Hunter's Café and glanced around as though expecting to see something or someone.

"Because you sounded a bit off then, and something's very obviously making you edgy now." Ben glanced up at the sky. The sun really wasn't bright enough to warrant Simon's reaction with the glasses. Come to think of it, Ben had never seen him out during the day without them. "You're not worried about that murder Forge told me about, are you?"

"A little," Simon admitted. "I'd feel better knowing who

was responsible and that they've been dealt with. Doesn't it worry you that that man was killed after he spoke to you?"

Ben shrugged. "Yeah, a bit, but I'm trying not to think about it. I can't help but wonder if the same person is responsible for the death of your friend too."

"I hope not." Simon swallowed and grew quiet.

"They'll find the person who killed her." Ben tried to sound reassuring. He slipped his hand into Simon's. "Forge strikes me as someone who knows what he's doing."

"Yes, he's been doing this a long time." Simon squeezed Ben's hand and smiled. He licked his lips and swallowed again.

"Why don't you just come out and say whatever's bothering you?" Ben suggested. "I promise I don't bite."

Simon paled. "I don't either," he said hurriedly.

"I don't mind if you do." Ben flushed bright red as soon as he'd spoken. "Sorry, that just kind of came out."

"There's no need to apologize, and I'm not doing this very well." Simon took a deep breath. "We need to talk, and I'd prefer we did it somewhere more private. Would you like to come back to my place? I promise, if you want to leave afterwards, I won't stop you."

"Why are you so sure I'll want to leave?" Ben frowned. Was Simon going to finally share whatever secret he'd been keeping? "I'm sure, whatever it is, it won't be that bad." He managed a laugh. "After all, it's not as though you're an axe murderer or something, right?"

"I've never used an axe," Simon said.

"Very funny," Ben said, although Simon's expression didn't seem to suggest he was making a joke.

Simon shrugged.

Ben slid his other arm around Simon's waist and pulled him close. "Look, I know you're nervous about whatever this is, but I'm not planning to go anywhere. I trust you. I don't know why, but I do. I like being with you, and I'd like to see where this goes. Hell, I want it to go somewhere." He kissed Simon softly.

"You might not after tonight." Simon leaned into Ben, the hardness of his erection very obvious even through his coat. Whatever this was about, Simon wanted Ben as much as Ben wanted him.

"Yeah, but don't make that decision for me already." Ben kissed Simon again. Warmth flowed through him, and he groaned aloud.

Simon broke the kiss abruptly. "We can't do this here," he said, trembling. His skin was flushed, and he was breathing heavily. He started to lead Ben back to the car. "Please."

"Okay. But once we've talked and you've told me whatever..." Ben felt himself grow bright red. God, he sucked at this. "You're okay, right? You've been tested? I haven't been with anyone for a couple of years, and—"

"I'm not contagious, Ben." Simon opened the passenger door of the car for him. "You're not going to catch anything from me, I promise."

"I wasn't implying you were," Ben said. "I just wanted you to know I was okay in case we wanted to continue this when we get to your place." He shifted uncomfortably. That kiss had really got him going, and he was hard as hell. "I want you, Simon, and I'm not going to pretend I don't, but if you're not someone who jumps into bed after a few dates, that's okay."

Had they only known each other a couple of weeks? It felt much longer than that, almost like they'd always been a part of each other but like a shadow just out of reach. It was weird, but in a good way.

"Follow your instincts," his granddad had always told him. That's what Ben was doing now, with Simon. Wasn't it?

"I want you too, Ben," Simon said quietly. "I haven't been able to think about anything else for days. It's one of the reasons I haven't asked you out again since dinner the other night."

"Only one of the reasons?"

Simon fumbled for his keys and dropped them, his hand shaking when he picked them up. Ben went to help him, and their fingers brushed together. Heat surged through him, going straight to his cock.

"Declan was right," Simon muttered, jerking back as though he'd been burned. "I am a bloody idiot."

"He's your friend who lives in Europe?" Ben fastened his seat belt, taking care to keep his distance from Simon. He hoped the conversation would help distract them from what they both wanted until they got to Simon's apartment. He bit his lip in an attempt to control his growing excitement. At this rate, they'd be lucky if they made it through the front door.

"Yes." Simon grew quiet again, his attention seemingly focused on the road, although a couple of times it seemed he was about to say something but changed his mind.

Finally, they pulled into a long driveway in the grounds of an enormous old house with a rusty iron fence. It looked run-down and in serious need of attention. Paint peeled off the windows, and the flower garden was a mix of weeds and overgrown bushes. "This is where you live?" Ben asked. It reminded him of something out of one of the old Hammer horror movies.

"Welcome to Boggs's Castle," Simon said, already getting out of the car. There were two other vehicles parked in front of the house. One was a classic Mustang, the other a battered Jeep, which meant that at least one, if not both, of Simon's friends were home.

Once out on the pavement, Ben craned his neck, looked up, and counted four more floors above the front door. "You said castle before," he said, "but I didn't take much notice. It's a lot smaller than I expected, but I'm no expert. I've only seen one once, and that was some time ago. Is it a real one?"

While the silence between them on the drive over had taken the edge off his physical desire, another distraction wouldn't be a bad thing. This was ridiculous; he had more control than this. Simon wanted to talk first, and Ben wasn't going to embarrass himself like some hormonal teenager who couldn't keep it in his pants.

"Boggs insists it is a real castle and gets upset when anyone implies otherwise." Simon lowered his voice. "I made the mistake once of saying my family home was bigger and asking if perhaps this was originally a gatehouse. It's not a mistake I'll repeat."

"Boggs as in the name of the city?" Ben glanced at Simon, certain he'd heard that wrong, but Simon just nodded. "I hope that wasn't a roundabout way of telling me the place is haunted by one of its founders." He hadn't put two and two together before about the name of the house.

Was that what Simon wanted to talk about? That he lived in a haunted house and thought it might scare Ben away?

"Yes, it is haunted, and he *is* one of the city's founders." Simon pointed to the first floor, or was that what was called the second floor here? Ben still hadn't managed to figure that one out. A balcony with an iron railing around the edge of it extended out from the brickwork. "That's my apartment. Forge lives on the floor above, and the one above that is for guests. Lucas has the top floor. It keeps his mess in one place that way, and whatever else it is he does up there." He grimaced.

Ben took an instinctive step backward.

"Don't worry. It's perfectly respectable on the inside, or at least the floors that aren't Lucas's are. Having it appear run-down on the outside discourages a lot of unwelcome visitors."

Ben took a deep breath. "Okay," he said, torn between wanting to turn around and walk away and the thought that this was all rather cool and definitely worth exploring further. "Lead on." If Simon wasn't afraid of this ghost, then Ben wouldn't be either.

The steps leading up to the impressive double wooden doors seemed sturdy enough. A huge stone container sat on the ground floor balcony, and Ben noticed what appeared to be an old birdbath or fountain peeking out from under the eaves.

As soon as Simon's key turned in the lock, Ben heard barking. Simon stepped inside and dropped to one knee to pat a big dog. With his other hand, he motioned Ben to come forward. "Moose, this is Ben," Simon said. "He's a friend."

Ben held out one hand and let the dog sniff it. Moose wagged his tail and slobbered all over Ben's hand. Moose definitely had some German Shepherd in him, and he seemed friendly enough, although Ben doubted he would have been so accepted if he hadn't been with Simon. "Hi, Moose," Ben said. "Nice to meet you, boy. He is a boy, right?"

"Definitely a boy, yeah," a familiar voice confirmed. Ben looked up and saw Forge watching them. "Hey, Ben. Good to see Simon's finally got the sense to bring you home with him."

"Hello, Detective Forge. Is Moose yours?" Ben glanced around, and his eyes widened. Simon's comment that the castle was respectable on the inside was a serious understatement. The decor looked immaculate, the wooden floors and staircase polished, the slats on the shuttered doors restored to their original glory.

"Yeah, he is, and it's just Forge." Forge gave a low whistle, and Moose trotted over to his side. "C'mon, boy, you can slobber over Ben some more later." He grinned. "You guys don't want us hanging around while you sort out the important stuff." Forge gazed at Simon for a moment.

"No, we don't." Simon's focus shifted to somewhere behind Forge, but when Ben looked, there was no one there. "Not even if you knock."

"I think you just upset him, questioning his good manners like that," Forge said dryly. "Don't worry, Ben. This will all make sense once Simon's explained it. Won't it, Simon?" He turned and walked away before Simon could answer.

"Huh?" Ben frowned. What the hell was he missing? Or was the ghost just the beginning of whatever this was about?

"That wasn't even subtle," Simon muttered. "Don't mind him. He's just trying to make a point."

"Who was he talking about?" Ben decided what the hell, and followed Simon up the winding staircase to the next floor. "Forge hasn't seen the ghost as well, has he?"

"I meant what I said about leaving if you wanted to." Simon walked a few steps down the hallway that led off the landing to his floor and stopped in front of a door. "None of these doors have locks, and no one will stop you if that's what you decide to do."

"You sound as though you've already decided that's what I'm going to do." Ben shook his head. "I haven't, and you talking like I have is getting bloody annoying." As weirdness went, so far it wasn't anything he couldn't handle. So what if this place was haunted? Simon, Forge, and Moose didn't seem fazed by it, and that had to be a good sign, right? It would also serve to make life a bit more interesting. He hadn't met a ghost before, but that didn't mean they weren't out there.

"When I've told you, you'll understand why." Simon opened the door and stood back to allow Ben to enter first.

Ben made a frustrated noise. "Did you even listen to a word I just said?" He walked into the apartment, and his jaw dropped. "You *live* here?"

The large room reminded him of a stately home he'd once visited in Christchurch. The polished hardwood floors were covered with Oriental-style rugs, and the room itself was furnished in solid wood, the style of which wouldn't have been out of place in the early years of the previous century. Tasteful artwork adorned the walls, and a couple of comfortable leather sofas faced each other in the center of the room. A grand piano stood near the window. Ben walked over to it and struck one of the keys. He didn't play, but his mum did and the Bach fugue open on the stand was one of her favorites.

"I like to be comfortable. The piano was my uncle's. It's the one he taught me to play when I was a child. Those are some of my happiest memories," Simon said. "I've wanted to bring you here and show you."

"There's no TV." There was, however, an expensive

stereo system, and the back wall was lined in bookcases filled with both books and CDs.

"I don't watch it." Simon leaned back against one of the bookcases and crossed his arms. "You're the first person I've invited here for a very long time."

"Thank you." Ben rubbed his palms against his jeans, his mind helpfully supplying the thought that Simon's bedroom was behind one of the doors on the far side of the room. Now they were in the apartment and had some privacy, his desire for Simon was growing again. Distraction only went so far.

"We need to talk." Simon took off his coat and hung it on an old-fashioned coat stand by the door. "Can I take your jacket?"

"Sure." Ben handed it to him. Their fingers brushed. Simon was trembling, and very flushed. "You okay?" Ben asked softly when Simon finished hanging the jacket.

Simon nodded. He took Ben's hand, brought it up to his lips, and kissed it. "I want you, Ben."

"I want you too, Simon," Ben said, but Simon shook his head.

"You need to know what you're getting into first." Simon's voice was hoarse. "Come, sit with me." Without letting go of Ben's hand, Simon led him over to the sofa.

Once they were seated, Ben glanced up and froze. "What's wrong with your eyes? Or are you wearing contacts?"

Simon's eyes were completely brown, no white showing at all.

"I'm not wearing contact lenses." Simon released Ben's hand. "It's a part of what I am," he said, watching Ben closely. "Usually it's easier to control it, but not now. Not this close to you, when I want you." He shrugged. "All things considered, it seems foolish to waste energy trying to right now."

"Is that why you wear dark glasses?" Ben frowned. "Does it hurt? There is something wrong, isn't there? That's what you're trying to tell me, isn't it?" He moved closer to Simon, his hand resting on Simon's knee. "Look, if you're sick, that's okay. We'll get through whatever it is, together." Ben could feel the heat of Simon's skin through his pants. Was he running a fever? He leaned forward to place his other hand on Simon's forehead, but Simon shook his head.

If Simon thought that would scare him off, he was wrong. Ben wasn't in the habit of running out on his friends once they ran into some kind of trouble, and he wouldn't now.

"Sick?" Simon laughed. "I wish it was that easy. I haven't been sick in nearly one hundred years." He wet his lips with his tongue, and Ben could have sworn there was something weird about his teeth he hadn't noticed before.

"One hundred years? Stop the crap, please, Simon. You don't have to make anything up. Just tell me the truth."

Simon made a choked noise. "I'm a vampire," he said so quietly Ben almost missed it. "I'm a vampire," he repeated, louder this time.

"No, you're not," Ben said. Surely Simon couldn't believe what he was saying. "Come on, how bad is this thing you won't tell me? If you're going to keep lying, at least find something a bit more believable. Vampires don't exist. They're not real."

"It's the truth. I'm not lying to you. We do exist, and this is real." Simon took Ben's hand in his own, shifting it from his leg, and placed their joined hands over his heart. "I'm aroused as hell, my heart should be pounding, and you can't feel it, can you? It beats a lot slower than yours. The whites of my eyes have completely disappeared, and I have fangs." He opened his mouth to show Ben. "Think about it."

"I've seen you out in sunlight," Ben protested, snatching his hand away. "Do you have any mirrors? Get me one and I'll show you your reflection. Wearing contacts and fake fangs aren't going to cut it, even if they do help you to believe in this delusion yourself." If he could show Simon how crazy this idea was by presenting him with something he couldn't deny, it might help.

"I don't have any. I never saw the point, as I don't reflect. They're also a reminder of what I am."

"What if I take a photo?" Ben had his phone in his jacket pocket. He went to get it, but when Simon shook his head, he sat down again. "Don't tell me. Your kind of vampire do show up on photos so it's not going to prove anything."

"I don't photograph." Simon smiled sadly. "You've already taken a photograph of me. Remember that day in the park when we first met? I didn't get out of the way of your camera in time."

"You're not a vampire. Stop scaring me." Fuck, it was just his luck, wasn't it? He'd finally found a guy he really liked and wanted to sleep with, and something like this happened. "There are easier ways to let a guy down, you know. I don't understand how you can act like you want me and then pull something like this." Ben wanted to be angry, but Simon really sounded and looked like he believed what he was saying. "Why don't we go downstairs and talk to Forge about this? He can help, I'm sure."

"Forge is a vampire too," Simon said. "All this time I've been psyching myself up to tell you what I am, and I never considered you wouldn't believe me."

"Do you blame me? Seriously? It's right out there." Ben

sighed. Of course, Forge was a vampire. How stupid he was to think otherwise. He wasn't about to ask what Lucas was. God knew what the answer would be for that one. "And no, he's not. I've seen him out in sunlight too."

"We don't combust in sunlight. It's a story circulated by vampires to give humans a security blanket. If humans think they're safe during the daytime, we have a better chance of surviving when they decide to hunt us, which they have done many times over the past centuries."

"You have an answer for everything, don't you?"

"It's the truth." Simon spoke calmly enough, but his eyes had a haunted look, a real fear. "You seemed to accept it when I told you the castle was haunted. How is this so different?"

"Because this is about *you*, and I—" Ben stood. Fuck this. "We'll get you some help, Simon, I promise." He wiped at his eyes, hoping Simon wouldn't notice the tears. God, why? He didn't want this crap. He just wanted to pretend it hadn't happened.

"And I what?" Simon lowered his gaze and spoke very softly.

"I was going to tell you tonight that I love you." Ben's thoughts rushed out of his mouth. He'd never been able to control his brain-to-mouth filters when he was upset. "I don't sleep with just anyone, you know. I thought we might have a future together. I wanted one. I've never felt like this towards anyone before I met you." He ran his hand through his hair. All this, and he still wanted Simon. They'd find him some help, a way of convincing him that none of his delusions were real. Forge would be able to help, and so would Lucas. They were Simon's friends. Why didn't they know about this? Why hadn't they warned him? Ben groaned aloud, wishing he could hit something, *hard*.

"I'm sorry." Simon didn't move from the sofa. His fingers curled around Ben's wrist, holding him, his grip like steel. "I had hoped telling you would be enough. Everything I've said is the truth. I promise. I can prove it. At least let me do that. Then you can leave, and I'll never bother you again if that's what you want."

"It's not what I want," Ben whispered, pondering his own sanity. He slipped free of Simon's grasp when it loosened but didn't move toward the door. "I still want to be with you." He managed a shaky laugh. How desperate was he, clinging to one final thread of hope this might still work out? What the fuck was wrong with him? His mind might be screaming at him to run, yet his body was still yearning to be with Simon, to touch him, to kiss him. "You said you can prove it. So prove it."

Simon stood and wrapped one arm around Ben, pulling him close. He gently used the edge of one finger to wipe Ben's tears. "I love you. I know that now I'm about to lose you," he whispered. "I wanted a future with you so much. I'm so sorry, Ben." He smiled sadly. "You're a good man, and thank you for allowing me at least this."

He leaned in and kissed Ben on the lips, deepening it when Ben moaned into it.

God, it felt so good, being in Simon's arms like this. He'd get Simon some help, whatever it took. He at least could do that much, couldn't he?

Simon's embrace tightened, and he let out a sob.

Cannon fire sounded overhead. Dirt trenches fortified by wood surrounded him on either side. Men screamed. Someone fell into the trench next to him, the man's body hitting the ground with a dull thud, his sightless eyes staring straight ahead.

Ben whimpered. He knew what this was, but he didn't

know how. They were snippets in his mind of a lifetime that wasn't his, a movie of jerky, unconnected scenes. But instead of watching from a safe distance, he was there, smelling the stench of death and blood, experiencing it for himself like a living nightmare.

He held a slender dark-haired man who lay still, unmoving, dead. "Stephen!" Despair turned to fear. He looked up and saw a young man smiling down at him, his piercing blue eyes as cold as ice.

"Run, Simon," the young man whispered. "Run but I'll find you. I'll always find you."

The scene shifted.

An older man in an old-fashioned suit shouted at him. The woman in the long dress cried and begged the man to stop. "Get out. You're not my son. He's dead. You're a monster."

The images came faster.

Blood. He was surrounded by blood. He couldn't escape the smell. Another man, another death. "I'm not yours, John. Leave me alone!" Ben screamed the words, but the voice was unmistakably Simon's.

He wanted to escape. He couldn't do this. He didn't want to think about it, didn't want to feel. He wiped his hand across his mouth. It came away covered in blood. He let the girl in his arms fall to the floor, tried to cry out, but only managed a whimper.

Ben yanked himself free from Simon's embrace. Tears ran down Simon's face. He was shaking, something akin to terror in his eyes.

"Simon?" Ben barely managed to form the word. He felt the world spin; his legs barely held him. He staggered over to the sofa and sat down. "What the hell just happened?" It had felt so real. It was real. It had to be. But how?

Simon backed away. "I didn't want you to see any of that. I'd hoped… I wanted you to know what I am, to just believe me so I wouldn't have to. Not if you didn't want… us." He pulled himself together, his shoulders slumped. "This is what I am." He sounded exhausted, resigned. "This is what happens when we first give ourselves to our soulmate."

"But why now? We've kissed before, and I didn't see anything."

"You hadn't told me you wanted me then. That's how it works. In saying the words, you invited me in, just like you invited me into your home. If you were a vampire, I would have seen your life too."

"I'm not a vampire," Ben said flatly. No denying what he'd just seen. Images from a time long past.

"I know that," Simon said. "But as I told you, I am."

"Everything you told me, it's true, isn't it?" Ben felt numb. He knew he should be afraid, but he couldn't make himself feel anything. A slow thump started in his head. "I saw blood. I… you were drinking blood."

"I won't hurt you. I don't do that anymore."

Ben stood. He shivered. Simon was a vampire. He'd seen death, so much death. How many people had he killed? "I'm not running," Ben said, his voice wavering. "I just can't deal with this, not all of it, not like this. I'm sorry. I need…"

He needed some time to get his head around it.

"I won't hurt you," Simon repeated, his voice flat. Tears ran down his cheeks as he wrapped his arms around himself.

"You already have," Ben whispered, ashamed of his reaction, of the hurt on Simon's face. "I'm sorry. I can't..."

He ran for the door and slammed it behind him. He wasn't sure how he made it down the stairs, his vision blurring with tears. Even the air outside felt hot and constricting. His body was on fire, he couldn't think straight, he didn't know what to do or where he was going.

He didn't care.

He ran.

CHAPTER EIGHT

Ben leaned against a wall, gasping. He glanced around, trying to get his bearings, but had no clue where he was. He'd run from Simon's like the hounds of hell were after him, ignoring the weird looks from the people he'd passed.

So much for telling Simon he wouldn't run. Ben bit his lip. *Damn it!* He closed his eyes, and an image came to his mind of Simon with tears running down his cheeks, looking as though he'd been punched in the gut.

Ben had reacted exactly the way Simon feared he would.

"I'm so sorry," Ben whispered. How could he have done that to the man he loved? Ben groaned aloud. Despite what he now knew, he still loved Simon and cared about him. Knowing what he'd done made him feel sick to his stomach.

He had to go back, yet he couldn't help but shiver at the thought. Simon was a vampire, something that wasn't supposed to exist. A creature of the night, an evil—

He couldn't believe Simon was evil. Ben touched his cheek, remembering the gentleness of Simon's caress, the way his lips twitched into a smile, and the emotion behind his words when he'd told Ben he loved him.

Every instinct in Ben screamed at him that Simon was a good man and someone he wanted to be with. Yet he couldn't get his mind around what he'd seen when they'd kissed. All that blood and death. Simon had not only drunk blood, he'd enjoyed the taste of it and killed the woman in his arms to get it.

Simon had also been horrified at what he'd become. The memory of the emotions hit Ben in a sudden wave. He dropped to his knees and vomited into the gutter by the side of the wall.

Ben had not only seen snapshots of Simon's life, but he'd experienced it, emotions and all. How could Simon live with those memories, with the knowledge of what he'd done? Yet, being appalled by his actions hadn't stopped him.

Above Ben, a sign winked off, leaving him in semidarkness. He stood, wiped his hand across his mouth, and swallowed, tasting bile. Where the hell was he? He shivered and remembered he'd left his jacket at Simon's apartment.

The sign started to glow again, softly at first and then growing to a harsh light accompanied by a loud crackling noise. He looked up, curious, before the light died once more.

Knuckle Bone Bar.

It was weird, as bar names went, but perhaps in the light of recent events, he needed to seriously reconsider his definition of weird. A drink sounded good about now, despite common sense reminding him that a beer probably wouldn't be a good idea, especially as he'd just thrown up. He inwardly shrugged. In the grand scheme of how the day was going, what did it matter? To be honest, he didn't care.

He opened the door of the bar and walked in. The conversation stopped, and he could have sworn every head in the place turned to stare at him. He swallowed, suddenly feeling uneasy, like he was encroaching on something he knew nothing about.

"Don't be bloody stupid," he muttered and forced himself to approach the bar. The place seemed tidy enough, and music played over loudspeakers. He didn't recognize the tune. The bartender was clean-shaven, heavyset, and he wore his hair slicked back. He had a tea towel slung over his shoulder.

Ben cleared his throat. "I'll have a beer, please," he said.

The bartender's nostrils flared, and he glared at Ben. He was about six foot and not someone Ben would want to take on in a fight. "We don't serve your kind in here," he said.

"My kind?" Ben asked. What the hell was he on about? Surely it wasn't Ben's accent? No way the bartender would know Ben was gay, and if he did, well, that wasn't a good enough reason not to serve him. "Look, I know I'm not from around here—"

"Don't play the innocent with me." The bartender leaned over the bar, his glare decidedly much more unfriendly than it had been, something Ben wouldn't have initially thought possible. "Go back to your bloodsucker."

"My *bloodsucker*?" Ben felt the color drain from his face. What the hell? How did this guy know about Simon, let alone that Ben knew him?

"He can smell vampire on you," said a familiar voice softly in Ben's ear.

Smell? Vampire?

Ben spun to see Lucas by his side. Lucas shook his head when Ben started to speak and placed one hand on his shoulder, holding him firmly in place.

"He's with me, George," Lucas told the bartender.

George's expression changed immediately, as did his demeanor. His earlier aggression disappeared, to be replaced by contrition and fear. "My apologies, Dr. Coate, I had no idea." He glanced around nervously.

"It's fine, George." Lucas shrugged. "I probably should have picked somewhere else to meet, but—" He leaned in and lowered his voice. "—I thought I could rely on your discretion."

"Oh, you can, Dr. Coate, you definitely can."

Lucas smiled. "Of course I can." He gestured toward a table in a far corner, his manner suddenly very serious, and his tone suggesting arguing wasn't an option. "Go sit down, Ben. I'll be over in a moment."

"O-okay," Ben said. He walked over to the table, feeling as though he was under a microscope with the amount of attention he was getting. Lucas had said the bartender could smell Simon. How could that be possible? Ben sniffed at his shirtsleeve, but couldn't smell anything. Lucas had said the bartender could smell *vampire*. That meant Lucas knew what Simon was. He had to mean Simon, didn't he? Simon was the only guy Ben was close to, the only vampire who'd been close enough to leave any kind of scent. Wasn't he? Ben glanced around, suddenly nervous. What was this place, and what was the bartender's issue with vampires? And how did he even know they existed?

Perhaps staying here wasn't such a great idea after all.

Before he could act on his growing instinct to run, Lucas placed two beers on the table and sat down opposite him. Ben reached into his pocket for his wallet and frowned. He'd left it, and his phone, in his jacket pocket.

"You're quite safe here, Ben, as long as you're with me." Lucas pushed one of the beers toward Ben. "I wouldn't

recommend wandering in here on your own again, though."
He put his bottle to his mouth and took a swig.

"What is this place?" Ben didn't touch the bottle, although his mouth felt dry. He licked his lips and swallowed.

"It's a werewolf bar," Lucas said. "Werewolves have a long history of not getting on with vampires. We're taught as children to fear them, and some of their ideas are quite alien to us." He shrugged and took another swig of beer. "Being different doesn't make them the bad guys, but not everyone gets that, unfortunately."

"Yeah." Ben frowned. "Hey, hang on a minute, did you just say 'we' and 'us'?"

"Yep." Lucas put down his beer. "Why else would I be in here? I certainly don't come in for deep conversation with George."

"You're a *werewolf*?" Ben grabbed his beer and took a long drink. Was everyone in this city some kind of supernatural creature?

Lucas grinned. "I'll have you know my family is very old and powerful and can trace their lineage back centuries to the royal family." He sighed. "Stuck-up, old-fashioned bigots, the lot of them. Except for me, of course."

"Royal family?" Ben spluttered into his beer.

"Werewolf royal family, of course." Lucas seemed amused by Ben's reaction. "Nothing to do with you humans." He studied Ben for a moment. "So what kind of state did you leave Simon in?"

"What makes you think I left him in any kind of state?" Ben said quickly.

"Well, if you're anything to go by..." Lucas leaned back in his chair. "You look like shit, you stink of vampire, and your heart rate was elevated as hell when you walked in here. Do you want me to go on?" His expression softened before Ben could answer. "He finally got up the nerve to tell you, didn't he?"

"He told me he was a vampire, yeah." No point denying it, as it was obvious Lucas already knew. Ben shivered at the memory. "He told me, and I didn't believe him, so he showed me."

"The whole not reflecting, weird eyes, and fangs thing?"

"No. I was stupid enough not to believe him when he tried that." Ben picked up his bottle again and began to drink. Lucas leaned across the table and took it away from him. He was a lot stronger than he looked and moved quickly. "Hey, that's *my* beer!"

"It's not if you're going to drink it like that," Lucas said firmly. "I'll get George to make us some coffee instead."

"I don't want any coffee," Ben snapped. To his horror, he felt tears start to form. He scrubbed at his face.

"Give me your phone," Lucas said.

"I don't have it. I left it at Simon's."

"Figures." Lucas reached into his pocket and pulled out his own. He punched in numbers. "Let's hope he picks up a call from me, then, shall we?"

"You're phoning Simon?" Ben tried to grab the phone from Lucas. "You can't!"

"Yes, I can. If I know Simon, and I do, he's going to be beating himself up about this." Lucas shook his head. "You told him you were coming back, right?"

Ben swallowed. "Yeah." Or had he told Simon he wouldn't run? Just before he had. "I think so."

"You *think* so?" Lucas shook his head again. "I swear I should have just locked you two in a room together and left you there until you fucked each other silly. I wanted to, but Forge convinced me it wasn't a good idea, and that you were old enough to sort this out yourselves. Wait till I tell him how wrong he was."

"You have no right—" Ben couldn't believe what he was hearing.

Lucas held up one hand to quiet him and put his phone on speaker when Simon finally picked up. "Feel free to join the conversation at any time," he said. "Hey, Simon. I have something of yours."

"What do you want, Lucas?" Simon's accent was stronger than usual. "This had better be important or I'm throwing this infernal device at the wall."

"I thought you might like to know I'm having a beer at the Knuckle Bone with Ben."

"You took Ben into a werewolf bar? Are you crazy?" Simon's voice rose several notches.

"He wandered in here by himself, and as crazy goes, I think you two are more in line for that award than me." Lucas sniffed. "I'm being nice here and letting you know your boyfriend's fine, by the way. We're having a nice chat, and then I'm sending him back to you."

"He's all right? He's... coming back?" Simon said in a choked voice. There was a muffled sound on the other end of the phone.

Ben grabbed Lucas's phone. "I'm coming back," he said. "I'm so sorry I ran. I needed time to get my head around... you know... it." He swallowed, knowing he was responsible for the pain in Simon's voice. "I meant what I said when I told you I loved you."

"I love you too," whispered Simon. "Do... do you want me to come get you?"

"Yeah, because that would be really smart," Lucas said, snatching the phone back. "An upset vampire coming into a werewolf bar? Think about it. I'll bring him home when we're done. Go make some tea or some of that revolting milk you drink and play nice. Bye, Simon."

He cut the connection before either Simon or Ben could say anything further.

Ben studied the table. "I've hurt him really badly. I know I have."

"Yeah, you have, but it's a lot to take in. It's not like you've been raised with this stuff like me or had a hundred years to think about it like he has." Lucas pushed back his chair. "I'm going to grab us some coffee. Stay here until I get back, or I'll hunt you down and drag you back." He tapped his nose, no doubt a reminder that he would have no problem carrying through on his threat. "We need to talk before I take you home, okay?"

"Okay." Ben wasn't stupid enough to run with a were-wolf after him. Not that he knew much about what one was capable of, but he liked to think he had decent survival instincts, at least about that.

A few minutes later, Lucas sat down again with two steaming cups of coffee. "It's just coffeepot muck, but it's free and doesn't taste too bad. Don't waste your time savoring the smell, though."

"It smells okay to me," Ben said. He took a tentative sip. It tasted okay too.

"Further proof that my sense of smell is far superior to yours." Lucas took a sip of coffee and grimaced. "I think my taste buds probably are too. This stuff is worse than I remember it. I usually come in here for the beer."

"How did you and Simon meet?"

"I ran him over with my car. Horrible thud noise. It scared me half to death." Lucas put his cup back onto the table and eyed it with something akin to suspicion. "You can drink mine as well, seeing you like it so much. You probably need it more than I do anyway."

"You ran him over?" Ben banged his cup down. "How can you say that and sound so casual? You could have killed him!"

Lucas chuckled. "Protective sort, aren't you? That's going to work really well with Simon being the same way. You can argue over which one of you is going to play protective over the other one's ass on a given day. Promise me I can watch?" He grinned. "He's a vampire, remember? It takes more than being hit by a car to kill him."

"Why did you hit him with the car, then?" Ben gripped the side of the table with one hand, his knuckles whitening.

"I wasn't trying to kill him, so you can put that thought out of your head. You're cute when you get riled up. I need to remember that." Lucas winked at him. "He stumbled out onto the road in front of me."

"Why would he do that?" Ben wasn't convinced by Lucas's explanation. Sane people didn't run out in front of cars.

"He was badly injured and wasn't watching where he was going." Lucas rolled his eyes. "Geez, you sound like Forge. I had to convince him I hadn't done it on purpose too. What is it with people thinking I'd go around deliberately running someone over? I'm a nice guy, most of the time."

"How badly injured?" Ben felt himself go cold at the thought of Simon lying on the road in a pool of blood.

Lucas waved one hand. "He's vampire, so it wasn't a big deal, or so he says." He shrugged. "Still takes a while to heal, though, even if it's way faster than normal, and he wasn't going too far with his leg broken in several places." Lucas narrowed his eyes. "If you want the rest of this story, you need to stop interrupting me, okay?"

"Okay."

"Anyway, that was about ten years ago, just after I finished med school. I hadn't met many vampires before then, but I knew what he was immediately." Lucas tapped the side of his nose. "There's no mistaking the smell of them or the stench of blood about them, however long it's been since they've last drunk from a human. I ended up helping Simon and Forge on the case they were working, thinking it was a one-time deal, and then they started calling on me." He sighed dramatically. "That's how it always starts, you know. One favor turns into another, and then I moved into Boggs's Castle after my father threw me out."

Ben stayed quiet, listening, fascinated by the story and trying to connect the pieces. So Forge and Simon had known each other for years, and then Lucas had moved in later. How old was Simon? Lucas had said something about a hundred, which would fit with what Ben had seen when he and Simon had kissed. Had the fighting he'd seen taken place in the First World War or the Second? Or bits of both?

"This is the part where you're allowed to ask questions," Lucas told him.

"Oh, okay." Although Ben was tempted to ask Lucas what he knew about vampires, he decided he'd prefer to talk to Simon about it. "So your father threw you out?"

"Yeah. Apparently I didn't meet his expectations. He wanted me to take over his seat on the council when he retired, and I went off to med school instead." Lucas's usual cheery tone darkened. "Then I became friends with a couple of vampires. I think that was the last straw. I tried to explain that vampires weren't that bad, that Forge and

Simon were the good guys and my friends, but he didn't listen. You'd think being on the council he'd know that, but it appears that expecting vampires to risk life and limb to do your dirty work and keep things safe is entirely different from actually being friends with one." He met Ben's gaze. "I knew I was doing the right thing, and I don't regret any of it. Simon *is* one of the good guys, Ben. He's a good man and a loyal friend, and he loves you. Any idiot can see that. I haven't seen him this into anyone, ever."

"Do you know about Stephen?" Ben closed his eyes, remembering what he'd seen and the grief Simon had felt when Stephen had died. There had been something between them; that was obvious.

"Nope, before my time. Forge has known Simon a lot longer than I have, but if you have questions like that or about vampires, you need to talk to Simon." Lucas frowned. "How did you find out about whoever this guy is if Simon hasn't talked about him? I know Forge wouldn't say anything." His eyes widened. "You saw something, didn't you, when you and Simon were making out?"

Ben nodded. "Yeah. I saw stuff when we kissed. That's how I found out Simon was telling me the truth about him being a vampire."

Lucas let out a low whistle. "Shit," he said. "I've heard about it, but I've never known anyone well enough to talk to them about it."

"Heard about what?" Ben frowned. He'd presumed everyone in a relationship with a vampire got to experience what he had, once they'd exchanged the words *I want you*. Given Simon's reaction, he'd expected it to happen. He'd also called Ben his soulmate. Did that have something to do with it?

"The vampire soulbond. A vampire meets his or her

soulmate, and they have this instant connection," Lucas said, confirming Ben's thoughts. "It's supposed to be about way more than just having great sex. I came across a reference to it when I was doing some research. I asked Simon and Forge, but neither of them would tell me anything much." Lucas leaned in closer. "You could tell me, though, yeah?"

"No." Ben shook his head. "If Simon wouldn't talk about it, there must be a reason why. I can ask him about it, but it's up to him."

"That figures." Lucas gave a mock sigh. "So there's still no chance of a three-way with you guys, I suppose? Once you've made up and fucked like bunnies, that is?"

"Definitely not." Ben pushed back his chair and stood. He'd done enough talking. "Thanks for the conversation and the beer and coffee, but I need to go now."

Lucas grinned. "Do you have any clue where you are and how to get home?"

"No." Ben blushed. "No clue at all." He cleared his throat. "Could you show me?"

"I'll do better than that. I'll walk with you and get you safely to wherever you want to go. Simon would have my ass if I did anything less." Lucas drained the beer bottle he'd taken from Ben earlier. "Waste not, want not."

"When I asked you to show me, I didn't mean the way to my place," Ben said, just in case Lucas had any doubt. "I want you to take me to Simon."

It was time to go back to the man he loved and try to patch this up. It was time to go home.

CHAPTER NINE

Simon glanced at his watch again. It didn't take that long to travel the distance between the Knuckle Bone and the castle. Where the hell were they?

He stopped his pacing, picked up his glass, and drained it.

His mouth still felt dry. Hunger rose in him that no amount of blood would quench. Although he hadn't drunk human blood in years, he still needed some kind of fix when he was on edge. He stared at the empty glass, reminding himself he drank animal blood because he had no choice if he wanted to survive. So why reach for it now, hoping it would steady him?

God damn it!

What the hell was Ben going to say when he found out about the addiction?

It couldn't be any worse than his reaction when he'd discovered Simon was a vampire.

"I meant what I said when I told you I loved you."

Ben had said he was coming back. He wouldn't lie about that. Lucas was with him and would keep him safe.

Simon sat down on one of the couches and held his head in his hands. Ben had only seen a fraction of Simon's life when they'd kissed. What would happen when he saw the rest? Was it fair to expect him to have to do that?

The front door of the castle opened. The minute creak sounded loud to Simon's ears. He froze, listening. Lucas and Ben were talking in a low whisper. Ben's heart was thumping.

Ben's footsteps on the stairs were heavier than Lucas's, who could move almost silently when he wanted to. Simon ran a hand through his hair; his fingers shook. Reliving some of the nightmares of his past he'd tried so hard to forget hadn't done much for his state of mind either. He hadn't expected to see what Ben had. Perhaps that was one of the other differences when a vampire soulbonded with a human? Instead of seeing their life, you got your own reflected in glorious Technicolor.

It didn't follow the rules he knew. Two vampires soulbonded when at least one of them was contagious, and he wasn't, although he had been when he'd first noticed Ben. Perhaps that was enough to trigger it? Ben, being human, wouldn't be able to mark him, but the emotional connection and physical drive were unmistakably what he'd heard would happen.

Simon stood and took a step toward the door, then a step back. He wanted this, wanted Ben so badly, but was it right to bring him permanently into this world?

He was already a part of it. After what Ben had seen, he wouldn't be able to go back now. It didn't work that way. Knowing the truth, even if you remained human, left its own scars. Simon had known a few who'd been able to walk away seemingly unscathed, but they hadn't already had the insight Ben had received through the soulbond.

The knock on his door was quiet, tentative. "Simon?" Ben called. His voice had a reserved quality Simon hadn't heard before.

"The door's not locked." Simon undid the top button of his shirt. His skin felt flushed, and he'd discarded the constriction of the tie around his neck when he'd begun pacing.

Ben stepped into the apartment. His gaze rested on Simon, who was still standing several feet from the door. "I'm so sorry," Ben whispered.

"So am I." Simon closed the distance between them at the same time Ben did. He pulled Ben into a tight embrace and held him. Ben's heart was racing, and his scent filled not only Simon's nostrils but permeated the air around him. Simon brushed his lips against Ben's. Ben responded by deepening the kiss and running his hands up and down Simon's back.

"I still want you, Simon," Ben said when they finally broke the kiss. His voice wavered. He sounded nervous. "I know what you are, and I still want you." He traced one finger over Simon's lips. Simon trembled. Ben's touch sent fire through his body. "I guess that means I love you."

"I guess it does." Simon managed a smile. "It's asking a lot, Ben. If we go any further, there's no going back. Once the soulmate bond is complete, it's forever."

Ben brushed a lock of Simon's hair from his face and then cupped his cheek. "I won't pretend I'm not scared. I know I'm getting into stuff here I know nothing about, but I trust you to show me the way."

"I'm not sure I'm someone you should trust," Simon said. Ben's fingers against his face felt so good. He leaned into the touch. Ben's skin was flushed, and his eyes were glazed. "What you saw was only a part of it. I've done a lot of bad things."

"We've all done things we regret, and that's the important thing, right? That you regret it?" Ben swallowed. "That stuff I saw? Is that going to happen every time we kiss, or is it just part of completing this bond thing?" He gave a shaky laugh. "I'm doing it right, yeah? Telling you I want you. If we're going to do this, I want to do it properly. No going back."

"You only have to invite me in once." Simon blinked back tears. Ben really wanted this, wanted him. "I—"

"I'll ask all the stupid questions later, okay?" Ben hesitated. "This isn't going to turn me into a vampire, is it?"

Simon shook his head. "No. I couldn't, not even if I wanted to." He swallowed. God, no. He didn't want that. Not now. Not ever. "I-I'm not contagious."

"Then don't waste time talking. We'll do that part later." Ben threaded his fingers through Simon's hair, leaned in and kissed him again, hard.

Ben tasted like coffee and beer, but to Simon it was like tasting nirvana. Ben opened his mouth wider, and Simon groaned, his tongue stroking Ben's. Ben moaned loudly.

A building burned. Simon tightened his grip on Forge as he and Declan staggered into the cold night air.

Ben stumbled. Simon caught him, lifting and holding him as Ben's legs wrapped around Simon's waist. Ben's free hand ran down Simon's neck to his collarbone, caressing the exposed skin.

The images came faster. Neither Simon nor Ben slowed their touching of the other.

Lucas's car hit with a dull thud. Pain screamed through Simon's leg. Reassuring words were whispered in his ear.

His mind was spinning, a whirlwind lifting both of them higher, out of control.

He was drinking beer with Forge. Moose was a puppy sitting at their feet. Boggs laughed at a joke. Lucas pulled a face.

Simon could hear Ben's heartbeat, his breathing. Feel his desire, his body heat. His love. Ben broke the kiss and buried his face in Simon's neck, his breathing coming in gasps. "Simon," he whispered.

The park always seemed surreal at twilight. He watched Ben from a distance, trying to summon his courage to approach him, knowing he couldn't. Not yet.

Ben asked if he could take Simon's photograph. Simon panicked and walked away. He couldn't let Ben discover the truth.

They were kissing. Ben said, "I know what you are, and I still want you. I guess that means I love you."

And then suddenly the images were gone, and they were holding each other, clinging to each other, shivering.

"Oh God, Simon." Ben was shaking. "I wish... I wish I'd been there for you," he whispered hoarsely.

Only a minute had passed, but it had felt like a lifetime. What they'd seen was *his* lifetime. Simon carried Ben over to the couch and sat down so Ben was on his lap.

"I'm glad you weren't." Simon met Ben's gaze, afraid of what he might see, but found only love and compassion. Any fear Ben felt was for Simon, not for himself. "It wasn't all bad." There had been more good than bad toward the end.

"Life tends to be a mix, yeah?" Ben's eyes widened. "I can feel you." He brushed his fingers across Simon's face. "Not just like this, but in here." He pointed to his head and his heart. "I felt fear just then, but it wasn't mine."

"It was mine," Simon admitted. "Are you all right with that?"

"Do I get a choice?" Ben shook his head as though clearing it of cobwebs. "It's part of this soulbond thing?" Simon nodded. "Is this bit forever too?"

"I don't know. Things are different because you're not a vampire. I guess we'll both find out as we go along."

"I can live with that." Ben grinned. "Questions later, remember? You're distracting me." He licked the side of Simon's neck and grazed the skin with his teeth. He shifted in Simon's lap, rubbing himself against him. "Not only vampires bite," he whispered in Simon's ear.

The words went straight to Simon's cock. He'd always loved being bitten, teeth against his skin, the mix of pain and pleasure that threatened to send him over the edge. It was why he'd never dared to give into it, to risk his vampire showing when he lost control. He didn't have to worry about that now. Ben knew what Simon was; he didn't have to hide.

"Bedroom," Simon growled low in his throat. He wasn't having their first time on the couch.

Ben tightened his legs around Simon's waist, kissing him again as Simon stood and carried him into the bedroom. By the time they reached the door, Ben was already undoing the buttons on Simon's shirt. Simon lowered him onto the bed and took a moment to savor the sight in front of him. By God, Ben was breathtaking. His dark hair was mussed, his cock straining against the material of his jeans, his vision fogged with desire.

"Come here," Ben opened his arms. "Don't just look. I want you to touch." He reached for the top button on his jeans. Simon shook his head. "I know you want to. I can feel it, feel you. I like this. A lot."

"So do I," Simon confirmed. "I *want* to undress you." He climbed onto the bed and knelt over Ben. "I *want* to touch you. All of you."

Ben nodded. He swallowed. "Fuck."

"Oh yes, God yes." Simon dipped his head and slowly licked around the collar of Ben's shirt. The first button opened easily, exposing tanned skin and dark chest hair. Simon moaned. He ran his tongue over his teeth, lingering on his fangs, but he wasn't hungry for blood. Not now.

The second button was more resistant. Simon didn't have time for this. He bent over and used his fangs to rip open Ben's shirt down to his waist, buttons flying in all directions.

Ben reached up for Simon's fly, fumbling with the belt. Once it was off, he yanked open the zipper and pulled down Simon's trousers and underwear in one go. "Much better," he murmured.

"Not yet." Simon undid Ben's belt and the zipper. Ben's cock strained against the cotton boxers he wore underneath. Simon's mouth watered. He dipped his head and swiped his tongue against it.

"Off. Now." Ben grabbed the waistband of his boxers and pushed them down, raising his buttocks to get them past his hips. Once they were off, he eased Simon's shirt off his shoulders and let it fall to the floor. "Singlet's got to go as well."

"Singlet?" It took Simon a moment to realize Ben meant his undershirt. He pulled it over his head and then crawled on top of Ben. Ben traced one finger down Simon's chest before holding him close.

Ben wriggled under him, rubbing their cocks together. His breath hissed. "Fuck. This feels even better than I thought it would." He twisted his fingers through Simon's hair, bringing his head down for another kiss.

The kiss silenced any more words between them. Simon managed to open the drawer of his bedside cabinet and fumbled through it. He broke the kiss reluctantly when he couldn't find what he was looking for.

"There's lube in my jeans pocket." Ben blushed at Simon's raised eyebrow. "I came prepared and hoped like hell you wanted the same thing I did."

"I do." Simon slid off the bed and rummaged through Ben's jeans. He discarded the packet of condoms. "I'm a vampire. We don't need these; vampires don't carry disease."

"Okay." Ben held out his hand for the lube.

Simon climbed back onto the bed and handed the lube to Ben, watching him. Ben squeezed a good-sized amount onto his fingers and beckoned. "Come here," he said. "Lie next to me so I can reach you." He kissed Simon again, deep and slow, and began spreading the lube onto Simon's cock, his hand matching the rhythm of their kiss. Simon whimpered and pushed into Ben's hand. He was hard as hell and wanted to be in Ben badly.

"Your turn," Ben said when he broke the kiss. He spread his legs. "Take me. I'm yours."

"Mine," groaned Simon, fighting the urge to take him right then and there. He prepped him as quickly as he dared. Ben wasn't a vampire. He was human. Simon didn't want to risk hurting him. He bent and kissed the tip of Ben's cock, then ran his tongue down the length of it. Ben was hard and already leaking.

"Now, Simon," Ben growled. "I want you *now*."

"You have me." Simon dropped the tube to the floor at the side of the bed. He gasped as he entered Ben, his need merging with Ben's, their joined desire overwhelming, drowning him.

"Simon!" Ben's voice rose to almost a scream. He began to buck his hips and wrapped his legs around Simon, drawing him in, harder, faster. "Oh God, yes," he cried.

Simon kissed him, swallowing the scream, their tongues stroking each other's, their breathing speeding up.

Not just desire, but love, acceptance, becoming one. Ben broke the kiss, gasping for air. "I love you, Simon," he whispered, his hips bucking as they moved faster, faster, a whirlwind of emotion.

Heat pumped through Simon, spreading through his body. He gasped and sped up his strokes, his fangs grazing the side of Ben's neck. He could feel Ben's heartbeat, fast and irregular, his blood loud in Simon's ears.

"Ben!" He heard himself shout Ben's name. And then he was falling, shivering, wrapped around Ben in an embrace he never wanted to end.

Tears fell to land on Ben's chest. Ben rolled with Simon so they were facing each other and kissed Simon gently. "I love you," he whispered.

"I love you too." Simon carefully pulled out and then caressed Ben's cheek. "That was amazing. You were amazing. Being in you feels so good. It feels right."

"It's like coming home." Ben smiled. "I felt you. It was like nothing I've ever experienced. I've had good sex before, but this was different. This makes that seem like nothing. Wow." He blinked and wiped his eyes. "If you don't mind, I think I'm going to bawl like an idiot now. Sorry."

"Bawl away," Simon said. "I'm not letting you go. You're mine now, as I am yours. This is forever."

Ben's next words were choked, his voice hoarse. Tears ran down his face. "Bonded to a vampire, huh? I like that idea." He stroked Simon's hair when Simon curled into him and rested his head on Ben's chest. "Not because you're a vampire but because you're you." He was quiet for a moment. His heartbeat had slowed to a steady thump. "We are bonded now, right? I have no idea how this works. I'm just going with the flow."

"Almost." Simon looked up at Ben hesitantly. "There is one more part to it." He wasn't sure how Ben was going to take this or whether he'd agree to it. "I need to mark you."

"Mark me? Why?" Ben frowned. "But then I get to mark you too, right?"

"Two vampires mark each other. You can't mark me. It would heal over, even though you're my soulmate. But the mark I leave on you, it's forever. It completes the soulbond."

"But if I were a vampire I could?" Ben had gone very still.

"You don't want to be a vampire," Simon said very quietly. "I wouldn't wish this on anyone, especially you."

"I'm not saying I would." Ben shrugged, but Simon could feel the hurt behind the action. "I guess this is the downside for you bonding with a human, right?"

"It's not a downside." Simon kissed Ben deeply. "There is no downside. Being with you, I feel more human than I have in a very long time. You've given me a gift in that. Please don't change who you are." He took a deep breath. "I don't have to do this if you don't want me to. I'll understand."

"No." Ben shook his head. "It's part of it, so you need to do it. I want to be bonded with you, at least as much as I can be. You said we'll find out as we go along. This is me finding out." He laughed shakily. "There's so much to learn about your world, and this is just the beginning, isn't it?"

"You're not doing it alone," Simon said. "We're doing it

together." He disentangled himself from Ben's embrace. The closer he got to doing this, the more nervous he felt. He hadn't bitten a human in years. What if he couldn't stop himself from tasting Ben's blood? "Spread your legs."

As soon as he'd spoken the words, he winced. He'd wanted this to be romantic, but instead it sounded so clinical, as though he was doing this because it needed to be done rather than something he desired.

He wanted Ben to wear his mark, to complete their bond.

"You're going for round two already?" Ben asked, his voice light. "I need a few minutes to catch my breath first."

Simon shook his head. "I'm going to mark you." He traced a small area on Ben's inner thigh. Memories of having it done to him against his will replayed through his mind, and he shuddered. This wasn't the same. Ben wanted it. Simon wished Ben could do it in return, wanting badly to wear his mark for eternity, just as Ben would wear his, or for at least as long as his human lifespan allowed.

"Simon?" Ben looked at him, fear in his eyes. "I just saw something." He swallowed. "Was that—"

"This is different, I promise you. It's different." Simon took Ben's hand in his own and squeezed it. "I'm sorry. I didn't realize you'd see that." He shouldn't have seen that. Simon lowered his gaze, suddenly feeling very raw and exposed. One rush of powerful emotion and it was as though there was nothing between himself and Ben. Was that how this worked? Or was it because he hadn't yet done what was needed to truly complete their bond?

"You need it to be different," Ben said. He sounded calm, but his eyes reflected his inner turmoil. "Do it, Simon. Do it now. Finish this, and put that part of your past behind you. John's gone. Don't give him any more power. He was an arsehole who deserved everything he got."

Simon nodded. Ben was right. John had taken what was supposed to be a beautiful thing and warped it into something ugly and terrifying with his insistence that Simon was his soulmate, however much Simon protested he wasn't.

This *was* different. It was a mutual giving of each other. "I wish you could mark me," Simon whispered. He bent his head and bit the inside of Ben's thigh.

Ben gasped and gripped the blankets under him, his knuckles white. "Bloody fucking hell," he hissed. His eyes glazed over. He was shaking, his breathing erratic. Simon felt a wave of desire, of pure pleasure rush over him, and then it was gone.

Blood welled up from Ben's wound. Simon swallowed, staring at it. He licked his lips, bent once more to taste, but caught himself in time. He shuffled back on the bed and let out a low growl.

"What's wrong?" Ben asked, slurring his words. He glanced down at himself. "Oh. I'm bleeding." His brow creased into a frown. "You're a vampire. What's wrong with a little blood?"

Simon shook his head. His mouth was dry. Ben had seen so much of Simon's life, but he didn't have a context in which to make sense of it. "I'll get something to clean it up," Simon managed finally. He slid off the bed and grabbed several wads of tissue from the bathroom. The bite was a clean one, but there would be a scar, the way it was meant to be.

Silence filled the space between them as Ben carefully blotted the rest of the blood. Another look at Simon and Ben walked into the bathroom and flushed the used tissue down the toilet. He returned to the bedroom, sat down on the bed, and opened his arms.

"Come here," he said.

"I'm an addict, Ben," Simon said, not wanting to look at him. He hadn't said the words in years, and only then to very few people. "I only drink animal blood now. Human blood makes me do really bad things. I can't be that person again. I was scared of biting you. What if I couldn't stop?"

"You're not that person now." Ben cupped Simon's chin, turning his head so they were looking at each other. "You're stronger than that." He kissed Simon long and deep. "When you bit me, it felt amazing," he said when they finally parted. He held Simon close to him. "A real high, but it was because it was *you*. I felt your love for me, how much you wanted me, and you blew me away."

Relief washed over him, and Simon felt himself relax, truly relax for the first time in years. He'd told Ben his real secret, the thing he was more scared of having discovered than the fact he was a vampire. He'd told Ben, and Ben still wanted him.

"I do love you and want you." He threaded his fingers through Ben's. "I can still feel you, but it's different."

His reaction to the blood had taken over, and he hadn't realized the difference in the bond until now. When he'd bitten Ben, something had changed. The connection between them felt calmer now, less raw, as though the edges of a fresh wound were knitting together to become whole.

"It feels good." Ben tapped the side of his head with his free hand. "I can feel you in here, but it's not as strong, and it's more... comfortable. Like knowing you're there, but I'm not drowning in it like I was before." He lay back on the bed, bringing Simon with him. "That mark wasn't just an outward sign of this bond thingy, was it? It completed it? Completed us?"

Simon nodded. He leaned his head on Ben's shoulder and wrapped himself around him. Ben had described the way it felt perfectly. "It completed us," Simon said. He smiled. "We're soulbonded, one."

CHAPTER TEN

"Where the hell do you keep the tea?" Ben muttered after opening several cupboards to no avail. The cups had been easy enough to find, but the tea was proving elusive. When he'd woken first, he'd had the brilliant idea of surprising Simon by bringing him a cup of tea to start the day.

He stood back and studied the kitchen, wondering if he was missing something really obvious. The wooden floors were cold against his feet. He wished he'd taken the time to put his socks on, instead of just grabbing his jeans.

"Try the cupboard to your left," said someone helpfully from behind him.

Ben jumped and turned quickly. It wasn't a voice he knew. His eyes widened when he saw a strangely familiar man in his fifties in a white suit. He'd been part of the memories Ben and Simon had shared the night before.

"My apologies, where are my manners? I'm Mr. Boggs." Boggs had a deep voice and spoke with a Southern drawl. "Welcome to our home, Ben. I've been looking forward to finally meeting you."

"Mr. Boggs?" Ben leaned back against the counter as

realization struck. "You're the… ghost." What had Simon said about him again? Oh yeah.

"Whatever you do, don't mention the American Revolution."

Boggs smiled. He had salt-and-pepper hair, and amusement in his hazel eyes. Ben decided he liked him already.

"Excuse me for not shaking your hand, but it's one of the drawbacks of not having solid form."

"That's okay." Ben took a deep breath, surprised with how he was taking meeting a ghost in his stride. After last night, it really didn't rate that high on the weird scale. "I hope you don't mind me using your kitchen. There isn't one in Simon's apartment, and he'd told me there was a shared one down here."

"Our home is your home now, Ben. You don't have to ask, unless there's anything you need." Boggs studied him for a moment. "I'm very pleased that Simon has finally found someone. He's been on his own for far too long."

"Hey, I haven't said I'd move in yet," Ben said. The way Boggs spoke, it sounded like a given. Not that the idea was one Ben was opposed to, but he and Simon hadn't even discussed it yet.

Boggs smiled again. He reminded Ben of one of his uncles, who always acted as though he knew something the rest of the family didn't, although it wasn't quite as annoying in Boggs for some reason. "Not yet."

"How long have you known him?" Ben took the opportunity to change the subject. Doing that worked with Uncle Martin when he got something into his head. The kettle boiled, and Ben remembered the tea. "I'm going to make tea while we talk. Is that okay?"

"It's perfectly fine, and thank you for asking," Boggs said. "I appreciate it." He shook his head. "Things were different before the war, you know. In those days people had manners and knew how to use them. I can tell—"

Ben interrupted quickly before Boggs could continue, remembering Simon's warning just in time. "You were going to tell me how long you've known him?"

"Ah yes, I was, wasn't I?" Boggs didn't seem upset by the reminder, which was a relief. The last thing Ben wanted to do was upset someone he'd only just met. "I've known Simon since he arrived in Boggslake. He's been living here at the castle for over sixty years now."

"That's the bit I still have to remind myself about," Ben admitted. He frowned at the cupboards, trying to remember which one Boggs had said held the tea.

"To your left," Boggs said.

"Thanks." Opening the cupboard revealed a caddy full of tea leaves and a china teapot. "I look at him and see someone about my age, but really, he's much older."

"I'm one hundred and seventeen, to be precise, although unfortunately, I'm physically stuck at twenty-two. It can be a right pain, especially when trying to order in a bar," Simon said from behind Ben. He slid his arms around Ben's waist and nuzzled at his neck. His lips were cool against Ben's bare skin.

"I didn't know you were there." Ben tilted his head so Simon could keep doing what he was doing.

Simon chuckled. "I can promise to be noisier in future if you'd prefer."

"I like you with ninja skills." Ben put the tea caddy on the counter and turned in Simon's arms. Simon brushed his lips against Ben's, kissing him good morning. Simon was wearing long dark blue silk pajama bottoms and a matching robe, which was tied loosely around his waist. The fine material clung to him in all the right places, and Ben could feel Simon's arousal through it when he pressed up against him.

A horny vampire. Ben could definitely live with that.

Boggs raised an eyebrow. "I can see you two still have much to discuss, although I would have thought you'd done quite a bit last night already. It was very late when you finally stopped talking."

"You heard that?" Ben flushed. They'd done a lot more than just talk, with several rounds of lovemaking in between bits of conversation.

"I wasn't eavesdropping, if that's what you're implying." Boggs seemed upset at the insinuation. "The house has a different ambiance when its inhabitants are awake."

"Sorry, I didn't mean to be rude." Ben sighed. It looked as though things like privacy worked differently here. "I'm still getting used to all of this."

"It takes a while." Boggs bowed slightly. Then the air around him seemed to shimmer and he disappeared.

"He... vanished." Ben couldn't help but stare at the spot where Boggs had just been. Apparently, ghosts didn't just leave a room the same way others did. "And how come I can see him? I couldn't last night, and he was there, wasn't he?"

"We hadn't completed the soulbond then," Simon said. "That's why you can see him now. There's probably going to be a few things you'll notice you didn't before."

"Like what?"

"I have no idea," Simon admitted. "I've taken all of this for granted for such a long time, sometimes I forget what it's like to not be aware of it." He brushed Ben's hair from his forehead and kissed him. "How are you feeling this morning? Last night was quite intense."

"I'm okay." Ben had asked a lot of questions, not just about vampires but about Simon's life and how he'd been turned. "What about you? I know it was difficult for you talking about some of that stuff, especially the bloodlust and that arsehole who turned you."

"It felt good being able to get it out," Simon said. "I should have done it a long time ago." He smiled. "I love you, Ben. I still don't quite get how you can hear all of that and see so much of it and still want to be with me, though."

"Hey, we've been over that already." Ben gave Simon a playful whack on his buttocks. "I love you. That means I accept you for who you are, even if I don't like some of the stuff you've done." He placed a finger over Simon's lips to stop him interrupting. "You're a vampire, and there's a lot of shit that goes with that. It's not as though you asked to be turned, and you certainly didn't decide to do all that bad stuff on a whim. You lost it after someone you cared about was murdered in front of you. Hell, anyone would have snapped after that." Ben's eyes narrowed. "It's a good thing John is dead, or I'd stake the bastard myself for what he's put you through. He's the monster in all of this, not you."

"I wouldn't have come anywhere near you if I thought there was a chance he was alive." Simon shivered. "I know he's dead, but there's something about this case that disturbs me."

"Like what? *You* told me he's gone. You're safe. We're both safe." Ben held Simon tightly against him. Simon had spent far too long looking over his shoulder because of that arsehole. John was a sick sadist who hadn't taken no for an answer. He'd played cat and mouse with Simon instead of turning him immediately or killing him, and then destroyed his chance of happiness with someone he'd dared to love.

No wonder Simon had been worried when Ben had told him about that guy in the café. It wasn't easy to get rid of that kind of knee-jerk reaction, especially considering the number of years he'd carried it around with him.

A loud, not very discreet cough sounded from the doorway. Ben turned in the direction of it without letting go of Simon.

"Sorry to interrupt, but I've got some information I think you guys need to see." Forge leaned against the doorway, watching them. He looked tired, and his clothes were rumpled, like he'd slept rough or not at all. Stubble covered the lower half of his face. "Meet us down in the Bat Cave when you're done doing what you're doing." He grinned. "And yeah, Ben, you're invited. Now Simon's finally come clean, it's time you were brought up to date on this case."

"Bat Cave?" Ben rolled his eyes. "Seriously?" That was one detail Simon had forgotten, or most likely chosen not to mention. "Whose idea was that?"

"Not mine," Forge and Simon said at the same time, a little too quickly.

Ben laughed. "Hey, I think it's kind of cool, actually. So... which one of you is Batman, and is Mr. Boggs Alfred?"

"He's another comics geek?" Forge asked. "Heaven help us."

"Yes." Simon grinned. "No one's perfect."

"Hey, I heard that." Ben gave Forge a wave. "We'll be there in a few, if that's okay. It's taking me way longer than I thought to make this tea, and I want a shower."

"Yeah, getting dressed might be a good idea. Or at least put on a shirt or you'll distract Lucas. Simon's already a lost cause. Actually, take your time, I could do with a shower and shave and something to eat first too." Forge turned and headed in the direction of the stairs.

"Do you want me to help with the tea?" Simon asked, already reaching over to boil the kettle again.

"No, I'll do it." Ben sighed. "I wanted to surprise you. You were asleep when I came downstairs."

"Your telephone woke me. I thought I'd better answer it in case it was something important," Simon said. "You didn't mind me doing that, I hope?"

"Of course not." Ben swished some boiling water around in the teapot, emptied it, and began to spoon in the tea. "Was it? Important, I mean?"

"It was your friend, Ange."

Ben nearly dropped the pot. "Ange?" She never rang. Texted, yes, when it was something important, but mostly, they stuck to Skype because of the cost.

"That was the name she used and what your telephone said," Simon confirmed. He retrieved milk from the fridge. "She seemed rather taken aback when I answered, and I got the impression she didn't want to speak with me. She told me to tell you she called and then hung up."

"That's not like her." Usually, Ange was very chatty with anyone new in Ben's life and gave them the third degree. "Something must be up. I'll phone her later." A thought occurred to him. She'd offered to dig up what she could on Simon. What if she'd succeeded? He'd have to either find some way of fobbing her off or tell her the truth. "Come on. Let's have this tea before it gets cold. We can take it back to your apartment." He took a deep breath, wishing he hadn't forgotten to tell Simon about this earlier. "There's something I need to talk to you about."

Lucas looked up when Simon and Ben entered the Bat Cave. He grinned. "You're wearing one of Simon's shirts," he told Ben.

"I think it looks good on him," Simon said quickly before Ben could say anything that would be used to tease both of them. Ben's shirt wasn't in any state to be worn again, as Simon had managed to rip more than just buttons in his haste to get it off the night before.

"Of course you do," Forge said. "That's why you loaned it to him."

"You said you had some new information on the case," Simon said to stop the conversation degrading any further. He looked around for Boggs, but although the ghost was nowhere to be seen, it didn't mean he wasn't listening. He'd add his opinion if he felt the need, or later after he'd taken some time to think everything through.

"Yeah. There were another couple of victims last night." Forge glanced at Ben. "How much has Simon told you about all of this?"

"I'm up to speed." Ben glanced around the room. His gaze settled on the board with the photos of the human victims. He walked over to it and studied it. "I know these people," he said slowly.

"You know them? How?" Forge asked sharply. "All of them, or just some of them?"

"Some of them." Ben pointed to four of the photos—they were the ones with no apparent connection to one another. The rest were all blood donors. "These three guys and that woman were regulars at the café where I work. They haven't been in for a while, though." He peered more closely at the crime scene photographs, and his voice shook. "I guess that's why."

Simon placed one hand on the small of Ben's back, offering discreet support and comfort. Ben leaned into his touch. Simon reminded himself that this wasn't someone targeting Ben. Ben worked in a busy café. It made sense that at least some of the victims would have frequented it.

"Do we have any more leads yet?" Simon asked. "Who are the new victims?"

"I've got an ID on both of them this time," Blair said, his voice coming out of the computer speaker on Forge's desk.

"Who's that?" Ben looked around. "Blair?"

"Alucard." Blair sighed. "Why am I bothering? You guys really don't get the concept of a secret identity, do you?"

"Yeah, but remember Nightwing and Robin call Batman Bruce when they're in the Bat Cave." Ben grinned when Forge and Simon both rolled their eyes. "Hey, Blair, I'm Ben. Simon told me about you." He glanced at Simon before continuing. Simon smiled reassuringly. He had a fair idea what Ben was going to say next. "I'm his boyfriend."

"Great to meet you, Ben," Blair said. "I think we're going to get on fine."

"You said you have an ID on the vics, Blair?" Forge said quickly.

"Yeah. They were both students at Lakeview University," Blair said. "Marla Wilcox wasn't reported missing until last night. The male victim disappeared a few weeks ago and hasn't been seen since." Blair paused, presumably referring to whatever notes he'd made. "His name's Brian Wallis. He's only a teenager."

Simon's mouth went dry. He knew that name, he was sure of it. "Are you sure it's him?"

"Yeah, it's him." Lucas mouthed the word *vampire.* "Blair sent me photos of missing kids matching the description I gave him, and we got a match." He rummaged around in a folder and pulled out a photograph. "Brian Wallis," he said, handing it to Simon.

"You know this guy, Simon?" Forge frowned.

"Yes," Simon confirmed. "He was one of my students, but he hasn't been for lectures since..." He trailed off as the obvious hit him. The last time he'd seen Brian at a lecture was a couple of weeks ago. Just before Simon had entered his contagious cycle.

"Simon?" asked Ben softly. "What's wrong?"

Simon stopped himself just in time. Blair might have let slip in the past that he suspected vampires existed, but Simon wasn't about to confirm it. "It's fine," he said. "This is just getting a bit too close to home, with it being someone I know, I guess."

"That's a bit of a coincidence, isn't it?" Blair asked. "There's stuff you guys aren't telling me, isn't there? Look, I can help. I thought I was helping."

Forge shrugged. Lucas shot him a look. Forge shook his head. "You are helping, Blair," Forge said. "The information you've given us on this case and others has been invaluable."

"But not invaluable enough to tell me the truth," Blair said. There was a moment's silence. "Look, I'll keep on this case and see what I can find. If you change your mind, you know where to find me. My next payment's due too." He cut the connection.

"That went well," Lucas said dryly. "Perhaps it's getting to the point we should tell the kid the truth. I wouldn't be surprised if he's got some sort of clue. He'd have to be an idiot not to, considering the last couple of cases he's helped us out on. We can't keep changing the subject or ignoring him when he asks something we don't want to answer."

"It's safer for him and for us if he doesn't know," Forge said. "We don't know enough about him to risk telling him."

"He doesn't know what you guys are, does he?" Ben

shook his head. "It sounds as though you trust him, but only so far. I'm surprised he hasn't asked loads more questions."

"That's it in a nutshell, yeah," Forge said. "We've been doing this a long time, Ben, and you're new to this. We don't tell just anyone about us. It's dangerous. Blair doesn't need to know. He's an informant, someone we use for information, nothing more."

"Yeah, it sounds like it too," Ben muttered. "Okay, I am new to this, but I'm not one for keeping my opinions to myself either. Just telling it how I see it."

"You've only been a part of this world a short time," Simon reminded him. "The rules are different here. They have to be or we'd never survive. It takes a while to get used to it."

Ben shrugged. "Yeah, whatever." He didn't seem any more convinced than when he and Simon had discussed telling Ange after they'd gone back upstairs. Despite Simon reminding Ben of his own reaction when he'd found out, he was still not happy about keeping it a secret from his friend. They'd known each other a long time, and she'd always been much more open to the existence of the supernatural than he had. In the finish, Ben had agreed to go along with Simon's wishes, but it was obvious he wasn't happy about it.

"Most humans are scared of what they don't understand," Forge said. "Suspecting that vampires and werewolves exist is a very different thing than having those suspicions confirmed. That's one of the reasons we're able to live alongside them in Boggslake. We don't make it obvious what exactly we are, but they know we can, and will, keep them safe. In exchange, they turn a blind eye to certain things, like how long some of us have lived here and don't appear to have aged a day. Upsetting that status quo has the potential to go really bad."

"There's nothing to say Blair wouldn't keep your secrets," Ben said.

"There's nothing to say he would," Forge said. "We don't know him that well, and it's been next to impossible to find out much about him. He's a damn good hacker, and he's used those skills to stonewall any attempts to run any kind of background check on him. All we know is that he's the son of one of my old FBI informants. He only contacts us through the Internet. Why should we trust him?" He shrugged. "You, on the other hand… you're an open book. Investigating you was child's play."

Ben glared at Forge. "You ran a background check on me?"

"Of course I did," said Forge. "Simon's my friend. I wanted to find out whether you were someone he could trust."

"It's his way of showing he cares," Simon said quickly. He could feel Ben's anger growing, a slow build of emotion at the edge of the connection they shared. Apparently, it wasn't just desire that bled through when emotions ran high. Simon slipped his hand into Ben's and squeezed it. "It's no different than your friend Ange investigating me."

Forge grinned. "One of your friends tried to run a background check on Simon?" He seemed amused. "I'd love to know how that went."

It wouldn't have been very successful. They'd spent a lot of time ensuring their current identities stood up to scrutiny, especially since the introduction of the Internet. Even if Ange had managed to get further than most because of any information Ben had given her, she wouldn't have been able to discover anything that would be of much use to her.

"Don't worry," Ben said. "I've promised Simon I won't tell her, however much I'm not happy about it." He sighed, his anger subsiding. "I'm sorry. I guess I'm still a bit worked up about it. There's a lot to learn about all this stuff. I don't like keeping secrets from friends, however necessary it is or however crazy they might think I am if I told them the truth."

"Just because we do what is necessary doesn't mean we like it either," Forge said. He cleared his throat. "Simon, what were you going to say before? I saw you catch yourself when you remembered Blair was listening."

An abrupt change of subject was a welcome distraction and about as close to moving on as they were going to get. Although Ben had backed down for the moment, Simon suspected the two of them would be continuing this conversation later. He wished he could just tell Ben that he didn't need to keep secrets, but the consequences of sharing this one had a habit of backfiring badly. Simon had experienced it more than once, and it hurt far more than the knowledge he was being less than honest.

"If Brian was turned about the time he stopped coming to lectures, that means his maker was contagious at the same time I was, so he or she is a vampire who was turned at the same time of year as me. They wouldn't be able to turn anyone else otherwise." Simon shook his head. If Brian had been a vampire before then, Simon would have been able to sense it. He reached out for Ben, pulling him close, taking small comfort in knowing he was near.

"It's not John, Simon. Leave that arsehole in the past where he belongs." Ben squeezed Simon's hand. "Maybe it's just some other vampire who happens to be contagious at the same time? There's a good chance of that, right?"

"It could be someone you've pissed off who wants to blame these murders on you," Lucas suggested. "Or perhaps it's some friend of John's who knows how he died and thinks something like this will freak you out? It would explain that guy at the café who talked to Ben."

"It's not John. He's dead and in hell where he belongs," Simon said. Ben was right about leaving the past behind. Their group had taken down a lot of supernaturals since they'd started working for the council. "I've made a few enemies over the years," he admitted. "I tend to keep a low profile when I'm contagious. It wouldn't take much to figure out when it was."

"Well, it sure as hell wasn't you who turned this guy," Ben said quickly.

"I wasn't suggesting it was." Lucas held up his hands in mock surrender. He seemed amused by how quickly Ben had leapt to Simon's defense.

"It might not be personal. I'll look into it further and see what I can find," Forge said. "A lot of vampires were made during wars, and there's no shortage of battles to choose from. Hell, Declan and I cycle at the same time, and it doesn't mean anything. Sometimes a coincidence is just that. Simon, you didn't know any of the victims before Cynthia was killed. Ben, was this kid a regular at the café too?"

Ben studied the photograph. "Yeah, I've seen him there, but that doesn't mean anything. We're close to the uni, so most of the students have at least grabbed a coffee at the café at one time or another."

"What about the human victim?" Simon asked. "Do we know much about her?"

Lucas took another photograph from the folder. "I'll put these up on the board once you've looked at them. Marla Wilcox wasn't one of your students, Simon. I checked."

"There doesn't seem to be any pattern to any of this," Simon said, studying the picture. Marla didn't look much older than Brian. She smiled at him from the photograph, another life taken too soon by violence. It didn't matter how long he lived, people still died before their time, and often at the hands of others of their kind. Marla might have been killed by a vampire, but it didn't necessarily mean a human wasn't behind this. "Did Marla come into the café too, Ben?"

"Yeah." Ben frowned. "That's weird." He gazed at Brian's photograph again. "I've seen these two together. They knew each other, and I got the impression they were more than just close friends. How could someone turn on a person they care about like that?"

"That's what we need to find out," Forge said. "Brian was a new vampire, so he might have still been learning to control the bloodlust, but his maker should have been taking care of that." It was the responsibility of a vampire's maker to ensure their protégé knew how to survive in this new world and the rules that went along with it.

"Cynthia hadn't fed off a human in nearly two hundred years," Simon reminded Forge. "Her husband said she was terrified. He could feel it."

"Hmm." Lucas tapped the end of a pencil on the side of his desk and then stirred his coffee with it. "So you think someone might have found a way to control these vamps and their bloodlust?"

"Maybe," Simon said cautiously. It wasn't a possibility he wanted to dwell on, but it wasn't one that could be dismissed outright either. "I'll ask around the university and see if anyone has seen any strangers hanging around. It might give us a clue to finding Brian's maker. He or she might be able to shed some light on what happened to Brian after he was turned."

Forge strode over to the far wall and opened one of the

cupboards. "I think it's time Ben learned to take care of himself, don't you, Simon? Have you told him how to kill one of us?"

"Hang on," Ben protested. "Do you want to rephrase that? I'm not killing anyone, especially one of you."

"If a vampire suffering from bloodlust comes at you, you won't have a chance to play nice." Forge glanced at Simon. "This is about survival, and you need to know how to protect yourself." He retrieved a Taser from the cupboard and a couple of stakes. They were part of the stock they kept in hand just in case: foot long, wooden, and sharp enough to pierce through skin with enough force behind the blow. "You were talking about trust before? This is me trusting you, making sure you know this." He handed Ben the Taser. "This is one of Lucas's designs. It won't kill a vamp, but it will take one down, and it damn well hurts to boot." He winced. "We tested it to make sure it works."

Ben took it and turned it over in his hand, studying it. "Point and pull the trigger, right? I can handle that." He shook his head when Forge tried to hand him a stake. "I don't want that. This will do."

"Take it, Ben," Simon said. "If a vampire comes at you, you'll need every advantage you can get. Lucas has amped the electrical charge in these Tasers so they are much more powerful than conventional ones." As much as he didn't like the thought of it coming to that, he dreaded the idea of something happening to Ben. "We're much stronger and faster than you are, and there isn't that much that will take one of us down. You could use darts instead of a stake if you want. We could dip them in—"

"I'm not using silver." Ben reluctantly took one of the stakes from Forge.

"I see you have told him what he needs to know." Forge

gave Simon a look of approval. "We don't keep silver here anyway. It's too dangerous so we would need to source it somewhere else." He shivered. "Its touch burns like acid. As a poison, it's a painful way to die."

"That's why I wouldn't use it." Ben didn't look happy. "The chances of needing this stuff isn't that high, right? Especially if I don't invite anyone in and all that."

"Don't invite anyone in you don't know," Forge confirmed. "It's too late once they're over the threshold and you've discovered the nice Avon lady is actually a vampire. There was someone about five years ago who used that one. She stacked up several dozen bodies before we caught up with her."

"And if the person behind this isn't a vampire?" Ben asked.

"Then you Taser them, get hold of one of us, and we'll worry about the details later," Forge said. "You know how they work, right? Someone hit with one of these loses the connection between their brain and their muscles so they can't control them." He paused. "We're hoping that should give us enough time to take them down."

"You're *hoping* it will?" Ben had gone pale. "So what happens if the Taser doesn't work?"

"Run like the hounds of hell are after you, because there's a good chance they are," Forge told him grimly.

CHAPTER ELEVEN

After checking the difference in time zones, Ben sent a quick text and waited for a reply. Although this conversation wasn't something he could avoid forever, it didn't mean he was looking forward to it. Despite his growing realization that Simon was right about keeping the whole vampire thing a secret, it still didn't sit well with him having to lie to Ange.

But it wasn't Ben's secret to tell. It was Simon's.

He hadn't been home since he and Simon had soulbonded, apart from grabbing a fresh uniform for work. For the time being he'd keep the apartment but didn't want to sleep alone after everything that had happened between them. Finding out about the murders and the apparent connection to the café hadn't helped his state of mind either, although he'd slept well enough. He felt safe curled around Simon, until Simon's nightmare had woken both of them.

If Simon was agitated enough, his memories still bled through to Ben, although that part of their soulbond seemed to have mostly settled down.

He smiled at the memory of watching Simon sleep after he'd calmed again, and the smile and good morning kiss that had come later. Soulbonding hadn't decreased Ben's need to touch Simon and be with him. To be honest, he wasn't sure how much of it had been down to that. He didn't really care. Being with Simon made Ben feel complete. It was like he'd been missing a piece of himself all his life and hadn't realized it until now.

His mobile played "Slice of Heaven" a couple of times before Ben registered it had done so. He hadn't expected Ange to reply for at least another hour, given the time difference. Or was today one of those days she didn't have an early tutorial? He'd completely lost track. He'd thought of texting her sooner, but the time difference meant risking waking her at some ungodly hour. He'd learned the hard way that she used her mobile as an alarm and kept it by the side of her bed. It wasn't a mistake he'd make twice.

He made a cup of tea while his laptop booted up. Perhaps he could find another way of explaining about Simon and the supernatural situation without exactly lying? Her text didn't suggest anything out of the ordinary, but then it was often difficult to gauge mood that way. She hadn't tried to contact him again since she'd spoken to Simon the previous morning, and Ben had worked the early shift today so hadn't been able to text her before now.

That was his excuse, and he was sticking to it.

"Hey, Ben," Ange called out from the computer. "How's it going?"

He settled on the couch and sipped his tea. "Hey, Ange."

"I spoke to Simon yesterday. He said he'd tell you I rang."

"He did." Ben took another sip of tea. "Sorry I didn't get

back to you before now. I worked this morning, and things got a little busy yesterday."

"Busy?" Ange raised one eyebrow. "So busy he's answering your phone for you now?"

"I was downstairs in the kitchen making tea," Ben said.

Oh crap.

"Uh-huh." As he'd thought, Ange latched on to his reply and ran with it. "I'm going to presume you weren't home then, as *your* kitchen isn't downstairs."

"I spent the night at Simon's." Ben took a deep breath. "This is the first time I've been home since then." This was ridiculous. He didn't need to explain himself to her.

"You've slept with him?" Ange's eyes widened. "Ben, you don't know anything about him. You don't usually sleep with guys you've only just met."

"I know everything I need to know about him." Ben put down his tea. "Sometimes you meet someone and you just know they're the one. Simon's my one. I love him."

"It sounds serious." Ange bit her lip. "You're being careful though, yeah?"

"Yes, Mum," he said, trying to make a joke of it. What the hell had she found out? Her tone suggested she wasn't just making sure he was using a condom. "It's okay, Ange, really. Simon and I have talked. We don't have any secrets. I trust him." He smiled. "You'd like him, really you would. He's got a good sense of humor, and he's really caring and gentle." It was hardly the way he'd ever thought he'd describe a vampire, but that was only a part of who Simon was. "We have those in-depth conversations like you and I have. I never thought I'd find a guy who gets where I'm coming from like he does. He's not afraid to ask when he doesn't either. I connect with him like I've never connected with anyone before." While it was also true Simon had a tendency to brood, no one was perfect. Finding someone seemingly without fault would have driven Ben nuts anyway.

Ange twirled a lock of her hair around her fingers. She seemed nervous. "I need to tell you some stuff. Promise you'll listen?" She glanced away from the screen and then back again. "Don't get me wrong. I'm happy for you, really I am, but I'm also worried about you."

"There's nothing to worry about," Ben told her. He was soulbonded to a vampire who belonged to a group of supernaturals who were investigating a series of grisly murders right on his doorstep. Definitely nothing to worry about.

The murders had nothing to do with Simon, and she wouldn't know anything about them. Simon had assured Ben there wouldn't be anything for Ange to find when she investigated him. They'd made sure their backgrounds checked out if anyone ever took the time to look. Even a brilliant hacker like Blair would have difficulty finding any hint of the truth.

"You know how I said I was going to look into Simon?"

"You didn't need to do that," Ben pointed out.

"I'm being a concerned friend, and you're listening, okay?"

He didn't see the point in reminding her he hadn't actually promised he would listen. Aggravating her would only serve to get her spidey sense tingling, and that was never a good thing as once she got an idea in her head something wasn't quite right, she wouldn't rest until she discovered the truth. Lois Lane had nothing on Ange Duncan in that regard where her friends, and especially Ben, were concerned.

"Okay," he said instead. The best thing to do would be to listen and then try to do some kind of damage control.

"Yeah, so I looked into him. As far as I can tell, every-thing checks out." Ange glanced away from the screen again. "I'm sending you a photograph. Take a look at it for me?"

"Okay." Ben frowned. What was she up to? Vampires didn't photograph, so there wouldn't be any recent photos of Simon. Unless she had a copy of his university ID or his driving license? Simon's friend Declan had provided those, as he painted photographic quality portraits that could be passed off as the real thing, especially after a decent session with the right computer software.

He clicked on the file as soon as it came through. A picture of Simon stared back at him, but he was wearing old-fashioned clothing, similar to what Ben had seen when they'd bonded. He swallowed, not sure how to react. Without thinking, he traced the outline on the screen, and his expression softened.

"Weird, huh?" Ange said.

"What's weird?" Ben asked, her words jolting him back to reality.

"Well, as I said, your boyfriend checks out. But I couldn't shake the feeling I was missing something, so I talked to Josh." Ange nodded sagely, as though her last state-ment explained everything.

"You talked to Josh? I told you that wasn't necessary."

"Yeah, I know you did. As I said, I had a feeling. You've always told me to trust them, so I did. Josh suggested I check out Simon's family tree and all that. See if that threw light on any of it." Ange grinned. "That's what I love about librarians. They're really good at going sideways with a problem and sorting it out that way."

"It makes them just as dangerous, if not more so, as hackers," Ben said slowly.

"Of course it does!" Ange said, as though there was never any doubt. "So anyway, that picture you're looking at is one Simon Hawthorne. He was born in 1894 and died during the First World War, aged twenty-two."

"He's probably a relative," Ben said quickly. No way he was telling her that this was his Simon and what she'd discovered matched exactly what Simon had told him. Except for the dying part. He hadn't died but had instead become a vampire. According to Simon's father, the former would have been preferable and as far as he was concerned his son was dead. "That explains the likeness. They do look very similar. I'll ask him about it."

"All I can find of your Simon is his picture on the university website. It's a very small picture and not a very good one. You were right about his not liking his photograph taken." Ange rolled her eyes. "Whoever took it needs to be shot. I couldn't tell whether he looked like this guy at all, so thanks for confirming that."

Ben swore under his breath. "So he looks like some relative he was named after. What else?" There had to be something else, or she wouldn't be worried about him.

"Well, that's when it gets *really* weird," Ange said. "Remember you told me all that stuff you talked about when you went out to dinner that night?"

"The stuff you dragged out of me under protest to help with your so-called investigation, you mean?"

"Yeah, that." Ange leaned back in her chair. "As I said, really weird. This Simon and your Simon don't just look alike, but they both had brothers called Andrew who died at sea. This one lost his when the *Titanic* went down."

"You're fishing. If Simon was named after a relative, it could be his brother was too. Both their names aren't that uncommon, and some families like to pass names down generations." Ben rolled his eyes and tried to sound nonchalant. "Sometimes coincidences are just that. It's not the first time, and it won't be the last. History is full of it."

"I suppose so."

"Well, what else is it going to be?" Ben said. "Think about it. They'd hardly be the same person, would they? He'd have to be over a hundred, and I can tell you now if he was I think I'd know. I've slept with him, and not just once. When I look at him, I see a really sexy guy about my age." He snorted, reminding himself he wasn't exactly lying. Everything he'd said was true. It wasn't his fault she didn't have the same context he did for the information. "Unless you're suggesting he has a portrait in his attic."

"No, I'm not suggesting that." Ange sighed. "I'm sorry, Ben, but there's something about this that isn't adding up. What if he's not who he says he is and is an axe murderer or something? He could have built a false identity and used this other Simon's life to do it."

Ben let out a sigh of relief. At least she wasn't going anywhere near the truth. "He's not an axe murderer. He shares a house with the city medical examiner and a police detective. I think they'd know if there was something up."

"I suppose." Ange shook her head. "I'm sorry. This sounds crazy, doesn't it? It sort of worked in my head much better." She leaned in closer. "I'm allowed to be worried about you, aren't I? This has happened so fast, and it's not like I can even meet him for myself with you being half a world away. I know it's possible to fall for someone this quickly, but I never expected you to do it."

"Yeah, you're allowed to be worried about me." Ben picked up his cup and took a gulp of tea. God, he hated not being able to be honest with her. "I'm sorry I worried you, and I know you only did this because you care."

"You're not angry?"

"No, I'm not angry." Ben forced a smile. "I'd be worried about you if the situation was reversed and you hooked up with a guy I knew nothing about. I know this has happened quickly, but it's all good."

"Good." Ange seemed happier, but something in her eyes made Ben not so sure. Hopefully, the more she heard about Simon, the better she'd feel about the fact he and Ben were together.

"Hey, while I think of it, can you do me a favor?"

"Sure. I probably owe you one after this."

"You remember that fruitcake Mum makes? I thought I had the recipe, but I can't find it. Can you email it to me?"

"You want to make fruitcake? Seriously?"

"I can bake!" Ben reminded her indignantly. "I want to grab the ingredients before I meet Simon for dinner tonight. He loves fruitcake, but he's having trouble finding any. It's not that popular here, so I thought I'd make one for him."

"Aww, that's sweet. You really do love him, don't you?" Ange asked softly. "I've never heard you talk about a guy like this before. That look you got when you saw that photo I sent said it all."

"Yeah, I really do love him."

Ben heard a knocking noise, and Ange turned in her seat. "Oh hell, is that the time?" she said. "Hang on a minute, will you?" She got up and walked out of the room, then returned a few minutes later. "My neighbor's here. I'd forgotten she was coming over to watch last night's *Coro Street*."

"You're watching *Coro Street* at this hour?" He checked the time on his laptop. It was only nine in the morning in New Zealand. While he knew she was addicted to the long-running British soap opera, this was ridiculous.

"Her flatmate is in one of his moods and shut himself in the living room to play the piano. She decided it was a good idea to get out for a bit." Ange grinned. "You said Simon played, yeah? Has he played anything for you yet?"

"He played some Chopin nocturnes for me last night," Ben said. "He's very good." He wasn't about to mention what they'd done on top of the piano after that.

"He must be, considering how red you've gone." Ange laughed, more relaxed than she'd been since they'd started the conversation. "Hey, Ben, look after yourself, okay? You know I'm here for you if you need me, right? Not that I can do much at this distance, but the thought's there."

"Yeah, I know." Ben smiled. "Thanks, Ange." He reached over and cut the Skype connection before she could reply.

Their conversation had gone better than he'd thought. He leaned back and closed his eyes. Now he was with Simon, he'd have to start watching what he said around her. Thank God she lived half a world away. At least having some distance between them would make it easier. He'd just avoid anything that might make her ask questions.

Simple as.

Right?

Ben quietly snuck into the back of the lecture hall and slid into a free seat. Simon glanced up and smiled but didn't falter in his lecture.

Although they'd arranged to meet at Ben's apartment later, Ben had finished the errands he'd wanted to run and decided to surprise Simon at work. Lakeview University boasted some beautiful old buildings with an interesting mix of different styles of architecture, although they complemented each other well. Ben had managed to get some good photos.

Finding Simon's office hadn't been difficult, but Simon's assistant, Juliet, had given him the third degree once she'd discovered who he was. Apparently, Simon had mentioned him several times and insisted he be added to what she called the white list: people she had to put through immediately if they were trying to contact him. She spoke fondly of Simon and seemed quite protective of him. To Ben's amusement, she asked him to make sure Simon was eating properly. He had a tendency to skip meals and drink too much coffee.

Ben had nodded and promised he would.

"That concludes today's lecture," Simon told his students. "Next time we'll be looking at the Allied bombings of Berlin towards the end of 1943."

The students began packing up their papers and laptops. Ben walked slowly toward the front of the lecture hall, but hung back when a blond girl approached Simon and began to talk enthusiastically.

"I always thought the war wouldn't be that interesting, but you've changed my mind, Professor Hawthorne," she said. "You bring it to life in your lectures, especially with the way you talk about how it all affected the everyday lives of those who were there." She giggled a little. "Why, I'd almost think you *were* there, with the way you talk about it. I've never heard of a lot of those details you've told us."

Simon looked up at Ben and smiled. "Thank you, Mary. I'm pleased you're enjoying the lectures, and I'm looking forward to seeing your next assignment."

"Thank you, Professor." Mary turned to see what Simon was looking at. "Oh, I'm sorry. Did you want to see the professor? I don't remember seeing you in any of his classes before."

"This is my first time," Ben said, somewhat hesitantly. He wasn't sure whether it was common knowledge at the university that Simon was gay, and Ben didn't want to out him. Melanie from the café might know, but she wasn't taking this particular course, and she might not have said anything.

"Ben's not a student here, Mary," Simon said softly. "He's my partner, and if I'm not mistaken, he's here to pick me up for an early dinner."

"Oh, I'm sorry, Professor, I didn't mean to intrude." Mary glanced between them, then smiled broadly. "I'll see you on Friday in the tutoring session. Enjoy your dinner."

"I'm the one intruding," Ben pointed out. "Nice to meet you, Mary."

"Thanks, you too." A couple of girls waved at her from the top of the stairs, and she ran toward them. When she caught up with them, she whispered something, and all three teenagers grinned broadly in Ben and Simon's direction before leaving the lecture hall.

Simon smiled. "She thinks we make a cute couple."

"You heard—" Ben stopped just in time from stating the obvious.

"I have very good hearing, remember," Simon said. Now they were alone, he pulled Ben close and kissed him soundly. "This is a nice surprise. I wasn't expecting to see you until later."

Ben kissed him back, lingering before breaking it reluctantly. "You don't mind? I didn't mean to out you like that."

"I outed myself," Simon reminded him. "It's fine, Ben." He began packing his lecture notes into his briefcase. "I'm not hiding our relationship or that part of myself. There's too much I already have to keep secret." He looked up at Ben and smiled. "The only reason I haven't outed myself before now is that I didn't have any reason to. I haven't been with anyone for a long time, and I've never felt about anyone the way I do about you."

"You loved Stephen and Albert," Ben said softly. Neither of them had been Simon's soulmate, but that didn't take away from how important they'd been to him or how much he'd loved them. "I can tell by the way you speak of them."

"Coming out back then wasn't an option," Simon said. "It's not a crime to be gay anymore. I can be open about the fact you're my partner. There was a reason Stephen and I had our trysts in no-man's-land. There was less chance of being caught." He fastened the clasp on his briefcase. "You don't mind me talking about them, do you?"

"Of course not. They're part of who you are. You've lived a long life. I'm not about to get jealous of someone who died—" Ben stopped abruptly. God, as insensitive went, he was being a real jerk.

"A long time ago?" Simon shook his head. "Unfortunately, it kind of comes with the territory. You don't have to tread softly about that kind of thing. I don't want you to. I want to be able to talk about it—about them—with you. I've spent far too many years avoiding it and not dealing with it. I don't want to go back to that again."

"Okay." Ben managed a smile. He hated seeing Simon hurt, and his memories of those two men were very bittersweet. "You know I'll listen anytime you need to talk about anything, right?"

"I do." Simon slipped his hand into Ben's. "I need to stop by my office, and then we can go for dinner. Walk with me?"

"Of course." Ben grinned. "I met Juliet earlier. She's quite a force to be reckoned with, isn't she?"

"She can be." Simon opened the door for him when they got to it and waited for Ben to exit the lecture hall first. It was one of the things Ben loved about Simon; he was always the perfect gentleman. "So how was your day? Did you manage to catch up with Ange?"

"Yeah. Everything's sweet as." Ben tried to keep his tone casual. "It went a lot better than I thought it would, even if she thinks you're really someone else and you've based your identity on some guy who died in 1916."

Simon raised an eyebrow. "That's a new one. She's made connections no one else has before. I'm impressed."

"I wasn't." Ben shrugged. "She seemed to take it okay when I said we'd talked and I trusted you. It should take care of the questions for a bit." He cleared his throat. "So, anyway, Lucas came into the café today."

"Lucas? I hope he behaved himself."

"He still flirted with me, if that's what you mean." Although Ben now knew a lot of that had to do with Lucas being a werewolf, it still made him uncomfortable. "I told him I was only interested in you, and he grinned and told me not to spoil his fun. That's all it is, isn't it? Fun?"

"Does it bother you? I can talk to him if it does." Simon stopped in front of the door to his office and opened it, then stepped aside to let Ben go first. "To Lucas, flirting is as natural as breathing. It's part of who he is. He does respect our relationship, despite his constant hope that he might score a threesome."

"Because that's going to happen." Ben followed Simon into his office. Juliet's office was next door to his, but she was nowhere in sight. He wondered if she'd gone home for the day.

"It's not," Simon said. "I don't share well, and I certainly have no intention of sharing you." He set his briefcase down on his desk on top of a big pile of papers and pulled Ben close to kiss him hard. Simon scraped his fangs down Ben's neck. Ben moaned softly. To his disappointment, Simon then stepped back and grinned. "Hold that thought for later tonight."

"You have an evil plan in mind, don't you?"

"Yes." Simon's pupils dilated, his eyes reflecting his vampiric nature. He used his tongue to trace the outline of his fangs. Ben felt himself harden instantly. Fuck, Simon was hot when he did that.

Ben made a strangled noise. "Perhaps you should just get on with your evil plan now? Give me a taste of it or whatnot?"

"Maybe." Simon dumped some of the papers out of his briefcase. "I have a surprise for you when we get home."

"What kind of surprise?"

"If I told you, it wouldn't be one, would it?"

"Tease," Ben grumbled. He knew from Simon's grin that he'd just have to wait.

"Patience is supposed to be a virtue," Simon said.

"I'll remind you of that tonight when you're begging me to go harder and deeper and *now*." Ben was pleased with himself for not blushing. He ignored the fact the words had come out hoarse and barely above a whisper.

Simon's eyes glinted. He smiled, his expression totally predatory. He looked Ben up and down, his gaze lingering on Ben's cock. "You'll be too distracted to remember." He kept his voice low.

"If you say so." Ben felt the heat rise to his cheeks. Time to change the subject, or they'd be caught in Simon's office quite literally with their pants down. Having sex at Simon's workplace wasn't on his to-do list for today. He glanced at Simon's desk, imagining him on his back, his trousers down around his ankles, his fair skin flushed, his fangs—

Oh God. That visual really wasn't helping.

Simon swallowed. He glanced at his open office door. "You were going to tell me what happened at work," he said calmly, as though they'd just been discussing the weather.

How did he do that? Get Ben all hot and bothered and then carry on as though he hadn't? Vampire self-control, Ben had decided the first time Simon had done it.

Bastard.

"Do you mind if I have some water?" he asked, noticing the water jug and glasses on a small table to the side of Simon's desk.

"Of course not. Help yourself," Simon said.

Ben drank noisily while he collected his thoughts. "We had our first weekly competitive darts match today. I've told you I was starting that up, yeah? It's been quite popular." He grinned smugly. "Lucas decided he'd play. I kicked his arse."

"You didn't tell him you were the reigning champion of your local?"

"Of course not. Where would be the fun in that?"

Simon laughed. "I wish I'd seen it. I'll be sure to ask him about it."

"I'm sure he'd appreciate your interest." Ben took another drink of water, drained the glass, and wiped his hand against the back of his mouth. He frowned. "Something else happened today," he said. "It was a bit weird."

"Weird?" Simon's eyes narrowed. "How so? You are being careful like we talked about, aren't you? You're carrying the Taser with you at all times?"

"Yeah, I'm being careful." Ben had almost forgotten

about the incident until he'd finished his drink. "There's a guy at work I don't know that well. I went out the back after the darts game, and I saw him about to shove a dirty glass into his backpack. Brad glanced around like he was nervous, and when he saw me, he dropped the glass. It shattered and went everywhere. He swore at me and got really angry. I offered to help him clean it up, but he was having none of it."

"That is weird," Simon agreed, "and rather an overreaction. You don't get into trouble for accidental breakages, do you?"

Ben shook his head. "No. Ron's really good about that kind of thing. That's the other thing. Now I think of it, he didn't have it when he left the counter, and it wasn't there before the darts match. The only place he could have got it was the kitchen. But why take a dirty glass?"

"Has this Brad done anything else unusual?"

"Not as far as I know," Ben said. "You don't think it's got something to do with this case, do you?"

"It's difficult to tell," Simon said. "I'll talk to Forge and get him to take a closer look at Brad. Often it's something that seems totally unrelated or insignificant that holds the clue to solving a case. It wouldn't be the first time."

"Okay. Let me know if there's anything I can do to help, okay?"

"Be very careful. I haven't had any luck in finding Brian's maker. No one seems to have seen anyone who has no apparent reason to be here." Simon walked over to the door, closed it quietly, and turned the key in the lock. Ben was in his arms before he realized what was happening. "I don't want to lose you," Simon whispered, his breath hot in Ben's ear.

"I'll be careful," Ben whispered back. He shivered as Simon ran his tongue over his earlobe.

"I love you, Ben." Simon backed Ben against the desk and used his free hand to shove the papers onto the floor.

Oh God. They were really going to do this, weren't they?

Ben groaned loudly. "I love you too." He pulled Simon against him. Simon's cock felt hard through his dress trousers. He reached for Simon's belt, but Simon beat him to it, yanked Ben's jeans down, and lifted him onto the desk.

"Let me," Simon growled, low in his throat. "You're mine, and I love you. Let me show you just how much." He kissed Ben hard, pulled off his sweater, and ripped his shirt off his shoulders, breaking the kiss to graze Ben's skin with his fangs.

Oh fuck. Ben trembled, his heart speeding up. The feel of Simon's fangs against his skin never failed to excite him. He'd never have believed how good it felt or what a turn-on even the thought of it was.

Ben's moan was muffled by a hand over his mouth.

"No noise," Simon whispered. "Can you do that?"

Ben nodded, his mouth dry. He wanted this, wanted Simon. He could be quiet.

Simon removed his hand. He bent his head and took Ben's cock into his mouth.

Ben stifled a scream. *Fuck, oh God. Oh yes.*

"Now," he managed. "God, now. Please, Simon."

Simon looked up and met Ben's gaze.

Desire, love, and need.

Their emotions merged, grew, one feeding the other. Simon bent his head once more.

Ben's world narrowed to the two of them. Fire ran

through him, overwhelming him. He gasped, reaching for Simon.

Want. Love.

Mine.

He opened his mouth. No words came out. He couldn't think. Couldn't focus.

Simon scraped his fangs gently across the underside of Ben's cock. Ben lost it completely, surrendering to Simon, giving in to the pleasure, the love between them. Nothing mattered but this, but them.

Nothing else at all.

CHAPTER TWELVE

"You can't keep giving me shirts, Simon," Ben said as they walked into Simon's apartment. He'd wanted to stop off at his own apartment to pick up a T-shirt to wear for the evening, but Simon had insisted they go straight back to the castle after dinner. Ben had taken off his ripped shirt before they'd left for the restaurant, but it was beginning to get a little breezy with just his sweater on, especially now with it getting later and the temperature dropping.

"Sure I can." Simon grinned and then looked a little sheepish. "Do you want me to stop ripping them?"

"No! Umm, I mean, I don't mind. Really I don't. It's kind of hot, actually, knowing you want me that much."

"I do," Simon said, "want you that much." He snaked his arm around Ben's waist, pulled him close, and kissed him soundly. "I also think it's only fair that I replace the shirts I've destroyed." His face fell. "I did like that one on you, though."

"I thought you liked it better off," Ben reminded him. He enjoyed this side of Simon. Now Ben knew the truth and Simon didn't have to keep secrets, he seemed much more at ease and his mood was a lot lighter, almost playful at times, especially when they were alone.

"Well, yes." For a moment Simon's eyes turned fully brown, and Ben glimpsed the vampire who lurked beneath. Ben felt a sudden rush of nervousness from Simon.

"You okay?" Ben asked, frowning.

"Yes, I'm fine," Simon replied. He licked his lips, another sign of how nervous he was. That, or he was becoming aroused. "I have something to show you."

"Yeah, you said that." Ben brushed his lips against Simon's. "Whatever it is, there's no need to be nervous about it. I already told you I don't bite unless you want me to."

Simon groaned and rubbed himself against Ben. Yeah, he was definitely aroused and growing more so by the moment. "I love it when you bite me," Simon said hoarsely. He swallowed, grabbed Ben's hand, and led him toward the bedroom.

As soon as they entered, Ben noticed something new. He frowned and glanced at Simon. "It's a mirror," he said slowly. "But I thought you didn't like mirrors."

Simon flushed bright red. He glanced at the mirror before meeting Ben's gaze full-on. The freestanding mirror was beautifully carved and, if Ben's suspicions were correct, could be angled to catch a reflection from whatever direction its owner desired. It was at the foot of their bed, facing it.

"I don't, but, umm, there was something I wanted to show you, rather than tell you about."

"Show me?" Ben frowned, trying to work out what Simon might be referring to. "But you don't reflect in a mirror." He sat down on the bed, and once Simon had joined him, they looked into the mirror. If it were to be believed, Ben was alone.

"Not usually, no." Simon shook his head when Ben turned to look at him. "I want to show you this, rather than explain it. Whatever happens, I don't want you to look at me. I want you to look at the mirror."

"Not usually?"

"Keep looking at the mirror." Simon reached for the bottom of Ben's sweater and pulled it off. Barechested, Ben turned to look at him, but Simon gently cupped Ben's face and turned him back toward the mirror.

"Okay, I get it. Keep looking at the mirror." Ben kept his eyes fixed on the mirror obediently. Simon's fingers were cool against Ben's skin. He felt warm breath against his neck, and his eyes began to close.

"No, Ben," Simon chided. The enjoyable sensation disappeared, and Ben made a frustrated noise. "You stop looking and I'll stop touching you."

"That's not fair," Ben complained, but he opened his eyes anyway. His sweater fell to the floor, seemingly by itself. He felt Simon's mouth close over one of his nipples, and Ben gasped. In the mirror, the nipple hardened without reason. He shivered. A slow blush began to creep down his body.

Simon slipped off the bed to kneel between Ben's legs, his hair tickling Ben's stomach as he leaned forward to dip his tongue into the indent of Ben's navel.

"God." Ben ran his fingers through Simon's hair, holding him there. It looked as though he was caressing the air, although he could feel Simon's breath and the wetness of his tongue. Ben's belt began to undo by itself, and as he watched, his zipper eased itself down. He groaned loudly. "Bloody hell," he gasped.

He wondered if Simon knew how arousing that was.

Simon moaned softly.

Yeah, he did. He definitely did.

"Lift your hips," Simon said. Ben heard his boots unzip. As soon as they were off, his jeans and underwear joined them in a pile out of sight of the mirror.

Ben swallowed, the blush spreading farther down his body. He turned his head around, away from the mirror. "I'm not sure…" he started to say. It was weird looking at himself naked in the mirror. It wasn't something he made a habit of.

"You're beautiful," Simon whispered. He looked up at Ben, his eyes completely brown. "Maybe I'm not distracting you enough?" He bent his head, took Ben's cock into his mouth, and scraped the underside of it gently with his fangs.

"Bloody fucking hell," Ben yelled. Simon eased Ben up onto the bed, gesturing for him to lean back on his elbows. He curled his tongue around Ben's cock and sucked. Ben stared at the mirror, unable to divert his gaze. Seeing his cock get wet felt arousing as hell. He wriggled, trying to push into Simon's mouth. Simon let Ben's cock drop from his lips and crawled up him, kissing him. Ben groaned loudly, his hands roaming over Simon's body, pulling at his clothes, wanting them off.

"Keep looking at the mirror," Simon reminded him when he broke the kiss.

"Get undressed first." As much as he loved undressing Simon, Ben loved seeing Simon undress more, and he wouldn't be able to if he kept watching the bloody mirror.

"Are you telling me what to do?" Simon licked his lips and took a deep breath.

"Yeah, I am." Ben rolled them over so he was on top and

began undoing Simon's shirt. "Do you have a problem with that?"

"Fuck, no."

Ben's hand stilled on Simon's buttons. "That's the first time I've heard you swear like that," he said slowly.

"Do you have a problem with it?" Simon stared back at Ben, almost defiantly, his cock hard against Ben's groin. He rubbed himself against Ben, a moan escaping his lips.

"You're getting off on this, aren't you?" Ben shifted position, up onto his haunches, still sitting over Simon. "Tell you what. I'll look at the mirror if you do exactly what I say. Okay?"

Simon made a half-strangled groaning noise. "Okay." He reached up to pull Ben down to kiss him again. Ben shook his head.

"I didn't say you could do that, did I?"

"No." Simon bit his lip. His eyes darted from Ben to the mirror. "I want... need... to lose control. Please."

"You're okay with this?" Ben wouldn't do this unless Simon was okay with it. Not after everything he'd been through with John. Ben wasn't sure why he'd suggested it in the first place, but something in Simon's eyes told him it was okay. Raw need rushed through him. Need and trust. "This is me, Simon. I will never make you do anything you don't want to."

"I know." Simon's breathing sped up, although Ben still couldn't hear his heart. His own was thumping. "I love you, and I trust you." Simon glanced again at the mirror. "You promised you'd keep looking. You'll be able to see everything in there."

"I can't see *you*," Ben murmured. "I don't care about the rest."

"Trust me as I'm trusting you." Simon fixed his eyes on Ben. "Please. It's important."

"Okay." Whatever the hell was up with this mirror thing, it obviously mattered to Simon. That was enough for Ben. "Take your clothes off for me, but don't touch yourself. Then I'll keep looking at the mirror," Ben said. "I promise."

Simon nodded. His hands shook as he finished undoing his shirt. The fine light-brown hair dusting his chest stood out against his pale complexion. Simon shrugged his shirt off and undid the belt of his trousers. The fly unzipped quickly a moment later. Ben sat back so Simon could finish undressing. Watching his clothes come off was like seeing a present unwrapped, a beautiful present that Ben wanted so badly to touch and taste.

"You're the beautiful one," Ben whispered. He used one hand to part Simon's legs, crouched down on his knees between them, and then ran his hand up Simon's inner thigh. He moved to cover Simon for a moment and kissed him lightly on the lips. "No more talking, hmm? I want you to enjoy this."

Simon opened his mouth to reply, then stopped and nodded.

"And yes, I'll look in your mirror," Ben promised. He could do this by feel. He'd already memorized Simon's body so he didn't need to see, although he wanted to, badly.

God, he wished he could capture Simon on film. Sometimes his memory wasn't enough. He worried it would fade and fail him when he really needed it. Already, he couldn't imagine his life without Simon in it.

"Could you move so your head is at the foot of the bed?" That way Ben could see the mirror without compromising what he wanted to do. "Perfect."

Ben lowered his head and licked the tip of Simon's cock.

Simon hissed, and groaned loudly. The noise went straight to Ben's groin. He dipped his head again, this time taking Simon's cock into his mouth. At the same time he used his free hand to stroke himself. Simon stiffened under him and bucked his hips. He thrust into Ben's mouth, the blankets on either side of him scrunched up hard, as though some invisible force was gripping them tightly.

Intense desire flooded Ben. Simon panted, moaning his name. Ben forced himself to keep looking at the mirror. He could see himself stroking his cock, his mouth moving in time with his hand as he sucked furiously, his body flushed. God, he wanted to see Simon, not just feel him and taste him.

Simon bucked his hips again, jerking once, twice. His fingers wound through Ben's hair, holding him in place. Simon's leg brushed against Ben's thigh. Ben sped up his strokes. Heat built in his groin. He moaned loudly.

In the mirror, an outline began to form. Simon's grip on Ben tightened. He thrust frantically into Ben's mouth.

Love. Desire. Need.

Ben was drowning. He sucked hard.

Simon screamed, "Ben!"

And then suddenly there were two of them in the mirror, Simon's skin flushed and wet with perspiration. He thrust into Ben's mouth, his fingers white where they gripped Ben's hair, his mouth open in a silent scream.

Ben let go of Simon's cock. It fell from his mouth.

He glanced away from the mirror, wanting the reality of what he'd just seen. Simon was his. They were touching each other, loving each other.

Simon arched his back, his hand loosening from Ben's hair to pull him close as he lost control. He writhed under

Ben, his thigh rubbing frantically against Ben's already dripping cock. Ben followed a few moments later.

When Ben looked into the mirror again, he was alone. He shivered in Simon's arms, both of them wrapped around each other. Simon was breathing hard and trembling.

"Simon?" asked Ben gently when he could find his voice again. He kissed Simon's forehead. To hell with the sticky mess between them. "What just happened?"

"You blew me away." Simon sounded dazed.

"Yeah, that was the idea." Ben frowned. "I don't mean that. I saw you. I saw you in the mirror. Just for an instant, but you were there."

Simon smiled. He made a contented, satisfied noise. He sounded and felt more like himself. "Yes." He traced his fingers across Ben's shoulder blades. "I told you to keep watching the mirror, didn't I?"

"Yeah, you did." Ben snuggled in closer. It felt good being with Simon like this, and he didn't want to move. Besides, he wasn't sure he could, just yet. He felt utterly spent. "I've never done anything like that before. It was kind of kinky, but in a good way." He brushed his lips against Simon's. "So are you going to answer my question, or do I have to fuck it out of you? I'm up for round two later if you are."

"I'm sure you are." Simon chuckled, then sobered. "I know you wish you could photograph me, so I wanted to at least give you this." He placed a finger on Ben's lips to stop him interrupting. "What you saw is called a shimmer. When a vampire's adrenaline is very high, we become visible just for a moment. It never lasts, though."

"So there is a way of taking a photograph of you," Ben said slowly.

"You're not taking that kind of photograph of me!" Simon protested. "Someone might see it."

"I'll see it," Ben said softly. "You were amazing. You taste good too. I think we'll have to explore this further."

"You want to?" Simon had something akin to amazement in his voice. "I just wanted to show you. I never thought—"

"That I'd want to do it again?" Ben still wasn't sure how he felt about seeing himself naked and masturbating in a mirror, but if a glimpse of Simon, or better yet a photograph Ben could keep, was the result, he was all for it. "I know it's crazy, but I want something of you. I know I carry your mark, but this is different. I like to photograph beautiful and unique things, and you're more beautiful and unique than anyone or anything I've ever seen."

"You really think that?" Simon had grown very still. "I'm not beautiful, Ben. I'm a vampire."

"Yes, but you're *my* vampire." Ben kissed Simon slowly and tenderly. "A vampire is only a part of who you are. I look at you, and do you know what I see? A man I want to spend my life with. A gentle, caring man whom I love with all my heart and I know loves me too."

"Oh, Ben." Simon closed his eyes. When he opened them, they looked normal. The hint of vampire was gone. "I love you with everything I am." Tears fell down his cheeks. Ben kissed them away. "You are half my soul. You know me for what I am, and yet you still accept and want me." His voice dropped to a whisper. "That blows me away far more than any sex could."

"Though the sex is good too, yeah?" Ben teased.

"Yes, it is. Very good." Simon loosened his embrace. "There was something else I wanted to give you. The mirror was only a part of it."

"You've already given me more than enough, Simon," Ben protested.

"Let me do this, please?" Simon disentangled himself from Ben and walked over to the chest of drawers sitting in the corner. Ben turned and changed position, propping himself up on one elbow so he could watch Simon. He swallowed, wanting to touch Simon again, to be inside him, for them to be as one. Fuck, he was hot. Watching him naked like this made Ben hard again. Although, he had to admit, watching Simon with his clothes *on* had the same effect.

When Simon walked back to the bed, he carried a bag made of a brown cotton material. Whatever was in it was square and quite bulky. Ben sat up and moved over so Simon could sit next to him.

"What's that?" he asked.

"It was a gift from my Uncle Edwin." Simon handed it to Ben. "It's been sitting in that drawer for a long time. It's only right it should go to someone who will appreciate it."

"I can't take something that was a gift from your uncle," Ben protested. "Whatever it is, he meant it for you, not me."

"Wait until you see it before you decide," Simon suggested. He leaned back against the headboard, watching as Ben fumbled with the bag and drew out its contents.

"Oh wow," Ben said. He carefully turned the vintage Brownie camera this way and that. It was older than the one his grandfather had, by at least a couple of models. "I've seen pictures of these. It's very old." He slid open the clasp holding the bellows closed and examined the camera more closely. The unfolded bellows were still intact, as were the protective metal struts on either side of them.

"It was new when I got it," Simon said. "Uncle Edwin bought it for me before I left for France. It was the latest model at the time." He smiled, yet there was sadness in the memory. "You're a photographer. I only used it once or twice. After I was turned, I shoved it in a drawer and didn't want to look at it. But I couldn't bring myself to get rid of it either. That and the piano are the only ties I have to him."

"You should keep it, then," Ben said.

Simon shook his head. "He'd want you to have it. You can use it and keep his memory alive. I'm not sure whether the film is still available for it. You'd have to find out. It was supposed to be possible to write on the exposed film. I never tried that, though." He watched Ben run his fingers over the bellows. "Have you used an old camera like this before?"

"My granddad had a later model of the same camera," Ben said. "He brought it with him when he visited Boggslake." He laid the camera down carefully on the bed. "I've got a photo he took with it while he was here, actually. It's in my wallet. Hang on and I'll get it."

"Do you know where it was taken?" Simon asked. "Perhaps I could help you find out. Your grandfather was here in the fifties, yes?"

"Yeah." Ben fished his wallet out of his jeans pocket and pulled out the photograph. "It was taken in the park, around the same place where I met you. It's one of the reasons I was there. I wanted to find out where it was taken. Granddad was never too clear on the details, just that the photo was important. This one's a copy. He's got the original."

He handed it to Simon, who stared at it and went very still. "I remember this," he said slowly.

"You know where it was taken, then?" Ben frowned, feeling an echo of something akin to shock. "Simon?"

"I know where and when it was taken," Simon said very quietly. "I remember it being taken." He turned it over, but nothing was written on the back.

"The inscription on the back of Granddad's copy says

Boggslake 1951," Ben said. "What do you mean you remember it being taken?" Simon's reaction scared him a little. "Are you okay? You look like you've seen a ghost."

Simon's hand went to his lips. When he spoke, his voice had an urgent tone. "What's your grandfather's name, Ben?"

"Frank," Ben replied. "His name is Frank Connell."

"You're Frank's grandson?" Simon made a choked noise. "Oh Lord." He kept staring at the photograph.

"You knew him?" Ben couldn't believe what he was hearing, although logically he knew it wasn't that out there. Simon would have been in Boggslake at the same time, and when Ben's granddad had visited, he wouldn't have been much older than Ben was now. It was so easy to forget that Simon was anything other than the man he appeared to be, but then something always seemed to happen to remind Ben that Simon was a vampire and over a hundred years old.

Ben hadn't lied when he'd told Simon he wanted to spend his life with him. It was just there were still parts of *Simon's* life that took a bit of getting used to. Ben wondered if he ever entirely would.

"He was my friend. A very good friend." Simon looked embarrassed and glanced down. "I thought I felt something for him, and I kissed him."

"But Granddad's straight," Ben blurted out. "He was happily married to my grandma for fifty years before she died." Words kept tumbling out of his mouth, his mind struggling to comprehend what Simon had just told him. "He told me to come to Boggslake and that I should follow my instincts. He never said anything about finding you. Did he know about you? Not that you're gay but that you're a vampire, I mean."

Shut up, Ben, you're babbling like an idiot, he told himself sternly.

Several things his grandfather had said, or rather not said, suddenly clicked into place. But how could he know Ben would meet Simon when he came to Boggslake? At the first opportunity, Ben was going to pick up the phone and talk to him. To hell with the expense.

"I know he's straight. I found that out right after I kissed him." Simon flushed, his eyes glazed over in memory. "It wasn't my brightest hour, but Frank was very understanding." He gave Ben back the photograph of the empty park bench. "You said you wanted a photograph of me, and all this time, you've been carrying one." He smiled when Ben looked puzzled. "I was sitting on that bench when he took it. I had no idea he had until he confronted me with it after he had it developed. It was how he found out I'm a vampire."

CHAPTER THIRTEEN

Simon glanced around Miller's Café as he entered. Ben looked up at the sound of the bell over the door, caught Simon's eye, and smiled.

"I'll be done soon," Ben said quietly, not raising his voice, although Simon was still on the other side of the café. For the most part, he'd learned about vampire hearing very quickly, especially after Forge's teasing. However, Ben was still very loud when he and Simon made love, and Simon didn't want that to change, at least when they were in the *supposed* privacy of his apartment.

Instead of replying in kind, as Ben wouldn't be able to hear him, Simon nodded and slipped into a seat that gave him a good view of the counter.

A few minutes later, Ben set a cup of coffee down in front of Simon. "It's on the house," he said when Simon reached for his wallet. "I'm staying back a few minutes longer to help out in the kitchen, so Ron suggested you might like one while you wait."

"Tell him thank you." Simon glanced toward the back of the café, but saw no sign of its owner. "I'm a bit early even for the time you were supposed to finish, so I knew I'd have to wait."

Something akin to annoyance came off Ben in waves. Simon frowned.

"*Someone* decided to rearrange stuff in the kitchen," Ben explained before Simon could ask. He didn't need to ask who that someone was.

"Why?"

Ben lowered his voice. "How the bloody hell should I know? There's no rhyme or reason why that woman does what she does." He rolled his eyes when Melanie came out of the kitchen and waved cheerfully at both of them. "I've never met anyone so oblivious either."

"I'll make you forget all about it tonight," Simon promised. He brushed his fingers lightly against Ben's and let his eyes go completely brown for a moment.

"You're very distracting when you do that," Ben said.

"I know. That's why I do it." Simon grinned. Ben was rather transparent and vocal about what he liked. It was something Simon loved about him. "You'd better go back to work before you get into trouble for fraternizing with the customers."

Ben laughed. "I was planning to do a lot more than fraternize with you once we get home." He winked and walked away. His mood appeared much lighter than it had been a few minutes before. Simon picked up his coffee and took a sip. It was made just the way he liked it. He savored the taste and leaned back in his chair, letting his mind wander back to the night before.

Sharing a bath had been an intensely erotic and intimate experience, but it wasn't just the memory of their lovemaking that brought a smile to Simon's lips. He'd leaned back into Ben's arms, both of them naked in the soapy water. There'd been no need for conversation, just a feeling of being safe and loved. Ben loved to touch and be touched, as did Simon.

Being with Ben had brought with it something Simon had never really experienced before. For the first time in decades, it didn't matter who or what he was. He didn't have to hide from Ben, as Ben accepted him, personality quirks and all. It wasn't just about the vampire. Ben looked at him, saw into his soul, and had opened his in return.

It was humbling as hell, yet very liberating too.

Simon took another sip of coffee. A glimpse of someone out of the corner of his eye jerked him back to the present with a sharp reminder of the reason he'd come to the café before Ben had finished work.

One of Ben's coworkers was wiping down the counter. He was a young man in his late twenties, tall, slender, and wearing glasses. His hair was black, and he needed to get it cut, as it kept flopping forward over his eyes.

Brad Cooper.

Forge's investigations had unearthed some interesting information about Brad. Just over a month ago, Brad had nearly been evicted from his apartment for not paying his rent on several occasions. He owed money to more than one local loan shark, and they were demanding immediate payment. A week later, he'd suddenly cleared all his debts and bought himself an expensive new phone, TV, and sound system.

The café didn't pay that well. In fact, it paid minimum wage, as did most jobs of that kind.

It only took a slight jerk, and within moments, a growing puddle of coffee spread over Simon's table. He stood and walked to the counter. "Could I trouble you to clean my table, please?" he asked Brad politely. "I seemed to have spilled my coffee."

Brad glanced up and visibly jumped when he saw Simon standing there. His heart rate rose sharply. He looked nervous. "S-sure," he said. "I'll come do it now if you want."

"That would be appreciated, thank you, Brad." Simon kept his tone polite and his stance nonthreatening.

"How do you know my name?" Brad nearly dropped his cloth on the floor but caught it just in time. He followed Simon over to the table.

"You're wearing a badge," Simon reminded him. He waited until Brad had cleaned the table and then held out his hand. "I'm Simon Hawthorne. My partner, Ben, works here."

Brad's eyes widened. Although he was trembling, he shook Simon's hand. "*You're* Ben's partner?" He was breathing heavily, thin beads of perspiration dripping down his forehead.

"I believe I just said that." Simon let his eyes go fully brown for just an instant before smiling at Brad. He let go of Brad's hand.

"I need to go finish something in the kitchen," Brad spluttered. His nervousness bordered on fear. Simon had seen enough of those emotions in others to recognize them. Fear in particular had its own unique stench, yet it wasn't just fear he could smell. Brad had recently spent time in the close company of a vampire.

"What's wrong with Brad?" Ben ducked out of Brad's way when he dashed into the kitchen. "He looks like he's seen a ghost."

"More likely a vampire," Simon said as soon as Ben

moved close enough to hear. He waited for Ben to finish zipping up his jacket.

"You think he knows what you are?" Ben asked. He glanced back toward the kitchen, pointedly ignoring Melanie, who was now standing at the counter watching them.

"I suspect he does." Simon paused to open the door for Ben as they left the café and began walking toward the car. "He's been in close physical contact with a vampire recently. I could smell it on him."

"Are you sure? You didn't seem to know whether I'd been close to a vampire or not when I told you about that guy who looked like John."

Simon studied the pavement before replying. "Before we soulbonded, I wasn't thinking that clearly, and all I could smell was you. It overwhelmed everything else."

"Oh." Ben flushed. "But it's back to normal now?"

"Yes." Simon was amused by the disappointed look on Ben's face. "Also, for the vampire to leave his or her scent on him, he's got to have been at least hugged or been struck by one. Given his nervousness, I suspect the latter. So, all things considered, it does seem as though Brad could be involved with this case."

"You're not just talking about the thing with the glass, are you? Maybe he's been near a vampire but doesn't realize it? I didn't know you were a vampire before you told me."

"He was nervous when I approached the counter, and after I introduced myself, I could smell the fear on him." Simon unlocked the car and opened the door for Ben. "When most people get a glimpse of vampire, their reaction is one of disbelief quickly followed by fear. There was no disbelief there, just fear."

"You let him see what you are?"

"Yes." Simon climbed into the driver's seat and started the car. "Hopefully it's enough to send him scurrying to whoever his employer is. Forge has set up surveillance on him."

"Isn't that dangerous?" Ben asked. "Not just for him but for you? Do you really want whoever is behind this to find out you're onto him?"

"I can take care of myself, Ben." Simon rested one hand briefly on Ben's knee. Ben was forewarned and armed with a Taser. He also knew better than to invite a vampire into his home, and the human victims had all been killed by vampires. But for all of that, Simon still intended to be by his side as much as possible to ensure his safety until this was over. "My guess is that Brad is taking these glasses for whoever took care of his debt for him. He might not even know what they're needed for, but he's got to have some way to contact them, even if it's just a drop-off point." He'd already told Ben about the results yielded by Forge's investigation. "Lucas and I had an interesting discussion after you'd left for work this afternoon. He's been trying to figure out possible connections between the victims from the café and those who had donated to the blood bank."

"And?" Ben prompted.

"When someone drinks from a glass, they leave a minute amount of saliva."

"So what's the connection between saliva and blood?" Ben asked but then answered his own question. "DNA," he said slowly. "They're both sources of DNA."

Simon nodded. "You remember your high school science, I see."

"Yeah, and it came up recently in one of the comics I was reading," Ben admitted. "They were cloning and needed samples." He glanced at Simon. "You don't think they're collecting DNA samples, do you?"

"It's one possibility, but I have no idea why," Simon said. "Lucas is still working on that one. Although we don't have any proof about his theory yet, it's as good a clue as any, so we're following up on it."

"There's no blood missing from any of the blood banks, is there?" Ben seemed thoughtful. "You guys don't do that, do you? Steal blood from blood banks, I mean? I know you and Forge use those blood cube things, but what about other vampires?"

"No, we don't do that. It's too risky." Simon shrugged. "Besides, according to Lucas, if whoever is behind this is after DNA samples, even a small residue would be enough. He's looking into which medical waste firm has the contract to get rid of the needles used to draw the blood."

"Okay, so that's another one of those pop culture things that isn't right." Ben stared out the window into the darkness. "Thanks for picking me up tonight, Simon. It's getting cold out at night now. I wasn't looking forward to walking home."

"It's a full moon tonight. You shouldn't be out alone." Simon slowed down as they approached High Street.

"That's weird." Ben glanced at the Old Curio Shoppe, which was a couple of doors down from Scribbles Bookshop. "They've closed early."

"They do that every full moon," Simon said. "Remember I told you about the Supernatural Council?"

Ben nodded.

"The shop is owned by Jasper Coate, Lucas's uncle," Simon continued. "It's been in their family for generations. The council meets in one of the back rooms."

"Lucas said his father was the leader of the council. The

council is a mix of werewolves, vampires, and humans, right?"

"Yes." Simon parked the car outside Scribbles Bookshop.

"You've mentioned the full moon twice now." Ben frowned and looked up at the sky. "Is that why we're not going to the castle tonight? Does Lucas wolf out or something?"

"That's one way of putting it. This is the one night of the month where werewolves are forced into the change and have no control over their actions. It's dangerous to be around them, and more so for you."

"They'd smell you on me, like that guy did in the werewolf bar?"

"Yes." Simon hadn't been happy when he'd found out about that. Lucky for Ben that he'd stumbled into the bar Lucas liked to haunt, or things might have gone very badly. "Even Lucas isn't safe to be around on a full moon. He locks himself up each month. It's safer for him and for us. He can't access the lock while he's in wolf form, as it requires human dexterity and a password."

"He hasn't told me much about werewolves, and I haven't liked to ask too much. Does he only change once a month?"

"That's the only time he has no control over it," Simon explained. "The rest of the time, he can change at will, and it's still him, although communication can be problematic, as he loses his ability to speak while in wolf form. I'm still not sure what some of those wolf noises or the gestures he makes with his ears and tail mean."

"You're kidding, right?" Ben led the way up the stairs to his apartment once Simon had locked the car and retrieved his briefcase.

"No." Simon shrugged when Ben noticed his briefcase. "I figured if I'm spending the night, I'll go straight to work from here. I've got an early faculty meeting tomorrow and a couple of papers to go over before my first lecture. Do you mind?"

"Of course not. I was going to ask you to spend the night anyway." Ben unlocked his front door, then closed it behind them once they were both inside. "I haven't had a chance to finish that *Young Avengers* graphic novel Blair sent me. I can do that while you're working." He grinned. "Forge had a flip through the *Nightwing* one I sent Blair before it went. He looked through this one too when I put it down to refill my coffee."

Simon laughed. "If you're trying to convert him to comics, it's going to take a bit more than that." He took off his coat and hung it by the door, then placed his briefcase on the coffee table by the couch.

"A bit more than that, huh?" Ben hung his jacket up beside Simon's coat. "I saw you looking through those pictures of Billy and Teddy kissing." He put his arms around Simon and nuzzled the side of his neck. "I felt your reaction too."

"I might be persuaded to read your comics if I was sufficiently motivated, I suppose," Simon admitted. He moaned softly when Ben bit down gently. The thought of Ben dressed in one of those superhero outfits was very appealing.

"You suppose?" Ben's breath felt hot against Simon's ear. "I could picture you as Batman, you know. I think you'd be really hot."

"Just because I'm a vampire doesn't mean I have to be a bat, Ben."

"He's the one who hangs out with Nightwing."

"Oh." Simon swallowed. He'd seen the comic with that costume too. "Oh God." He growled low in his throat, grabbed Ben's hand, and pulled him toward the bedroom. To hell with the work he needed to do. It could wait.

Simon bent over the bed to kiss Ben softly on the lips. "I need to go to work," he said softly. "I'll see you afterwards. Enjoy your day off."

"Hmm." Ben opened his eyes; he was still drowsy. "You smell good," he mumbled, pulling Simon down for another kiss.

If Simon could have skipped this faculty meeting, he would have. Going back to bed with Ben was very tempting, but unfortunately, not an option. He'd woken early and showered, then drunk his coffee while he watched Ben sleep. They'd lain in each other's arms last night and talked until they'd both drifted off. Simon still couldn't believe he hadn't made the connection that Frank was Ben's grandfather. Now he knew, he could see the common traits they shared. Frank had accepted him for who he was, just as Ben did. He'd also liked to talk and had the same love of photography, although from what Ben said, his grandfather had never pursued it seriously, just as a hobby.

Ben didn't look anything like Frank, but something around the eyes when he laughed was familiar. In Simon's defense, Frank had been Australian, but when he'd returned home he'd met a New Zealand girl and settled in Wellington. Their daughter had married Ben's father, whom Ben took after in looks.

"It's your shampoo," Simon said after he broke the kiss. Damn it, he hated having to leave Ben like this. His hair stuck up on end, he had dark stubble on his chin, and he was naked under the covers. Simon smiled. "I love you."

"Yeah, I know," said Ben drowsily. "Love you too." He closed his eyes again, his fingers slipping out of Simon's as he drifted back toward sleep. Ben wasn't a morning person. It was difficult to get much sense out of him during what he referred to as the vampire hours.

Simon had chuckled at that one. He allowed himself one more glance at Ben, who now had both arms around Simon's pillow and was hugging it tightly. After picking up his briefcase, Simon retrieved his keys from the counter and headed for the door.

Not only had Ben invited him into his home, but he'd also given Simon the spare front door key the night before. Tonight Simon would treat him to a nice dinner out and his own key to the castle. He still wasn't sure how he'd let Ben talk him into phoning Frank tonight. It had been too long, and Simon still wasn't convinced Frank would want to talk to him. He wasn't the young man Simon remembered, and Simon dreaded hearing that in his voice.

He'd lost so many friends over the years, not just because they'd grown apart but because they'd grown old and died, while Simon hadn't. Immortality wasn't everything it was cracked up to be. He'd swap all of it for a lifetime with Ben and an opportunity for them to grow old together.

There was no point in brooding about something that wasn't going to change. Although Simon hadn't chosen to become a vampire, he was one, and it wasn't all bad. Certain aspects of Simon's nature definitely appealed to Ben, if the way he got aroused whenever he got a glimpse of the vampire was anything to go by.

The morning air felt much colder than the inside of

Ben's apartment. Simon reached into his coat pocket and pulled on his gloves. He still felt the cold despite being a vampire, but then he always had. The sun was barely up, so it didn't add any warmth to the air. Nor was it particularly bright yet, but at least that meant he didn't need to reach for his sunglasses.

Simon glanced up and down the street, but it was still early so there weren't many people about. A couple of men chatted under the shelter of one of the shop fronts. One of them looked up, and when he saw Simon, he dropped his half-smoked cigarette on the ground and stubbed it out with his boot before continuing with the conversation.

A quick focus of his vampire senses confirmed that both men were humans. He dismissed them as not being a threat and turned to walk toward his car.

The sharp prick on the side of his neck made him spin around quickly. His senses on alert, Simon scanned the area. The men he'd noticed earlier were walking toward him.

He felt his neck with his hand, and pulled out a tiny dart. It smelled of blood. His briefcase dropped from his other hand to fall to the ground.

Simon's fangs descended. The men ran toward him. Simon backed up and stumbled. His legs felt heavy. His vision blurred.

What the hell?

Blood. There had to have been something in the dart. The blood would have acted like a carrier. It was the only way any drug would work on him. That meant whoever had done this already knew what he was.

"Stay back," he warned.

One of the men laughed. "I don't think so, vampire," he said. He appeared to be unarmed. It didn't mean he was.

Simon felt the hard brick of a wall against his back. He bent his legs, ready to jump, when his vision blurred again, bringing with it a wave of sudden weakness.

In his present state, he doubted he could jump the height of his attackers, let alone the building behind him.

He had to lead these men away from Ben, away from here. If he could get past them, they'd never be able to keep up with him. He was a vampire. They weren't. He ducked to the right and nearly lost his footing. One of the men grabbed at him. Simon slammed his fist into the man's face and then kicked out. The man grunted in pain but kept coming.

"Bloody hell," muttered Simon. Not only was his speed waning fast but so was his strength. Normally, a blow like that would have sent his opponent flying or broken his jaw.

Whatever had been in the dart was working quickly. Too quickly.

Simon lashed out again. He grabbed the second man's jacket, yet the material slipped through his fingers. His body refused to obey him.

Run, you idiot. Run.

The strength drained from his legs. He collapsed onto his knees.

Two shapes towered over him.

He tried to crawl away. One of the men grabbed the back of his coat, holding him fast. Simon reached for his coat buttons to undo it, rip them off, anything to get free. The man pushed him forward. Simon hit the ground, the pavement scraping his face. He yelled a warning in his mind, reaching desperately for the one person he needed to keep safe.

For the one person who might hear him.

Ben!

Someone yanked Simon's arms behind him. Something hard and cold clicked around his wrists. His skin burned, like it was on fire. Simon bit his lip against the pain. He wouldn't go down. Not like this. He struggled, kicking out in all directions, desperation and instinct taking over. He fought the drug spreading through him, taking his strength, his consciousness. He couldn't hold off his attackers. He couldn't think, couldn't fight.

Only feel.

He caught sight of something wooden out of the corner of his eye.

No. God, not a stake. Please no.

He yanked at his restraints, ignoring the searing heat dissolving his flesh, burning his wrists, desperate to get free.

Pain exploded in his head.

He fell forward, his world swallowed up by darkness.

CHAPTER FOURTEEN

Ben woke with a start. He shivered despite the warmth of his apartment, snuggled down farther under the covers, and tightened his grip on Simon's pillow. For a moment, he could have sworn he'd heard Simon call his name, but that was crazy, wasn't it? Simon had left for work. Ben remembered the goodbye kiss and the promise to meet later.

He closed his eyes and rolled over in bed but couldn't settle. Something felt... wrong, for want of a better word. He'd had a nightmare, and it had woken him. That had to be it, right? He frowned, torn between wanting to remember the details and not wanting to go back to the feeling of pain and fear that had jerked him awake.

The bloody memory was too hazy to make sense of, as was often the way of dreams. He knew some people who could recall theirs, but he'd never been able to.

"Damn it," Ben muttered, swinging his legs over the side of the bed. So much for sleeping in; it wasn't going to happen now. He grabbed his boxers and sweatpants, then hunted around for his T-shirt and sweatshirt. He'd make himself a cup of tea and then decide on a plan of action for the day. Simon finished his last lecture midafternoon, so Ben had most of the day to himself. Entering the kitchen, he spotted the empty saucepan still sitting on the counter, a reminder that he wanted to have a go at making that fruit-cake for Simon.

Ben looked out across the street while the kettle boiled and glanced at his watch. Still being way too early, it was quiet outside. The shops opposite his apartment were in darkness, although that would change soon as their owners came downstairs to open up. They lived above their busi-nesses, and he'd chatted with them a couple of times.

He peered more closely at the street below and frowned. Wasn't that Simon's car? Yes, it was. That was weird. Simon wouldn't have just left it there, not with the way he fussed over the thing. Ben reached for his phone, dialed Simon's number, but didn't get a reply. He added setting up voice mail for Simon, and showing him how to use it, to his "to do" list.

The kettle boiled, and Ben poured his tea. He put the mug back on the counter after a couple of sips, unable to shake the feeling that something felt seriously wrong. After grabbing his shoes and a jacket, Ben jogged downstairs and headed toward Simon's car. Nothing seemed out of place, so why did his gut tell him he was missing something?

"Pick up," he muttered, giving Simon's number another go. He could hear the bloody thing ringing. Hang on, he could *hear* it ringing, not just through his phone but for real, although the sound was muffled. That definitely wasn't right.

A quick search of the area and following the sound led him to the shop front across the road, just behind the car. Simon's briefcase lay abandoned, almost hidden, in the gutter. Ben glanced around quickly, a cold chill going through him when he saw a stain on the pavement. He bent down and ran his fingers over it, then brought them up to his nose to smell it properly. Blood.

Oh hell.

Simon's phone rang again. Ben grabbed it and answered quickly, the words out of his mouth before he realized how stupid they sounded. "Simon, is that you?"

Of course Simon wouldn't be phoning his own phone unless he was looking for it and his briefcase.

A woman's replied. "Who is this? Where's Simon?" She sounded frantic.

Ben recognized the voice and checked the caller ID. "Is that Juliet? It's Ben."

"Hello, Ben, what are you doing with Simon's phone? Have you seen him? He was supposed to be here half an hour ago for the faculty meeting, and there's no sign of him. He's never late for those. I'm worried about him."

"His phone was in his briefcase, and I have no idea where he is," Ben admitted. "He left in plenty of time to get to the meeting." He decided against telling her Simon had abandoned his car. She sounded worried enough. "Look, I'll phone around and see if anyone's seen him and let you know. You've got my number, right? Phone me if you hear anything."

"Yes, I've got your number," Juliet said. "He gave it to me in case..." She trailed off. When they'd met, Ben had got the impression she was very fond of Simon. Her reaction now confirmed it.

"Talk to you soon," Ben said. "Don't worry, okay? I'm sure there's an explanation for why he's late." He cut the call before Juliet could reply, as he really didn't want to know what she'd meant by the "in case" comment.

There was no point hanging around on the street. Ben

tucked the briefcase under his arm and punched Forge's number into his phone as he headed back to the apartment. Forge picked up after two rings.

"Ben? It's early for you. What's up?"

"Something's happened to Simon." Ben fought to keep his rising panic out of his voice and failed. "He didn't show at work this morning, and his car's still here. Forge, I found his briefcase, and there's blood." He let himself into his apartment, slammed the door behind him, and leaned against the counter.

If something had happened to Simon... *Oh God*. Ben took several deep breaths, trying to calm himself. Something was wrong, terribly wrong. He could feel it. As illogical as the thought was, he could feel it. He knew he could.

"Ben? You still there?"

"Yeah, I'm still here," Ben said. "God, I hate this. I just want him to be safe, and I know he's not. As crazy as it sounds, I *know* he's not."

"Take deep breaths, Ben." Forge sounded calm, but Ben could hear the concern in his voice. "We'll find him. I promise. Do you want me to send someone to come collect you?"

Ben shook his head, although Forge couldn't see him. "No. I'll stay here. Just in case... you know." He didn't want Simon to come back to an empty apartment. Boggs was at the castle, so there'd be someone there for him.

"Yeah, I know," Forge said. "He'll be okay. Simon's good at looking after himself, and he's had a lot of experience doing it."

"That's what worries me," Ben said. Simon was not only very capable but a vampire. If something or someone had him, and if what Ben was feeling was only an echo of Simon's reaction to it, what the bloody hell was happening to him? He took a deep breath. "Hey, I don't know a lot about this soulbond thing we share, but I can feel him. He's... he's scared."

~

Simon forced his eyes open and bit back a groan. He felt groggy and his head hurt. He tried to sit up but couldn't move. In a panic, he realized he was lying on some kind of examination table, and his wrists and ankles were restrained. Someone had removed his coat and gloves while he'd been unconscious, his sweater too.

He yanked at the restraints. Pain rushed through him. His skin burned. He cried out, despite his best intentions not to. God, it hurt. He closed his eyes again and tried to calm himself.

"You're awake, I see," said a familiar voice Simon had never wanted to hear again. "I really wouldn't struggle, as you're only going to hurt yourself further."

"John." Simon opened his eyes again. No, it couldn't be. This wasn't real. But it had to be. Even in his worst nightmares, he hadn't imagined pain like this. He shivered and gritted his teeth. He wouldn't show his fear. He could do this. He could appear calm, even if inside every part of him was screaming to run, to get as far away from John as he possibly could. "It's been a while, but still not long enough."

John hadn't changed. The burns he would have received in the fire had completely healed, but then that wasn't surprising. Vampires didn't scar easily, even if severe wounds took a while to heal. The only thing that left a permanent scar was silver. John was dressed immaculy, in a dress jacket and tie, his black hair neatly trimmed into a modern style. His eyes were the same bright blue. They'd always reminded Simon of ice, and reflected John's state of mind. Cold, arrogant, and dangerous.

"You left me to die, Simon." John's expression was that of a disapproving parent. "It's not a very nice way to treat someone you love, is it?"

"I don't love you," Simon said, ignoring the logical voice in the back of his mind telling him that making John angry wouldn't be a good idea. "I've never loved you. Every time we have this conversation, I tell you that, and you still don't get it."

"My poor Simon," John said, shaking his head. "Everything I do, I do for us." His expression hardened. He held up one wrist. It was covered in scars, the skin puckered and discolored, the area completely devoid of hair. "Although I really should punish you for what you've done, I still can't bring myself to hurt you. At least, not too badly. Not as much as you've hurt me." He smiled. "There is silver in your restraints, which is the reason for the pain you're feeling."

"I already gathered that," Simon muttered. Struggling against silver would be not only painful but useless. It was the one thing that could hold a vampire. "Tell me something I don't know."

"I see we need to work on your manners too, my love." John leaned over Simon, grabbing his chin in a grip of steel when Simon tried to move his head away. Cold lips brushed against his. Simon's stomach twisted. It was all he could do not to gag and vomit.

John moved back when Simon spat at him.

"Don't touch me," Simon growled. "I'm not your love, and I'm never going to be."

"We'll see," John said. A smile played around his lips. "I hear you've been keeping company with very unsavory individuals. I must give my regards to your friend Forge again. I'm sure he'll be delighted to see me alive and well."

"Stay away from him," Simon said. "Whatever you want with me, it only needs to be between us."

Please don't mention Ben. He can't be dragged into this. Whatever happens, he needs to be safe.

"Nothing is ever just between us, Simon." John gestured off to the side, and a burly man was standing by him in an instant. Simon's eyes widened when he recognized the scent. The man was a werewolf. Why was a werewolf working with John? Simon could understand humans working for him. There were plenty who would do so for the right price, but werewolves were loyal to their pack. They'd never work for a vampire. Lucas was the only exception to the rule Simon knew of, and he didn't work for vampires—he worked with them because they were friends. John wouldn't be working *with* werewolves, at least not without a good reason. He'd made his derogatory opinion of weres very clear on several occasions.

"What's this about, John?" asked Simon. He could feel the effects of whatever he'd been drugged with wearing off and his strength returning. If he could buy some time, he might be able to find a way out of this.

"You worked with me once," John said. "I remember you after that last human of yours died. What was his name again? You killed so many of them. I was so proud."

"Albert," Simon said quietly. "His name was Albert." He wasn't proud of what he'd done after Albert's death. In his grief, he'd given in to the bloodlust he'd kept under control for so long. Just one drink had led to another, then another, and had taken not only his sanity but also his humanity. He still had nightmares about it.

But even then, he'd never worked with John. He never

would. Not that there was any point in reminding John of that, as he'd always believed his own warped perception of events.

"Oh yes, that's right." John leaned toward the man he'd summoned. "It's almost time, and our guest is not showing any signs of being very cooperative. Fetch another of your colleagues to help hold him still."

"What are you planning?" Simon couldn't stop his voice shaking. "What are you going to do to me? Whatever it is, it won't change how I feel about you. Nothing will."

"We'll see." John smiled. "You remember that other friend of yours, don't you? Cynthia, I believe her name was. She wasn't very cooperative either. You really need to do something about the company you keep, my boy."

"Cynthia?" Simon swallowed, his mouth dry. *Oh God.* "You did something to her, didn't you? What did you do to her?" He had to get out of here and warn his friends. He had to keep Ben safe.

Another tug at his restraints sent a fresh blast of agony through his body. He could smell his flesh burning where the silver touched it. He bit his lip, tasting blood. He wouldn't cry out and give John the satisfaction.

"Of course I did something to her." John seemed pleased Simon had figured that out at least. He gestured around the room. "This is my great experiment, Simon, and it has so much potential. Of course, others don't see the same future that I do, but that's the price some of us have to pay." He smiled, his eyes dilating to full blue. He'd always been an attractive man and not above using his looks to lull his victims into a false sense of security. Simon had never been fooled by it, but then their first meeting had been John standing over Stephen's dead body, wiping Stephen's blood from his mouth.

And of course Simon's refusal to be turned by John and to be with him had made John all the more determined to make sure it happened. He'd never been one for taking no for an answer.

Simon met John's gaze but said nothing. Better to let him talk, especially as he was obviously intent on doing so. Interrupting him wouldn't achieve anything but more pain. It never had.

"I'm building a future for us together, and this is just the first step." John brushed his fingers over Simon's cheek, caressing him. Simon flinched. "You were the inspiration for it, you know. I did love the way you embraced your bloodlust, after your *friend* died."

"After you murdered him, you mean." Simon couldn't resist the correction.

John slapped him across the face. Hard. "After I saved you from your misconceptions, you ungrateful whelp. You never really loved him. *I'm* your maker, your soulmate. *We're* one."

"You are not my soulmate," Simon muttered. His face stung where John had struck him.

"We'll see." John's fondness for that particular phrase was just as annoying as Simon remembered. "Anyway," John continued as though Simon hadn't interrupted him, "I found a way to harness that bloodlust. All I needed was an efficient delivery system." The werewolf returned and handed John a syringe full of clear liquid. He'd brought a friend with him, another werewolf. "Not just to deliver it but to target specific DNA. Imagine it, a vampire assassin who would kill whomever I wished. Oh, the power that comes with that." He grinned at Simon. "I know, isn't it brilliant? Especially now I've found a way to make it work. That's the reason for all the incidents you and your friends have been investigating, in case you hadn't guessed. I had to hone my methods, you see."

"Vampire assassins?" Simon didn't like where this was going at all, and that syringe wasn't helping.

"Oh, yes." John tapped the side of the syringe. "That's the thing with viruses. They're not only the perfect carrier, but an active one will also use its host's body to multiply until it burns out." He gestured toward the werewolves. They approached Simon, one on each side, grabbed him, and held him still. Simon struggled furiously, but all he achieved was to grind his wrists and ankles against his restraints.

His vision blurred, the pain growing in intensity.

He felt his sleeve being rolled up. "No!" he yelled. "Please. Don't."

"It's for your own good," John insisted. He found a vein and inserted the needle into Simon's arm, checked to make sure it was in, and then pushed down the plunger. "And don't worry. I'm not going to dispose of you like I did the others. Once you deal with this problem for me, there'll be nothing in the way of our new life together. I promise."

"Problem?" Simon looked up at John in horror. "What problem?" The werewolves let go of him, and Simon slumped back in his restraints.

"That human you think you're so fond of, of course." John smiled. "It's a shame the messenger I sent didn't scare him off. I had hoped it would at least have warned you to keep your distance from your human, but no." He shrugged. "The old gentleman played his part so well too, but loose ends are dangerous so he had to die. All loose ends must be dealt with, don't you think?" He gestured toward the werewolves. "Leave us, please. Simon and I wish to get reacquainted while the virus takes effect."

Bloody hell, so John *had* sent that man in the café Ben had told him about.

"Ben," Simon whispered. "Please, don't hurt him. I'll do anything you want. Just don't hurt him."

"Oh, *I'm* not going to hurt him." John placed the empty syringe on a tray on a nearby table. "It makes me very happy that you'll do anything I want. Everyone has their price, don't they? I had a feeling he might be yours."

Simon shook his head. "No," he whispered. He knew what was happening to him. He could already feel the beginnings of the bloodlust coursing through his body. He licked his lips despite himself. He wouldn't do this again. He couldn't.

"Oh yes," John whispered. "You're getting hungry, aren't you? I do love the way it works so quickly, more so on some than others, of course, but then it's something you've tried to put behind you for so long. Foolish boy, it's always been a part of you. I'm just helping you to embrace it. It's not good for us to deny our true nature." He ran his lips over Simon's neck. "You still taste so good." Simon tried to pull away, but he had nowhere to go.

John undid Simon's belt and then reached for the zipper of his trousers. He slipped his hand under the material.

"No," Simon said. "Don't touch me. Don't."

"I love you," John said, his breath hot against Simon's ear. "I'm going to mark you as mine. We'll have an eternity together. Isn't that a wonderful thought?"

Simon closed his eyes. His body was on fire; he could feel his self-control ebbing. He was hungry, but not for this. Never for this.

His eyes snapped open. He felt his fangs descend. John smiled. He yanked down Simon's trousers, licked his lips, and sank his fangs into Simon. Simon jerked back and tried to pull away. No! He didn't want this. He'd never wanted this. He wouldn't acknowledge what John wanted. A soul-mate bond that wasn't John's to take. A bond that Simon would never give him. He belonged to someone else.

To Ben.

Simon licked his lips. God, he was so hungry.

Ben, I love you. I'm sorry.

It should have been Ben biting him, marking him there, not John. Please not John. Not again.

I want you so badly. You taste so good. Ben, you taste so good.

"No," Simon screamed. "No!"

CHAPTER FIFTEEN

Ben picked up the phone on the first ring, then stared at it, not able to bring himself to say anything.

"Ben, you there?" Forge asked.

"Yeah." Ben flopped down on the couch. His hands shook. "You haven't found him yet," he said.

"Not yet." Forge made a frustrated noise. "That kid, Brad, was next to useless and has no clue what's going on, apart from the fact he's working for a vampire. He had a contact number, but it's to a burner phone, so impossible to trace."

"How much did you scare him?"

"It didn't take much," Forge admitted. "He's nervous as hell. Simon talking to him yesterday did enough of a number on him, from what I can tell."

"Simon's not that scary," Ben pointed out. "He told me he just gave Brad a glimpse, nothing more. It's not like he put the fear of God into him or anything."

Forge snorted. "Just because you think Simon's hot when he shows the vampire doesn't mean others are going to."

"I never said that!" Ben protested.

"Not in so many words," Forge said, "but yeah, you do."

"Bloody vampire hearing," muttered Ben. He and Simon were never going to have any privacy at the castle while... His thoughts trailed off, and he bit his lip. "It's been twelve hours. What if he's hurt? What if he's...?"

He couldn't bring himself to finish the sentence.

"That's never a good line of thought, so don't go there, hmm?" Forge's voice softened. "Are you sure you don't want to come over here? It would be better than you sitting alone, letting your imagination run wild."

"It's not—" Ben's phone slipped from his fingers to land on the couch as a sudden wave of pure terror hit him in the gut. He cried out.

Simon!

He tried to reach for Simon through the connection they shared, but there was nothing. It was like the awareness he'd had of Simon since they'd soulbonded had been snuffed out. Not that it had been that strong to start with, more like a vague feeling he wasn't alone or an echo of any strong emotions Simon was experiencing.

If what he'd felt was just an echo...

"Bloody. Hell," he muttered, his breath coming in gasps.

"Ben? Ben! You okay? What's going on?"

Ben slowly came back to his surroundings with the realization Forge was yelling into the phone.

"No, I'm not okay," Ben said, picking up the phone again. "Simon's in real trouble. I just felt..." Ben's stomach churned. He tasted bile. "There's nothing there. I can't feel him. Why can't I feel him?" He stared into space and wiped his eyes. He couldn't lose Simon like this. They were supposed to have a lifetime together, at least Ben's lifetime.

"Whoever's done this," he ground out, "I'll fucking kill them. I'll find them and I'll fucking kill them."

"No, you won't," Forge said. "You're going to sit there and stay safe until we find him. If you go running off into danger, Simon will kick my ass, and then he'll probably kick yours, once he's finished fucking you senseless."

Ben shook his head. "What if he's d-dead? What if that's what I just felt?" Cold crawled through him. He picked up a cushion and threw it at the wall. It hit the hard surface with a soft thud and did nothing to quell his frustration. "I can't just sit here and do nothing!"

"You're not doing nothing. You're giving him something to come home for," Forge reminded him. "I've known Simon a long time. He's one of the strongest people I know, and he's survived bad things before when a lot of others wouldn't. Stay strong a while longer, okay? Lucas is working on a lead. If we get anything, I'll let you know. Promise."

The phone went dead, and he threw it onto the couch. He'd never been good at sitting back and watching everyone else do what needed to be done. Part of him knew Forge was right, but it was getting harder to believe Simon was still okay.

He buried his face in his hands and closed his eyes. Stupid soulmate bond. It was next to useless in this kind of situation. If he was a vampire like Simon, it would be stronger and more helpful, at least from the little he knew about it. God, there was so much he didn't know, and no one to ask.

Unless...

Simon had talked about an old friend, Hugh. He was the husband of the woman who had died. Cynthia. They'd had a soulbond like Ben and Simon's, human and vampire.

Would he have some kind of clue as to how to decipher what was going on? It was worth a shot, right?

The address book on Simon's phone provided contact details easily enough. Ben started to punch in the number, then hesitated. Did he have the right to do this? Not only was he going through Simon's private stuff, but he was seriously debating calling a man who had just lost his wife and dredging up her death all over again.

"God, you're a dickhead," Ben muttered. He walked over to the counter and put Simon's phone down out of temptation's way. The street below him was in darkness now and as deserted as it had been that morning when he'd first looked for Simon.

Something brushed against him—not against *him*, but against his mind.

"Simon?" he whispered. He spun, but no one was there. That settled it. He was definitely losing the plot.

Whatever had reached for him didn't feel right either. It wasn't gentle and loving like Simon but something much colder and darker. Ben swallowed. He shivered.

He walked into the bedroom and hunted through his backpack for the Taser Simon had given him. This was crazy. Jumping at mental shadows wasn't going to do Simon any good. Ben managed a shaky laugh.

Definitely losing it.

A quiet click made him jump. He tightened his grip on the Taser and strode out into the living room. Where the hell had the noise come from?

Oh crap.

Someone was opening his front door. But how? Ben was sure he'd locked it. Positive he'd locked it. He'd also been careful not to invite anyone in, not even the pizza delivery guy.

"Simon!"

Ben lowered the Taser and ran toward the door. Of course! He'd given Simon a key the night before.

"Ben." Simon stood framed in the doorway. He looked like hell. His eyes were fully brown, his fangs extended. His coat and sweater were gone, and his shirt was untucked. There was blood on it. He still wore his tie, but it was askew, just like the rest of him. His skin was paler than usual, and there was something wild about his expression.

"What the hell happened to you?" Ben asked. "I was—"

Before he had the chance to finish his sentence, Simon closed the distance between them and pulled Ben close. "Ben," he said, but his voice held no love. It was flat, hollow, and for the first time since they'd met, Ben felt scared of him.

"Simon, let go of me," he said, trying to push Simon away. Something was wrong. Very wrong.

"I want you," Simon whispered. "You smell so good. I need you." He moved with vampire speed and shoved Ben against the wall.

Sudden sharp pain took Ben by surprise. "Simon! What the fuck are you doing?" Simon had his fangs in Ben's neck, and he was starting to drink.

Ben attempted to push him away again, but it was no use. Simon was too strong and too focused on drinking.

God, Simon was drinking from *him*. But Simon didn't do that. He didn't drink human blood. He couldn't. Not after everything he'd been through.

"Simon, you're hurting me." Ben's vision blurred. He felt his strength leaving him. He had to stop Simon before he lost too much blood.

Simon caught one of Ben's wrists, his iron grip holding Ben in place.

Fuck. Fuck.

Ben wriggled, limbs flailing in his desperation to be free. He managed to move his head just enough to see the inside of Simon's wrists. They were an angry red, the skin blistered and burned. Ben pulled Simon's free hand toward him and bit down. Hard.

"Ben?" Simon jerked back. He looked up at Ben as though seeing him for the first time. An expression of horror crossed his face. "Get out. Run! I can't stop this. Run!"

Ben ducked under and past him. He saw the Taser on the floor by the door. He must have dropped it when Simon grabbed him.

A low growl made him hesitate. Whatever reprieve Simon had given him was gone. The man Ben loved was gone. In his place was the vampire who had attacked him.

Simon started to move. Ben dived for the Taser, rolled, and fired. Simon screamed. His body jerked convulsively. He fell to his knees, forced himself to his feet, and started moving again.

"Stay down, damn it," Ben yelled. He fired again, and as Simon got to his feet, Ben headed for the large bookshelf on the far wall. The Taser was definitely having an effect, but it wasn't enough to stop him, although the second time had slowed him down way more than the first.

Simon staggered. It gave Ben the chance he needed. He drew on what was left of his strength and hoped like hell it would be enough. One tug at the bookshelf did nothing. It wobbled, but that was it.

"Stupid, stupid thing," Ben muttered. He yanked it again, this time with everything he had.

The bookshelf crashed to the ground, catching Simon as it fell, trapping his still body underneath. Blood pooled under his head, seeping into the carpet. Ben grabbed his phone and punched in Forge's number.

He'd dragged the unconscious Simon out from under the bookcase and was holding him in his arms before Forge picked up. Simon had to be okay. He had to be.

"Get over here, Forge, quickly, and bring Lucas. It's Simon. He's—" Ben choked on the words. He stroked Simon's hair, but Simon didn't move. He knew he should keep his distance, but he couldn't.

Simon was his. Ben loved him. Simon had tried to fight this. He'd told Ben to run.

"We're on our way," Forge said.

The phone went dead.

Whoever had done this was going to pay. Ben traced the angry wounds on Simon's wrists. He'd been tortured, at the very least. That much was obvious.

No, they weren't just going to pay. Whoever had done this was fucking dead.

Ben paced back and forth across the Bat Cave. What was taking Lucas so damn long? By the time Lucas and Forge had arrived at Ben's apartment, Simon had started to regain consciousness, but he was still groggy and definitely not himself. Ben was relieved Forge and Lucas were able to handle Simon between them so Ben didn't have to Taser him again. He was going to have serious nightmares about having to do that.

Once they'd reached the castle, Forge had held Simon down so Lucas could administer enough sedative to ensure he was no longer a threat. Ben had been told in no uncertain terms to make himself scarce until they knew what they were dealing with. He'd retreated to the Bat Cave with Boggs for company, but he was far from happy.

"Lucas knows what he's doing, Ben," Boggs said. He'd vanished for a few minutes and gone to check on Simon for Ben. "He's very experienced."

Simon was conscious and more lucid than he'd been and had asked to speak to Forge.

Not Ben. Forge.

Logically, Ben knew he couldn't see Simon until they'd figured out why Simon had attacked him, but it was driving him crazy knowing Simon was hurt and he couldn't be there with him.

"I know that." Ben touched his neck. Lucas had suggested he put a dressing on the wound, but as the bleeding had stopped, Ben didn't see the point. It was going to be obvious as hell as it was, without a bandage there as a reminder to Simon of what he'd done.

Lucas appeared in the doorway. He ran his fingers through his hair. His tone was more serious than Ben had ever heard before. "Forge is with Simon. He'll come speak to you in a few minutes."

"How's Simon? When can I see him?" Ben asked.

"I've given him a sedative and something to help his immune system fight this." Lucas sat down heavily. "He's been programmed to kill you, Ben, the same as those other vampires were sent to kill their prey. His body is fighting a virus; it's the carrier for this thing. It targets specific DNA. You were lucky he didn't kill you."

"He was fighting it," Ben said quietly. "I'd be dead otherwise." Now he had time to think, there was a lot to sink in. Despite what Simon had told him, Ben hadn't realized how fast and strong Simon was. It had brought home why Simon was so scared about losing control and hurting him.

"Staying away from him is the best thing you can do until he's recovered," Lucas said. "I know it's going to be hard, but he's got enough guilt to deal with as it is. Think of it as an influenza virus or something. His body will fight it, but it's going to take time."

"The other vampires didn't recover. They died!" Ben bit his lip and turned away, not wanting Lucas to see how upset he was.

"They were murdered. This isn't what killed them. Simon will make a full recovery, and he has a lot to live for." Lucas looked sad for a moment. "He loves you, and he's putting himself through hell. When this is over, you'll need to have a long talk with him. He's convinced himself you're going to want to leave him because of what he did to you. You know what he's like."

"That's crazy," Ben protested. "This wasn't him."

"He says it was." Lucas shrugged. "You can't be in the same room with him, but that doesn't mean you can't write him a letter or talk to him on the phone. I'll let you know as soon as he's up to it."

Ben nodded slowly. "In the meantime, could you give him a message from me? Tell him I love him and I'm not going anywhere. I'll wait. However long it takes, I'll wait."

"I'll tell him," Boggs offered. "I'm going to stay with Simon, as I think it's better both of you are here to listen to what Forge has got to say." His expression hardened. "This stops now. I'd join you if I could."

"That asshole's seriously got Mr. Boggs angry," Lucas said after Boggs disappeared. "Whatever we need to do to take this guy down, I'm in."

"He's mine," Ben said.

"He's a dangerous as fuck vampire, and you're not the

only one who wants him dead," Forge said as he came into the room. "Stand in line."

"He's mine," repeated Ben. He shot Forge a look. "I don't care what the bloody hell he is, *I'm* going to kill him. He hurt *my* Simon, and badly. He's mine." His eyes narrowed. "You know who he is, don't you? What did Simon tell you?"

"Nice show of testosterone there, guys, but first things first, hmm?" Lucas said. "We can decide who gets to do the actual killing later."

Forge met Ben's gaze with a level one of his own. "John isn't as dead as we thought he was. He's the one behind this, and he's the asshole who hurt Simon. Not only that, but he's got humans *and* werewolves working with him."

"Fuck." Ben sank into the nearest chair. "He's supposed to be dead. Simon told me he burned to death in some fire in the fifties."

"He wasn't too happy that Simon left him there to die either," Forge said dryly. He absently rubbed at his wrist. Ben caught a glimpse of silver-colored scars. "He's still batshit crazy and fixated on the idea he and Simon are soulmates. His excuse for this particular bout of madness is that he's building a future for them together."

Ben snorted. "Yeah, like that's going to happen." A thought struck him. "Is that why he sent Simon to kill me?"

"Yeah. Simon didn't say as much, but I got the idea that John thought if he killed you, it would set him back to how he was after—"

"After Albert died," Ben said. "Yeah, I know all about that." He'd seen some of how it had affected Simon too, through their soulmate bond. He shuddered.

"Well, I don't," Lucas pointed out. "I mean, I know the

general gist of it but not the details. It's not like I was there or anything."

"I was," Forge said grimly. "So was Declan. It wasn't pretty." He glanced at Lucas. "It's not something we're going to talk about, and just because Simon's not here, don't think he can't hear you." He gave Ben a long hard look. "He's asked me to keep you safe, and I intend to keep my word. You do realize we'll be going up against a vampire, right?"

"Yeah, I do realize that. I did get the memo." Ben returned the look in kind. "I also figure that gives me an advantage you guys don't have. I don't have the same issues with silver you do."

"I thought you said you weren't going to use that against anyone?" Lucas reminded him.

"I changed my mind," Ben said.

"He's stronger, faster, and has no qualms about killing you," Forge said. "I know you want to do this, Ben, but what's to stop him turning you against us if he uses his thrall on you? You could be more of a hindrance than a help."

"Vampire thrall doesn't work on me because of the soul-bond," Ben told him. "Simon and I talked about it, and he tried to use it on me." Simon had hated the idea of using it on Ben, and it had taken some convincing to get him to try. In the finish, Ben had argued it was something they might need to know in the future. It wasn't something Simon did often, as doing it for a prolonged period of time usually gave him a migraine.

"It's too dangerous, Ben." Forge's voice had taken on a steady, smooth quality, just as Simon's had when he'd tried to use the thrall on Ben. "You should stay home and let us handle it."

Ben rolled his eyes. "Nice try, but no. I already told you

that thrall thing doesn't work on me." There had to be some advantages to being bonded to a vampire, despite their sharing of emotions and the like. Not to mention the great sex. "From what Simon's told me, John is an arrogant bastard. I'm human so he won't be expecting me to be a threat. I figure we can use that against him. When you and Lucas go after John, I'm coming with you."

"Vampire thrall doesn't work on werewolves either," Lucas put in, "which makes me wonder if Simon's right about this John guy working with them. Werewolves don't usually work with vampires. I'm an exception to the rule. *And* we still have the small problem of not knowing where this guy is. Simon has no clue where he was taken, and he was out of it when he was dumped back outside Ben's apartment." He pointed toward a flashing light on Forge's computer. "Hey, looks like someone's trying to get your attention."

Forge hit a button on the keyboard to increase the volume. "What is it, Blair? We're kind of busy."

"This is important," Blair said, his voice tinny over the computer speaker. "There's a firm that deals with the medical waste for the blood bank. They've got the contract for most of the city's medical facilities, actually, not just that one place. I've tracked down the location of their warehouse."

"Saved by the flashing red light," murmured Lucas. "Wouldn't be the first time." He shrugged and grinned when Ben shot a curious look in his direction but didn't elaborate.

"Where's the warehouse?" Ben asked, already mentally going over a plan of attack in his head. He had the Taser and the stakes he'd been given.

"Sixteen Mitchell Street," Blair said. "I'll contact you

when I have more information." He cut the connection before anyone could reply.

"We have all the information we need," Forge said. "We move out now."

"I just need to stop by my apartment, then I'm set." Once Ben had collected the rest of his arsenal he'd be armed and ready to dust this arsehole.

CHAPTER SIXTEEN

"Definitely human," Lucas confirmed, after he got back from scouting the building, "so they won't spot us here as long as we keep our voices down."

"How can you tell?" Ben asked.

"They have their own unique smell." Lucas glanced at Ben. "No offense."

"None taken."

Ben peered around Lucas's shoulder to take a brief look at the two men standing outside the rear door of the warehouse. Although the wall wasn't well lit, the moon shed enough light to get a good look at them. Both were sturdily built and neither looked very friendly, especially the one sporting a fresh bruise on his jaw.

"If John's working with werewolves," Ben asked, "wouldn't it make more sense to have them on guard?"

Forge shook his head. "Having weres on guard would be a dead giveaway to any passing supernatural that something is going on, especially as this warehouse isn't owned by the pack. Lucky for us that makes it easier to get inside. If Lucas hasn't smelled them yet, they haven't gotten our scent either." He glanced at the guards, then back at Ben and Lucas. "I'll deal with these two, and then we'll go find John. My guess is if he's using these goons to guard this entrance, he'll be saving the rest of his minions to deal with whoever gets inside."

"Did he just call them minions?" Ben asked Lucas after Forge sneaked over to the warehouse. They'd left his car a block away and continued the rest of the way on foot so they wouldn't be so easily spotted.

"Yeah, he did." Lucas grinned. "There's hope for him yet." He hoisted his backpack onto his shoulder.

"What's in your backpack, anyway? Some kind of weapon?"

"It's for my clothes," Lucas replied with a wink. It was difficult to tell whether he was being serious or not, so probably better not to know. "So what's in that jacket of yours, anyway?"

"Stuff," said Ben, glad his jacket had lots of pockets. He had a couple of stakes in one inside pocket and something especially for John in the other. His Taser completed the ensemble, stuffed into the waistband of his jeans.

"Ready?" Forge asked from behind them. The guards were sprawled on the ground, both unconscious. Ben hadn't seen them go down.

"Ninja vampire," Lucas whispered. "Personally, I find it kind of hot."

"Yeah," said Ben distractedly. He groaned when Lucas grinned from ear to ear. "I didn't mean when Forge does it," Ben amended.

"Of course not."

According to the building schematics, the warehouse was split into two large sections, divided by a door. The area Simon had described was probably at the back so it could be more easily protected. The warehouse wasn't a big one, but more the size of a large hall.

Simon had only seen two humans—probably the ones Forge had just taken out—and two werewolves, but that didn't mean John didn't have other men working for him. He usually didn't fight his own battles and preferred others did the dirty work needed to keep him safe.

"Bastard," Ben muttered under his breath. Lucas shot him a look. Ben shook his head and shrugged.

Forge sneezed suddenly. "Damn allergies."

"I know you're a vampire," Ben pointed out. "You don't have to keep faking it. Vampires don't have allergies."

Forge shrugged. "Tell that to my allergies." He glanced between the warehouse and their hiding place. "Once we're in, there's no going back. If there are weres in here, they'll smell us before they see us."

Ben nodded. He bit his lip, not willing to show how scared he was. His hands shook. He shoved them into his pockets. Forge and Lucas might be used to this kind of thing, but Ben wasn't. He took a deep breath and thought of Simon.

Simon lying unconscious in his arms.

Simon's agitation when he'd woken, the almost over-whelming feelings of anger, fear, and despair Ben had felt through their soulbond.

They'd left him at the castle, heavily sedated, with Boggs keeping a close eye on him.

Ben could do this. He could do this for Simon. John needed to pay for what he'd done. He'd haunted Simon for long enough.

It stopped now.

"You okay?" Forge asked softly. "We can handle this if you're not up for it."

"I'm up for it," Ben said. "Let's go get this arsehole."

Without replying, Forge jogged over to the warehouse. Lucas ran to join him, Ben following a few steps behind. Forge pushed opened the door and led them inside. Ben blinked against the sudden light of the overhead fluorescents. On first look, the place appeared deserted, which was unlikely, considering the lights left burning.

Lucas lifted his head. He sniffed the air. "Company," he announced. "Weres and human." He growled, his eyes glowing yellow.

Slight movement caught Ben's eye, and he ducked out of the way behind a stack of packing crates just in time. A huge black wolf landed on the floor where he'd just stood and growled at him. Lucas stepped between them and growled back, baring his teeth. "Go find our prey," he hissed. "I'll deal with this one."

Lucas's features blurred, and he shook his head as though to clear it. Coarse fur grew rapidly where moments before there had been smooth skin. Still circling the wolf, Lucas pulled his shirt off over his head.

Another wolf pounced on Forge. He ducked out of its way at the last minute, moving at vampire speed, maneuvering the wolf closer to the wall. The wolf growled, and launched itself at Forge, hitting solid brick with a thud when Forge danced out of its way again.

"Move, Ben," snapped Forge. "There's more coming."

The double doors at the far end of the room burst open. Three large wolves bounded through. A low howl filled the room. Ben glanced quickly behind him. Where Lucas had stood moments before was now a large gray wolf. The other wolves, including the black one, backed off for a moment, as though unsure.

Lucas growled.

"Move," Forge yelled. "We'll deal with this. Go. Now." He stood next to Lucas and bared his fangs, his body tense, as though ready to pounce.

As the wolves leapt, Ben ran for the open door. A burly man stepped out in front of him. "Going somewhere, boy?"

"I'm not your boy," Ben said evenly, "or anyone else's." He pulled out the largest stake, which was just over a foot long and several inches thick. As weapons went, it wasn't perfect, but used the right way with enough force behind it, it had the potential to at least slow a bad guy down.

"Is that supposed to scare me?" The man snorted. "I'm not a vampire. You'll have to do better than that." He closed the distance between them and swung his fist at Ben.

Ben sidestepped, the blow barely missing him. He gripped the pointy end of the stake and swung it like a club. Hard. The man howled in pain but kept coming. Ben swung it again. The man dropped to the ground, and Ben hit him over the head before he could get up. He groaned and lay still.

Breathing heavily, Ben moved cautiously forward. Forge and Lucas had quite a fight on their hands with the wolves, and John hadn't struck him as an idiot. Surely he wouldn't have left himself with only one guard?

"Figures," he muttered when he found himself in a short corridor. Another man stood at the other end of it in front of a door. The scenario reminded him of the old science fiction shows he watched. There was always a corridor, and it was always guarded. They were usually dimly lit like this one too.

Ben rolled his eyes. He pulled out his Taser and hid it behind his back. "Excuse me," he said politely, approaching the guard. "I'm lost. I'm looking for Lake Erie, and someone told me it was this way."

The man gaped at him and then seemed to regain his composure. "How did you—"

Ben drew his Taser and fired it. The guard hit the floor with a satisfying thud. "Dickhead," Ben muttered. "Not that bright, are you?"

He stepped over the guard and cried out when a grip of steel closed around his ankle, yanking him onto the floor.

"Brighter than you, *boy*," the guard growled. He sounded groggy, but he hadn't lost consciousness.

Fuck it, the Taser should have brought him down. Why hadn't it? The guy was human, wasn't he?

The guard's eyes gleamed yellow like Lucas's had done. His body was already covered in coarse fur.

Bloody hell. Another werewolf. Why hadn't the Taser taken him down completely on the first go? He'd already begun his change. Had that protected him?

As Ben tried to wriggle free, the Taser slipped from his hand and slid along the floor, just out of reach. Ben kicked out with his other leg and the grip on his ankle loosened. Ben pulled free, rolled, and backed up quickly, using his legs to propel him on his bottom along the floor. He felt around for the Taser, his fingers touching thin air.

The guard, now in full wolf form, leapt for Ben.

Damn it. Damn it.

Ben reached inside his pocket and grabbed one of the silver-tipped darts he'd secreted there. The wolf collided with him before he could throw it, knocking the dart from his hand and sending it skittering across the floor. Ben scrambled after it, but the wolf grabbed Ben's ankle again, dragging him closer.

Ben fumbled in his pocket for another dart, his fingers shaking. Pain screamed in his ankle and ran up his leg as the wolf tightened his grip, reeling Ben in. Ben grimaced at the rank smell of the wolf's breath, and shoved the dart upward into the body hunched over him.

The wolf yelped in pain and backed away quickly. He—Ben couldn't bring himself to think of the wolf as "it"—gasped for breath, his paws scrabbling at the dart stuck in his chest. A smell of burning fur filled the air. Ben dived for the Taser and shot the wolf, who crashed to the floor, unmoving.

At least the darts worked against werewolves. Ben took a moment to catch his breath and calm his state of mind.

He climbed to his feet, still shaking. He hesitated for a moment, wondering if he should remove the dart from the werewolf and give him a chance to heal. Despite what the werewolf had done, Ben was no killer. He couldn't leave someone to die.

A quick tug and Ben retrieved the dart, then the one on the floor, and shoved them into his pocket. He'd need everything he had to take down John.

He gritted his teeth and limped toward the door to what was most probably John's laboratory. His ankle throbbed where the werewolf had held him. He focused on the pain, using it as a reminder of how John had tortured Simon.

"I told you I wasn't to be disturbed," someone said in a clipped British accent when Ben entered the room. The man was absorbed in paperwork and didn't bother to turn around. His next words suggested he hadn't taken the time to check who or what had disturbed him either. "Go lick your fur or something."

"Life isn't always about getting what or who you want," Ben said. He wanted to be sure this was John before he attacked, and it was difficult to tell from behind. The arsehole deserved to die for what he'd done to Simon, but Ben's hesitation with the werewolf had brought home the fact he couldn't bring himself to kill anyone else.

"You!" John exclaimed as he turned to face Ben. Seeing him up close, rather than an image in Simon's memories, Ben was struck by how the guy in the café could have been an older version of him. They had the same piercing blue eyes, although John's skin was unlined and his hair was black, not red with streaks of gray. It was creepy, to say the least.

Ben took a step backward, keeping a safe distance between them. While he knew safe was a relative term, considering how fast a vampire could move, he still liked the illusion of the word. "Yeah, me. Expecting someone else?"

"Did dear Simon decide to deliver you to me, instead of killing you?" John's expression brightened. He glanced around. "Where is he? He was always one for not doing exactly what he was told, despite how much I chastised him."

"Simon's not here." Ben shivered, remembering the images he'd seen when he'd been woken by one of Simon's nightmares. Chastised was not the word he'd use for it. Tortured was closer. "He's not coming anywhere near you ever again."

John snorted. "Simon knows what's good for him, and he's realized by now that his place is with me, not you." He waved one hand dismissively. "Go home, human, while I'm in a mood to allow it."

"You sent Simon to kill me," Ben pointed out. "Why let me go now?"

"Questions, questions." John peered at Ben more closely. "I've never understood his fondness for humans, but I suppose no one is perfect." He smiled, his eyes cold. "Do I have to explain *everything*? I'm not going to kill you. I already told Simon that. No, no, it's much better for everyone if he does that himself."

"Arsehole," Ben muttered.

"Tsk, tsk, they certainly don't teach manners to you young ones anymore, do they?" John frowned. "You're not having a good influence on my Simon, young man. He was quite rude to me the last time we met." He glanced at the door behind Ben, then turned back to his work.

"He's not *your* Simon," Ben snapped. He'd had enough of this psycho's small talk. "He's *mine*." He took a step closer to John. "We're soulbonded, and you're never getting your hands on him again. You hurt him, you bastard."

John turned again and growled low in his throat, his eyes becoming fully blue. He smiled at Ben, this time with his fangs extended. "You've wasted my time, human. As Simon's failed the simple task I set him, I'll just have to do it myself. He'll pay for this."

"No." Ben shook his head, the darts already in his hand. "He won't."

A sudden wave of fear caught him by surprise. He hesitated. No, he wasn't scared. This wasn't him. It wasn't him.

Simon had told him about some sort of glamour thing, that a vampire could project emotions onto others. It wasn't like Ben and Simon's soulbond, but more of a defense mechanism, designed to reduce an opponent to a quivering mess.

What if Simon had lied? What if they weren't really soulbonded? Ben stumbled back, his ankle sending a fresh wave of pain through him.

What the fuck was he doing taking on a vampire? Simon had nearly killed him. John wouldn't hesitate.

He couldn't kill John. He wasn't a killer.

Ben dropped to his knees, his vision blurring.

He clenched his fist. Simon had fought the bloodlust. He'd fought John every step of the way.

He fought John. I need to fight this for him.

This isn't my fear. It's the glamour. We're soulbonded. He's mine.

"You're no threat, *human*." John's gaze lingered on the incisions on Ben's neck. "Run back to my Simon. Let him finish the job he started."

Simon had bitten him. He's dangerous. *He could have killed me.*

I'm no threat to a vampire.

If he didn't stop John, he'd keep killing. The bastard had already lived several lifetimes, leaving a wake of murder and chaos behind him.

No more.

The sudden rush of anger cleared Ben's head. Not his. Simon's.

Ben grabbed the emotion, held on tight, and forced himself to stand.

"Not happening," he muttered and threw one of the darts at John.

John ducked. The dart hit the floor, missing its target. Ben drew back to throw again, but John caught his arm and twisted it back around his body, turning him in the same motion so Ben now had his back to him. Ben gasped in pain. John scraped a fang against Ben's cheek from behind.

Fuck, it hurt. Blood dribbled down his cheek, dripping onto his T-shirt.

Ben kicked out, desperate to be free. John tightened his grip, and Ben's arm felt numb as John twisted tighter.

Simon. I have to do this for Simon. Ben reached out frantically for Simon through their soulbond. Emotions flooded back.

Fear, determination. Love.

If Ben didn't break free, John would go after Simon again.

Focus on Simon. Not the pain.

"He's not *your* Simon," Ben growled. He pulled another stake from his pocket with his free hand, and shoved it backwards as hard as he could. "He's mine, you arsehole."

John yelled in pain, and stumbled back, letting go of Ben, who sidestepped quickly. John yanked out the stake and glared at Ben. "You'll pay for that."

Two darts struck John square in the chest. He yelled in pain and fell to his knees, the silver burning into his skin.

Ben pulled out his Taser and fired. John jerked, then fell onto his back. He stared up at Ben, the fear he'd felt now reflected in John's eyes.

"I'll let him have you as a pet," John pleaded when Ben leaned over him, stake in hand. "We could be a family." He twitched erratically as the silver spread through his body.

"Like hell," Ben yelled. "I love Simon. He's *mine*. He's never been yours. Never. Go to hell."

He shoved the stake in. Hard. John grabbed Ben's wrist, but Ben pulled free easily.

"Think about this, Ben," John said. "You're human. I can make you so much more."

"Simon loves me the way I am." Ben gave the stake another shove.

John screamed. The last of the color drained from his face, and his body crumbled into tiny flakes of skin and bone. Ben watched, a sick feeling in his stomach, but was unable to look away. The stake fell to the floor to lie in a pile of gray dust.

Ben dropped to his knees and retched. *Oh God.*

"It's okay, Ben. You did good." Forge had one arm

around him. Ben hadn't known he was there. "John's dead. The world's already a much better place." His shirt was ripped, and his chest covered in angry red claw marks. He and Lucas had fought their own battle while Ben dealt with John.

"I've never killed anyone before," Ben said, his voice coming out as a half croak. Oh God, that had been close. Too close. "I couldn't let him hurt Simon again. I couldn't."

His stomach heaved again, and he vomited over Forge's boots.

Forge pulled him close. "The first time's always the worst," he said.

"Does it get easier?"

"Nope, and the time to worry is when it does." Forge glanced over at the door as it opened. "Hey, Lucas."

"Damn it, I thought those wolves would never give up," Lucas said. "All done here?"

Ben leaned into Forge's embrace, shivering. "Yeah," he managed. Forge helped Ben to his feet, tightening his hold when Ben stumbled. "I don't feel too good," Ben said.

"Shock," Lucas said softly, glancing at Forge. "Do you want to do cleanup and contact the council? I'm going to take Ben outside for some fresh air."

"Sure." Forge frowned. "Something about this doesn't add up," he said almost to himself. "I would have expected to see more equipment for an operation of this size."

"We'll know more when we look over his notes," Lucas said. "I, for one, am going to revel in the knowledge he's gone." He indicated Ben and shook his head. "Let him have his moment, okay?"

"I'm still here, and I can hear you," Ben said irritably. John was dead. He was too tired to focus on anything else. It had been one hell of a day. "And it's not a moment. It's—"

Everything that John had done to Simon hit Ben as though someone had physically struck him.

Simon, I love you. I'm so sorry.

John was gone, but it wouldn't give back anything and everyone Simon had lost. Nothing could do that.

To his horror, Ben felt tears form in his eyes. He scrubbed at them quickly. God, he wanted Simon, and badly. If Lucas was right, they couldn't be together yet. Hell, he wouldn't even be the one to tell him John was gone.

He felt another flood of emotion through their soulbond.

Simon knew.

"It will be okay," Lucas said, "and you guys have each other and friends who care about you. Both of you. Remember that." He put his arm around Ben and helped him from the room out into the night.

EPILOGUE

"Oh yes!" Ben arched his hips and thrust into Simon harder, faster. He kissed Simon hungrily, his hands roaming over Simon's body, touching everywhere he could reach.

Simon threaded their fingers together. "Ben," he whispered when they broke the kiss. "Ben." Tears were flowing down his cheeks. Ben kissed them away.

He was drowning, losing himself in Simon, their bodies moving together, their need and desire for each other taking over completely. He couldn't think, didn't want to. All he wanted was Simon, like this, with nothing between them, touching. He could feel Simon's emotions, raw, desperate and needy. They mirrored his own. God, he'd missed Simon, missed being with him like this so badly.

Ben felt Simon tighten around him. The little control he had left disappeared completely, and Ben came hard, shaking. "Simon!"

They held each other, neither wanting to let go. Simon closed his eyes, shivering, his skin flushed and glistening with perspiration. "Ben," he whispered again, his voice breaking.

Ben pulled out and, keeping his arms around Simon, rolled them over so they were lying side by side. "It's okay, I'm here. It's okay."

Instead of answering, Simon gripped Ben more tightly. He was sobbing. Ben cupped Simon's chin and met his eyes. "I'm not going anywhere, Simon. I love you."

The last five days had been hell for both of them. Ben's dreams had been plagued by nightmares that weren't his own, and he'd taken to cuddling Simon's pillow while he slept, wanting some part of him close. It was the only way he'd managed to sleep at all.

The thought of John being reduced to a pile of dust when he died still made Ben sick to his stomach. It wasn't only the knowledge he'd killed someone but the thought of that happening to Simon. Of him dying, his body crumbling to... that.

"You should have left me for what I did to you." Simon averted his eyes from Ben's gaze. "I nearly killed you!"

"But you didn't." Ben placed a finger over Simon's lips. "You're stubborn, and you fought the bloodlust. I'm betting none of the other victims got that warning you gave me." If Simon hadn't let go when Ben had bitten him, he'd be dead by now.

"I could suddenly think clearly. I remembered us. Biting me is something you do when we make—"

"When we make love," Ben finished for him. He bent his head and gently nipped at Simon's shoulder. "I know you keep saying it was still you, but it wasn't." Ben kissed Simon's chest, over his heart. "It was the bloodlust, Simon. It wasn't you. You're a good person, and okay, your dark side is a little darker and more dangerous than some others, but they aren't vampires. You are, and it's a part of you. I love *you*. All of you, for better and for worse and all that."

"You really believe that, don't you?"

"Yeah, I do." Ben traced a pattern on Simon's chest with one finger. "I thought this week would never bloody end. I've missed you so much. The phone calls really didn't cut it." He bit his lip. "I moved into one of the guest apartments upstairs. I didn't want to go back to mine, and Lucas said it would be okay as long as I made sure I kept my distance, and… I couldn't face going home."

Simon brought Ben's finger to his lips and kissed it. He'd already asked Ben to move in with him, and Ben had said yes. "I knew you were there, and it helped. It was like I could feel you inside me." He sighed. "I'm not explaining it very well, am I? Having that sense of you didn't seem to trigger the bloodlust, though, thank God." He shuddered and glanced at the healing bite marks and ugly bruise on Ben's neck. "Not like at your apartment."

He went very quiet and still.

"I figure we have two ways of dealing with this crap," Ben said softly. He brushed his fingers across Simon's cheek. "Either we move on or we dwell on it. If we dwell on it, then John's won, hasn't he? I don't want him to do that, and I don't think you do either. He's ruined your life for long enough."

The marks on Ben's neck would heal, for the most part, the thin cut John had left on his cheek already had. The silver burns on Simon's wrists and ankles would leave him with scars that would never be completely gone. He'd told Ben that John had marked him, or at least tried to. The scar on his inner thigh had almost healed. It always did, but that had never stopped John from attempting to claim Simon as his soulmate. Only a mark from Ben would be permanent, and it was something he could never do, being human. Simon hadn't said much about it, but he'd flinched when Ben had touched him there, and jerked away.

The emotional and mental trauma John had inflicted on Simon might not be as obvious, but it would take a long time before he'd be able to put it completely behind him, if he ever did. Ben would feel happier knowing exactly who was behind all that happened too. Simon had agreed with Forge that he doubted John had been working alone, but so far, besides the werewolves, there were no clues as to who was behind it or why. As much as Ben wanted answers, for now they could wait. Simon had been through enough.

"Forge told me what happened. I could feel you were in trouble, but I couldn't do anything. You took one hell of a risk going to that warehouse with him and Lucas. You could have been killed!"

"Yeah, I know that, but he had to be stopped." Ben shrugged. He'd been damn lucky, and he knew it. "And you did do something. I felt you, and you gave me the strength to keep going. I couldn't have done it without our bond." Without that, and John's arrogance and his belief that a human couldn't pose any real threat, Ben wouldn't have been able to get close enough to kill him. "Did Forge tell you I threw up afterwards? I was a write-off for several days. Some hero." Ben had tried going into work a couple of days later, but Ron had sent him home again after his ongoing headache had escalated to the point of migraine. He'd never had one before, and never wanted to go through it again.

Lucas had tried to reassure him that it was probably a delayed reaction to the reality of what he'd done, and to his and Simon's enforced separation.

While he appreciated Lucas's attempt to make him feel better, Ben had been more focused on the fact he felt like crap, the toilet was his new best friend, and he just wanted a nice dark hole to crawl into.

His suspicions that Lucas was taking notes about the whole thing hadn't helped his mood either.

"You're *my* hero." Simon flushed bright red. "Please tell me that didn't sound as corny to you as it did to me. I usually phrase things a lot better than that."

"It was pretty corny." Ben chuckled. "But I'll put it down to the fact I just addled your brain with great sex."

"I've missed you." Simon kissed Ben softly. "I much prefer my life with you in it."

"Yeah, same. I don't want a life without you." Ben kissed him back and sighed. "I phoned Granddad yesterday." Once he'd started feeling better and more like himself again, he'd needed to do something, anything to take his mind off the fact he and Simon were still apart, and besides, he figured his granddad had some serious explaining to do.

"And?" Simon propped himself up on one elbow, his expression serious and more than a little worried. "What did you tell him?"

"Pretty much everything," Ben admitted, "although I left out the bits I thought might freak him out too much." He'd downplayed the stuff with John in particular. "You're not going to believe this, but he's been playing matchmaker!"

"He has?" Simon arched an eyebrow. "How? I know he encouraged you to come to Boggslake and gave you a copy of the photo he'd taken of me."

"All part of his plan, apparently." Ben still couldn't believe it, although he knew his granddad had a sneaky streak a mile-high. "I'd been feeling restless for a while and couldn't settle after I'd done my degree. He wondered if I was missing something but didn't realize it, and he hoped it might be you." His expression softened. "He was right about that. It was one of the reasons I decided to travel and come over here."

"Boggslake's not a big place, but it's still a long shot that we'd meet," Simon said.

"Yeah, well, that's why he gave me the photo. He knew you always came to the park to think and figured you probably still did. If you'd found someone already, no harm done, but he said he'd hoped you hadn't. He reckoned the two of us would probably get on, even though, and I quote, 'we're both as stubborn as hell.'"

Simon laughed. It was the first time Ben had heard him laugh since he'd been kidnapped by John. "Frank said that? Did he tell you about how bloody stubborn *he* can be?"

"Mum reckons he's where I get it from," Ben told him. "He denies it, of course."

"That figures." Simon smiled, and his eyes glazed over, which was usually a sign he was thinking about something that had happened years ago. "I should write to him and tell him thank you."

"He'd like that." Ben stroked Simon's hair, enjoying the feel of it between his fingers. "I've been thinking about something."

"Yes?"

"I've been wondering if there's a way I could mark you as mine." Ben met Simon's gaze.

"I wish you could too." Simon's voice held a mix of regret and sadness. He swallowed. "If I hadn't marked you that night—"

"I know," Ben said quietly. Although the bloodlust virus had worked through Simon's system and no longer affected him, they'd always have to be very careful. Lucas had warned them that with Simon's existing issues with human blood and now this, if he tasted Ben's blood, or even came into contact with it, the results could be very bad. "We'll treat this like any addiction. We'll be careful." When Simon had marked Ben, he'd stopped himself from drinking. He might not be able to again.

"You know if something happened and you were injured and bleeding, I'd have to call someone else for help and walk away." Simon shook his head. "I hate that. I didn't ask for any of this. I never wanted to be a vampire. Sometimes I wish I could wake up one morning and it'd all be a bad dream."

"All of it? There's a saying about throwing out the baby with the bath water, you know. Not everything about you being a vampire is bad. If you weren't, we would have never met." Ben lightened his tone, trying to make a joke of it. "You're way older than me, after all. Positively ancient."

"And I act like it too sometimes, don't I?" Simon sighed. "Sorry."

"Hey, don't be sorry. I kind of like you that way. I think it's hot." Ben grinned.

"I noticed," Simon said. "You're not exactly subtle about it."

"Why be subtle? It seems a bit of a waste of time when I could be having my evil way with you."

Simon growled low in his throat. He rubbed his cock against Ben's leg. "I like the way you think."

Ben slipped off the bed before they got into round two. There was something he needed to do first. Something important.

"Ben?"

"It's okay. I just need to get something." Ben picked his jeans off the floor and found what he was looking for in one of the pockets. He closed his hand around it so Simon couldn't see it and climbed back onto the bed.

"Ben?" Simon asked again.

Ben cleared his throat. "I said I wanted to mark you, right? I know I can't, not in the way it's usually done when two vampires soulbond, but it hit me last night that, as I'm human, why not do it in a human way?"

He opened his palm to reveal a thin band of gold.

"It's a ring." Simon stared at it and then glanced at Ben.

"It's for you," Ben said. Silver hadn't been an option, so it had to be a gold ring. He'd thought briefly about white gold, but it didn't sit right, probably because it looked too much like silver. It had taken him most of the morning to find the right one, and he was sure he'd driven most of the jewelers in Boggslake insane while he'd looked for it. "If you want it, that is." God, he hadn't expected to feel so nervous. "I just figured if you wore it, it marks you as mine, right? It shows people you're taken, which you are. This soulbond thing is supposed to be forever. That's what I want. You and me together. Forever, or at least for my lifetime."

Simon nodded. He opened his mouth and closed it again.

"Was that a yes?" Ben asked. "Look, don't worry if you don't want to. It's probably a stupid idea anyway."

"It's not a stupid idea, Ben." Simon's voice was hoarse. "I want this too." He held out his left hand. "I love you, and I like the idea of being marked by you. I wanted you to be able to so badly."

Ben grinned. "I love you too." He slid the ring onto Simon's finger. The gold looked good against his pale skin. Ben was glad he'd gone for the plain design, and Lucas had helped with the sizing. The ring was elegant, just like Simon. "There you go. You're marked now. You're mine."

"I think I always have been. I just had to wait a long time to find you."

"Worth the wait?" Ben couldn't help asking.

Simon replied by pulling Ben down on him and kissing him hard. "Oh yes, very much yes." He grinned. "Being with you is sweet as."

CONNECT WITH ANNE

Contact me at:
annebarwell.wordpress.com
darthanne@gmail.com

Anne Barwell lives in Wellington, New Zealand. She shares her home with Kaylee: a cat with "tortitude" who is convinced that the house is run to suit her; this is an ongoing "discussion," and to date, it appears as though Kaylee may be winning.

In 2008, Anne completed her conjoint BA in English Literature and Music/Bachelor of Teaching. She has worked as a music teacher, a primary school teacher, and now works in a library. She is a member of the Upper Hutt Science Fiction Club and plays violin for Hutt Valley Orchestra.

She is an avid reader across a wide range of genres and a watcher of far too many TV series and movies, although it can be argued that there is no such thing as "too many." These, of course, are best enjoyed with a decent cup of tea and further the continuing argument that the concept of "spare time" is really just a myth. She also hosts and reviews for other authors, and writes monthly blog posts for Love Bytes. She is the co-founder of the New Zealand Rainbow Romance writers, and a member of RWNZ.

Anne's books have received honourable mentions five times, reached the finals four times—one of which was for best gay book—and been a runner up in the Rainbow

Awards. She has also been nominated twice in the Goodreads M/M Romance Reader's Choice Awards—once for Best Fantasy and once for Best Historical.

Electric Candle
by Elizabeth Noble

When a vampire finds his soulmate, the bond is forever. It's love at first sight.

Or is it?

Homicide Detective Jonas Forge has been a vampire for centuries. He's fought wars, seen life go from the simple colonial days to the modern high-tech world. He's evolved with the times, adapted to each new era, blended into each new life. The one constant is his best friend, mentor, and lover, Declan. Even though not fated to bond as soulmates, Forge and Declan are happy and settled in their life together.

Until Forge's real soulmate falls, literally, into his life.

Forge isn't thrilled with the guy, despite the pheromones

attracting them to each other, and the feeling seems mutual. While trying to adjust to his clumsy soulmate and equally awkward feelings, Forge is also on the hunt for a serial killer witnesses can't identify who's leaving a trail of bodies in its wake.

Will the bond Forge is finally forming with his soulmate be destroyed when the hunter becomes the victim?